THE ADOPTED DAUGHTER

JJ BURGESS

INKUBATOR
BOOKS

Published by Inkubator Books
www.inkubatorbooks.com

Copyright © 2023 by JJ Burgess

JJ Burgess has asserted his right to be identified as the
author of this work.

ISBN (eBook): 978-1-83756-229-9
ISBN (Paperback): 978-1-83756-230-5
ISBN (Hardback): 978-1-83756-231-2

*'I think the king is but a man, as I
am: the violet smells to him as it doth to me: the
element shows to him as it doth to me.'*
Henry V
William Shakespeare

'Envy does not enter empty houses'
Danish Proverb

PROLOGUE

She kept her foot on the accelerator and sped through the village, but there was no way her old Mini Cooper could outrun the menacing black Land Rover that was closing in on her. Wind blew into the car through the smashed driver's-side window, and her twirling dark hair kept threatening to block her view.

She caught sight of the two men in her rear-view mirror and saw how dangerous they were. Violence and anger pulsated from the two brutes. And then she felt the crunch of glass under her feet, and her hand went up to her throat where they had tried to strangle her.

Despite the broken window, her brow was covered with sweat. Tears filled her eyes, her hands were shaking, and she thought she might vomit.

Two men were chasing her. No, this couldn't be; things like this didn't happen to people like her. She was struggling to make sense of the situation, but the one thing she knew was that if they did get hold of her, it would all be over.

The road became a quiet country lane surrounded by

fields, which was not good, but it was an empty road, so she kept her foot down and yanked the steering wheel through the tight turns.

She needed help. She needed to call the police.

Her handbag was over her body, and she yanked it off and dropped it onto the passenger seat. Keeping her right hand on the steering wheel, she dug through the bag with her left hand, her fingers scrabbling around various items.

"Come on!"

Where was her phone?

The Land Rover revved from behind, its bumper inches from hers. If she had to suddenly brake, it would smash into the back of her. This was tailgating taken to another level.

She couldn't locate her phone, so she tipped the handbag upside down onto the seat beside her. Then her head became a ping-pong, eyes moving quickly between the road and the seat, back and forth. Tissues, makeup, mirror, little notebook, mints. No phone.

She'd left it in the house! There was no way of contacting the police.

Up ahead, a line of cars had stopped for a set of traffic lights. This was the end of the village road; she could turn right here and get onto the motorway that would take her into Bristol's city centre.

The feeling of terror flooded through her, she would need to stop at any moment, and the two men would have a chance to grab her again. Her foot hit the brake, leaving a twenty-foot gap between her and the car in front. It was the only thing she could think to do: if the men jumped out, she could at least drive forward to stop them from grabbing her.

She watched the two men in her rear-view mirror, and they watched her. They were like predators, watching their little prey. She was drenched with sweat from the heat of the day. The steering wheel was hot to the touch, but she wouldn't let go of it; she clung to it like a buoyancy aid in the ocean. In the mirror's reflection she could see that the man in the passenger seat was holding something in his hand. Her eyes blinked rapidly and squinted at it. It was a claw hammer.

The traffic lights up ahead finally changed, and the cars in front started to move forward onto the main road.

And then her engine cut out.

"No! No! NO!"

She tore her eyes away from the rear-view mirror and grabbed the car key. She turned the key to the off position and switched it back on. The car choked and spluttered, but it didn't start.

"Please," she begged, the tears now rolling down her cheeks.

The cars ahead disappeared from view, leaving her old battered Mini Cooper and the Land Rover alone on the road.

She turned the key. Again, the car wouldn't start.

Behind her she could hear car doors opening and closing. They were coming for her; the two men were coming to batter her with their claw hammer.

"Please," she begged the car again.

A shadow came to the smashed window.

Her car door was yanked open.

PART I

1

NINE DAYS TO GO

"Professor Richard Barnes has been a stalwart member of staff at the university for fifteen years." Alfred, the dean of Bristol University, paused to make sure the crowd was listening to him. "Of course, he's been with us for almost twenty years, but the less said about his early days, the better."

Laughter erupted around the restaurant, and Alice could feel her partner, Richard, tense beside her. There came a wave of good-natured nods and knowing grins from friends and colleagues acknowledging the joke. Richard smiled politely back at them, and Alice wondered if he would snap and make a scene; could he keep his bitterness hidden?

"Of course, I'm joking." Alfred grinned through his grey beard. "When he joined Bristol University, back at the start of the new millennium, the biology department was a very different place. I can honestly say Richard was a real driving force in transforming the department into one of the country's best lecturing teams." Alfred tipped his glass of red wine to Richard in the crowd. "We owe you a big debt, Richard."

Richard nodded, grim faced.

"In addition to helping build the department, Richard has also done a lot for the field of biology itself. At the last count, there are over fifty papers and six books written, a great achievement. So please raise your glasses in a farewell toast to our dear friend and colleague," he encouraged as everyone dutifully raised their drinks, "to Richard, wishing you a well-deserved rest in your retirement! Cheers."

"Cheers!" the room chorused.

Richard smiled and looked around the restaurant. His leaving party was in the Lido in Clifton, near to the university. The Lido had been a Victorian swimming baths but had since been converted to an upmarket restaurant, although the outdoor swimming pool had remained, which added a novelty to the fine dining establishment. That evening, the usual dining tables had been cleared to make room for the fifty or so people gathered there. One side of the room was all glass, through which could be seen the lit swimming pool directly outside.

Alice joined in with the toast and watched Richard closely, wondering what he would do; if he would keep calm or if he would give into the bubbling undercurrent of rage at the unjustness of being asked to leave his job. She studied his face, looking for a clue. Even for Richard, he was looking handsome that evening. His thick grey hair had been swept back from his strong, lean face, and his tailor-made velvet jacket fitted him immaculately.

Alfred moved back into the crowd of lecturers and staff, and Richard stepped forward to replace him at the front of the restaurant. Alice could see a look of worry pass over

Alfred's face, and she wondered what he would do if Richard began a tirade of abuse aimed both at him and the university. A significant proportion of the room was relaxed, but others knew what had happened, and they were the ones who looked on edge, anxious at what could occur. One or two were even grinning with wild-eyed excitement.

Richard sipped from his glass of wine, savouring the audience's attention.

"I think the food will soon be ready, so I will keep this brief," Richard told the hushed room.

Alfred folded his arms and clenched his jaw. He had spilled some red wine into his grey beard, giving it a dark streak.

"The university has been a great place to work, and I've enjoyed my time working alongside all of you. As you know, my partner, Alice, and I will be sailing off to the Mediterranean soon."

Richard glanced over to where Alice was standing at the bar, and she couldn't stop herself from blushing as the guests turned to look at her. She had a face that always seemed sympathetic, eyes that were warm, and a voice that was soothing. People were often drawn to her natural kindness, and she had been a popular member of staff at the university until she'd left a few weeks previously. Despite being friends with most of the room, she didn't like too much attention, and she could feel her face turning crimson.

"Although after receiving my leaving gifts" – Richard waved to a table in the corner, which was littered with life-jackets and various pieces of nautical safety equipment – "I think I need to reassure you that I'm an excellent sailor."

The room reverberated with laughter.

"So please don't worry about me. And if things get too

rough, I'm sure Alice will try to pitch in." He waited for more laughter, but none came. Alice ignored the sympathetic looks at the put-down, as she always did.

"Well, you've got our email addresses, so if ever you find yourself around the coasts of Spain, France or Italy, please let us know, and we may sail over and join you for a glass or two of wine." He smiled brightly out at them.

A waiter appeared in the corner of the room.

"Ah, looks like the buffet is ready. So I'll just say, once again, thank you for all your support over the years, and I wish you all the best for the future."

The room applauded as Richard moved back into the mass of people. Alice watched him as he shook hands and received pats on the back. Several waiters were bringing platters of food out, and the warm, meaty smells filled the restaurant. Slowly, Richard made his way through the throng of people and back to Alice.

On the tables there were calathea plants that Alice had brought into the restaurant earlier that day for decoration, their large waxy leaves offering a green tone to the pale blue room. Calatheas symbolised new beginnings because their leaves turned over in the dark.

"Nice speech, darling," she said.

"Thanks." He looked around and made sure no one could overhear them. "Although I was tempted to tell them all what a complete bastard Alfred has been recently."

She laid a hand on his arm. "You would only have regretted it in the morning." At fifty-six, he was ten years older than her, but it was Alice who was often the more sensible of the two of them.

He looked down at her. She was wearing his favourite

dress for him, a blue and white floral one that showed off her hourglass figure.

In that moment she suddenly remembered when they had first met, all those years ago. She had been his new lab assistant, and she'd been so nervous around him, the great Professor Richard Barnes. For the past twenty years they had worked together within the biology department until Alice had finished her job last month. That morning Richard had given his last lecture, so now they were both jobless. No more university, no more pay cheques.

"Have you seen any of your old workmates here?" he asked.

"One or two. I've been getting the latest gossip."

"Yeah?" He looked around, staring across the restaurant at Alfred.

"Some things never change; it's still the same old politics."

Richard snorted. "You're telling me it is."

"Let's get some food," Alice said.

"Huh?"

"Let's eat."

"Okay."

She took his hand and led him from the bar and over to the side tables where the food had been laid out.

"They've done a lovely spread," Alice said, taking a place in the queue.

The tables of food were placed against the windows, and Alice looked beyond them at the outdoor swimming pool below. It was lit up in the summer's evening, and she stared down into the blue stillness. From her vantage point it looked shallow, but she knew her eyes were playing tricks on her. The water was deeper than it seemed.

"WINTERBOURNE, PLEASE, MATE."

"No problem," the taxi driver called back to them.

They got into the large car, Richard clutching his bundles of gifts, Alice holding a collection of retirement cards. She clipped on her seatbelt, but Richard was too drunk to bother.

The car set off from the city and began the fifteen-minute drive north to the village that bordered Bristol. It was late, but the summer sky was still light. Through the windows they could see the city of Bristol pass them by, ancient buildings made from the yellow Bath stone. There were two universities in the city, and it was a popular destination for bachelor and hen parties, and as they drove through the city centre, there were dozens of young people out walking the streets, shouting and laughing as they headed to the next bar. Alice noted some very short skirts and minuscule tops on the girls, and she stopped herself from judging them; years ago, she'd worn the same on nights out with friends, although at forty-six years old, her days of tiny outfits were no more.

"Did you see that git Alfred?" Richard slurred.

Alice looked across at him as he ran a hand through his hair. He had looked dashing that evening in his red crushed-velvet jacket. Even now, after twenty years, she still found herself attracted to him with his square jaw and dark eyes. When people met him, they had a hard time believing he was a university professor.

"You still haven't told me all of the details," Alice said. "Why exactly did they push you out?"

Richard looked out the window, the passing streetlamps flashing orange light on and off his face.

"I told you, Alfred was playing politics. He made some rubbish up about my admin not being correct."

They'd had this conversation several times already, but now she decided to push it. Perhaps it was the wine, or maybe her curiosity getting the better of her. Besides, he still hadn't properly told her his side of the story.

"Admin?"

He adjusted the pile of gifts on his lap, trying to get comfortable.

"You know, my expenses and stuff."

"Expenses?"

"Don't worry, it was nothing untoward, I'd done a few expenses slips wrong, and he jumped on them as an excuse to have me replaced. The important thing is, it's nothing that's going to interfere with my pension in a few years."

The car braked suddenly, and they jolted forward on the back seats.

The driver beeped the horn as two young men stumbled into the road, arm in arm, singing at the top of their voices.

"Pair of nutters," the driver commented, although it was said casually and without malice. Obviously, he was used to having drunks stumbling in the way of his car.

The driver beeped again, and there came shouts of, "Sorry, mate," from the two youths in the road as they moved away. The car set off again.

Alice turned back to Richard. It was the first time he had mentioned expenses being the reason for the university asking him to leave his post after twenty years. He was always like this: a closed book. For years she had accepted it, assumed it was part of his persona as a great professor. These days she just found it annoying, but she also knew she wouldn't get a straight answer from him no matter how much she probed.

"You sound drunk." She smiled.

He grinned out the window. "Yes, I had a few reds."

"Well, if ever there's a time for it..."

"My bloody retirement party is it."

Alice ran her hand over his shoulder. She'd had a few glasses of wine herself to celebrate an end of an era. With her small frame, she always felt the effects of the alcohol after just one glass of wine.

"I love you, you know," Alice told him.

The taxi driver's eyes flickered to them through the rear-view mirror.

Richard didn't turn from staring out the window as he squeezed her hand.

"Love you too."

EIGHT DAYS TO GO

RICHARD'S SNORING WOKE ALICE. Or maybe it was the stifling heat of the Saturday morning. They were due a heatwave that weekend, and it felt like it had already started despite it still only being 7 a.m.

Alice dragged herself out of bed, went to the toilet and then headed downstairs to put the kettle on. The bright morning sun was streaming in through the window as she made a pot of coffee. She'd had just the right amount of wine, her head felt okay, and any trace of a hangover was minimal. Richard wouldn't feel the same.

From the fridge she pulled out packets of fresh fruit and cut them up into small pieces ready for his breakfast. Once she was finished, she placed the fruit neatly in a large bowl and placed the bowl back in the fridge because he liked his fruit cold.

On the kitchen counter were the cards and gifts from last night's retirement party. Alice put the cards up on the mantelpiece in the lounge, and, as she did so, a photo of her mum looked up at her, and she was hit by a jolt of pain. It had been six months since her mum had died, but she still felt the loss strongly. Her hand caressed the photo, taken the year before on a walk through the New Forest.

"Miss you, Mum," she whispered to the picture.

Back in the kitchen she sorted through the gifts; there were two slim lifejackets, a yellow waterproof bag, a waterproof torch, a handheld beacon, a first aid kit and a rubber-handled knife. She picked the knife up and couldn't help but smile; there was nothing safe about that.

Moving quietly, she laid the gifts neatly out on the dining table, ready for Richard to go through them. It was exciting to think about leaving their home and sailing around the vibrant blue sea of the Mediterranean. When Richard had first suggested it, she hadn't been so sure, but his passion for the idea had become infectious to her. They had spent weeks poring over maps and planning the route they would take. Alice had even signed up for sailing lessons, although she still had a way to go to feel confident on the water.

She poured Richard a coffee from the pot and took it upstairs to him.

"Morning, darling." She put the cup on the bedside table.

He stirred under the covers.

"Uggh, how much did I drink?"

She laughed. "Enough."

Alice showered and then sat at her dressing table in the bedroom. She studied her hair and admired her new high-lights. She pulled out all of her makeup and got to work putting on her face. Alice pouted as she swept on her neutral-toned lipstick. Her mouth was so small that when she'd gone to the dentist a few years ago, they had struggled to take a moulding of her teeth because the mould was too big to fit in her mouth. Eventually they'd had to use a child's mould.

After a while Richard sat up and slurped at his coffee.

"That's good," he said.

He got out of bed and showered whilst Alice dried her hair.

"What time is lunch?" he asked her as he reappeared looking more alive.

"Not till twelve, but I thought we could have a look around the shops for an hour before."

"More shopping?"

"In just over a week's time I'm going to be living on a boat, so I need to get the shopping time in whilst I can."

"Fair enough."

He got dressed, and they went downstairs together. He poured himself more coffee from the pot, and she got his fruit from the fridge for his breakfast. Alice then made herself some cereal.

The front doorbell chimed.

"Why don't they just leave the parcel in the porch?" he complained through a mouthful of fruit.

"I haven't ordered anything, so it must be for you," she said.

He shook his head. "I haven't either."

They looked at each other. The doorbell chimed again.

She sighed. "Okay, I'll get it."

Alice walked down the hallway to the front door. There was a figure on their porch, blocking out the morning light. She opened the door to see a young woman standing there. The woman was tall and blonde, nervous and curious.

"Hi," Alice said.

"Hi, my name is Sally; umm, does Professor Barnes live here?" she asked with a Welsh lilt to her voice.

Alice smiled politely, her eyes taking in the young woman in front of her. She was wearing tight blue jeans and a black T-shirt; it was unisex clothing that her long legs and curvy figure made very feminine. Her hair looked dyed rather than natural blonde; the dark eyebrows were a giveaway.

"Richard," Alice called behind her.

She could hear him walking down the hallway.

"What's up?"

Alice stepped aside and pulled the front door open wider, like a magician revealing an assistant who had just reappeared.

"There's someone here to see you," Alice said.

Richard arrived and looked at the young woman.

"Can I help you?" he asked cautiously.

For a moment the young woman seemed speechless and just stared at him with an intense look on her face.

"Professor Barnes," she said. It wasn't a question.

He nodded.

"My name is Sally; I think I'm your daughter."

Alice and Richard stared at her, completely lost for words. A feeling of dread and sickness came over Alice, and it took all of her willpower not to slam the front door right then.

"Twenty-five years ago, you and my mum...my mum is Julie Long. She got pregnant and gave me up for adoption."

"I didn't. I'm not..." Richard began, struggling to find the words.

Alice looked from Richard and back to the woman on her doorstep. The summer sun was higher in the sky now, blasting heat and sunlight into the hallway.

Alice tried to control her emotions. "You'd better come in," she said.

2

EIGHT DAYS TO GO

The lounge was a long room that was painted white apart from one wall covered in blue and gold wallpaper. Two sofas faced each other at one end of the room, one on each wall. In the corner there was a black glass stand with a large, flat-screen TV on it. On the opposite side of the room, by a window, was an oversized grey armchair, as was the fashion when Richard and Alice bought it. Stood on a coffee table was a vase of white and yellow lilies, which gave off a strong scent that filled the room. Alice always liked to have fresh flowers in the house.

Richard sat on the left-hand sofa, Sally on the right. Alice sat in the armchair facing the two sofas, watching them both. Nobody spoke as they all studied each other, their voices lost in shock.

Alice cleared her throat. "Shall I make us all a drink?"

Sally looked up, there was a nervous glow to her cheeks, and her eyes kept jumping around the room. "Yes, please."

"What would you like?"

"Coffee with milk would be fantastic, thank you." The word *fantastic* sounded very Welsh.

Alice went to the kitchen, put the kettle on and exhaled loudly. Her head was spinning, and she couldn't help but hold onto the kitchen counter. Her half-eaten bowl of cereal was on the countertop, and Alice pushed it away, suddenly feeling horribly hungover from the night before, and she was unable to face eating, not that it would be appropriate to eat now. A young woman had turned up suggesting she was Richard's daughter. Alice felt sick.

Richard appeared behind her.

"Bloody hell," he said.

Alice couldn't look at him. "A daughter?" was all she could manage.

"If she's telling the truth," he whispered to her back. "How would we know?"

Alice shrugged weakly. "Oh, Richard, at least give her a chance to explain."

"Of course."

Alice turned from the counter to face him, and they stared at each other as the kettle boiled. It was strange to see Richard looking nervous and on edge; he was usually so calm and collected. Every day he lectured hundreds of students, and doing so had made him comfortable in his own skin: he was confident and able to talk to anyone. It was rare to see him so unsettled.

"She must be about twenty-four years old," he said, "and you know I've never been unfaithful." He was giving her the math; Richard and Alice had been together twenty years, so his alleged daughter couldn't have been conceived whilst they were together.

A small laugh escaped from Alice's mouth. "I know, but the thought hadn't even occurred to me."

He seemed relieved by this.

"What do you want to drink?"

"Coffee, please."

She turned to the counter and made the drinks, two coffees and a green tea for her. Richard located a tray in one of the cupboards, and she put the hot drinks on it. They walked back into the lounge, Alice leading the way. Sally hadn't moved; she simply sat looking around the room.

"Here you go," Alice said as she put the tray of drinks down on the coffee table between the two sofas. In doing so, she became aware of Sally's perfume, which was musky.

Richard resumed his seat on the sofa facing Sally and motioned for Alice to sit next to him. Alice pretended not to see; instead, she took her drink from the tray and sat on the single armchair again.

Sally sipped her coffee.

"So," Richard said, "what makes you think I'm your biological father?"

Alice winced at the word *biological*.

Sally put her coffee cup down on the table. "I was adopted just after I was born. By two lovely people, Jeff and Deidre. They never tried to hide anything from me, and I've always known I was adopted. Maybe I was six when they first told me." Sally looked from Richard to Alice. "Of course, it didn't really mean anything when I was little, and as I grew older, I just accepted everything without question. Anyway, I never thought about finding my real parents until recently."

"So why now?" Alice asked.

"My father died. Cancer. They were a lot older when they adopted me, so he was eighty-three when we lost him."

Alice watched Sally. She was aware her eyes were glued to this young woman who had suddenly appeared in their house, but she couldn't stop looking, couldn't move her focus elsewhere. Sally's blonde hair was tied at the back, but a few strands had worked their way free and fell around her face. Her black T-shirt seemed simple, but the cut and stitch of it suggested it was expensive.

"Sorry to hear that," Richard said. His voice was dry.

"Mum's still going strong, although she's in a home now. I guess you get to an age where you think about things differently. So I got in touch with my mum...biological mum... Julie Long. Do you remember her? She was a lab assistant at Cardiff University."

A jolt of shock hit Alice, and she tore her eyes away from Sally to glare at Richard. "A lab assistant?"

Richard's face turned ashen; it was as if all his confidence had drained out of him.

"You were sleeping with your lab assistant at Cardiff?" Alice asked, her voice louder and sharper than she meant it to be.

The sick feeling in her stomach grew. They themselves had met when she was assigned to Richard as his biology lab partner. Their meeting had been so romantic, so special. It was one of her most cherished memories – as Richard was well aware – but now Sally was saying Richard had been romantically involved with another lab assistant before her?

"Yes." He wouldn't look at Alice; his eyes were fixed to the floor.

Sally looked at Alice, her head tilted to the side.

Alice took a deep breath. "Richard and I have been together for twenty years, after we met at Bristol University. I was his lab assistant."

"Ohh," Sally replied. "I'm so sorry. I didn't mean to make things awkward."

"It's fine, Sally," Richard assured her. "I should have told Alice." He looked up at Alice. "Sorry, it was remiss of me not to mention it."

Alice realised her hands were clenched, and she tried to relax. She took a sip of her green tea, but it was too hot and burned her mouth.

"So, might there be any other lab assistants you've got pregnant?" It was petty, but Alice couldn't help it.

"No," he said to the floor.

"I'm so sorry," Sally murmured. "I didn't think..."

The moment of rage passed, and Alice took a deep breath. It took a lot to make her angry, and she felt the bitterness of jealousy spark in her stomach. Emotions were flooding through her, and she had to work hard at controlling herself.

"It's fine, Sally. Truly," she said with as much grace as she could muster. "It was before Richard and I met, so I shouldn't get worked up about it. Please do continue."

"Well, Julie Long's details, my mother's details, were on the adoption letter, and I managed to get a copy of it."

Sally reached into her bag, took out a folded piece of paper and handed it over to Richard. At first, he seemed reluctant to take it, but Sally didn't retract her arm, so he had no choice but to reach out for the paper. Slowly he opened it and scanned the page.

"Julie Long." Those three syllables were all he could manage.

"Well?" Alice asked.

He seemed to resign himself to talking, so he sat up straight and finally lifted his head to look at them both. "Yes.

I was a new lecturer at Cardiff University. I spent three years there. Julie and I were both single, and we started seeing each other. I knew she got pregnant, but we were both so young that she decided to have an abortion. It caused things to become strained between us, and we ended our relationship not long after."

"Did you push her into having the abortion?" Alice asked him.

A part of her, a big part, believed in manners and politeness, and she knew they should wait to have this conversation in private, but she somehow couldn't help herself.

He looked shocked. "Of course not! It was a joint decision. And as far as I knew, she'd had the bloody abortion. I was upset at the time; we both were. But then she left me, and I had to get on with my life."

Alice had to stop herself from bombarding Richard with the multitudes of questions that boiled up inside her. Instead, she sipped her tea, which was still too hot. She couldn't bring herself to look at Sally, although she could smell her musky perfume. Did she really have to wear so much? It was killing the sweet smell of her white lilies.

"Oh, I am so, so sorry. I should have thought this would all be overwhelming." The Welsh accent was already starting to grate on Alice. "As you can see from the birth documents, she did in fact give birth to me, and she put your name as the father. She was listed as a lab technician, and you, as my father, was listed as a lecturer. I traced her to the university, and from there, it was easy enough to find you. I'm twenty-five, so the dates all match up too."

Richard stared at the paper in his hands and shifted in his chair like a sciatica sufferer. After a moment he looked up at Alice.

"Well, this is all a bit uncomfortable." He smiled at her, switching the Professor Barnes charm back on, and despite everything, she already felt herself relaxing at his smile.

People always thought Richard's talents lay in his knowledge of biology, but Alice knew his real skills were his charm; she'd never met anyone whom Richard couldn't win over with his easy smile and soothing voice. It helped that he was so handsome too.

Alice couldn't help but give him a little smile in return. "Yes."

"Like I said, I'm sorry," Sally said. "For any upset caused."

"I think you're right, looking at this document, and hearing your story, it does sound like I'm your father." Richard paused. "Although – and I don't mean to be rude – might it be worth thinking about a DNA test?"

"Oh, of course." She smiled brightly at him.

"So I have a daughter? I must say, it's all a bit of a shock."

Alice watched Sally. She was pretty, in a sort of obvious way. She'd had a friend at school called Sally and had always liked the name, but it suddenly sounded cheap to her.

"So, where do you live, Sally?" Alice asked.

"Yes, please tell us about yourself," Richard added.

"Oh, well. I live in Cardiff with my boyfriend, Ryan. I'm a nurse..."

"A nurse? Good for you."

"Thanks. I'm a midwife nurse at Heath Hospital."

"A midwife! I can't imagine delivering all those babies."

Alice watched them talk, flooded with emotions so strong they clawed like acid in her stomach. The worst of the feelings she was battling was jealousy, she wasn't used to it, and it was horribly consuming.

"We have a dog, Dudley. We enjoy taking him for walks

in the Brecon Beacons. Ryan has a big family, so we spend a lot of time with them."

They talked for a while, mostly Richard asking questions, Sally answering them and Alice watching them both. She smiled and nodded but felt as if she was on autopilot. The story of the Cardiff lab assistant had thrown her, and despite the polite smile, all she really wanted to do was throw her tea at Richard's head.

Eventually, the conversation ran out of steam.

"Thank you for sharing all of that with us," Richard said. "Perhaps we can swap email addresses and get in touch again once we have processed all of this." He sounded as if he were wrapping up a job interview.

"Of course. Honestly, I don't have any expectations from you. I just wanted to make contact. I really appreciate your time and you talking to me."

Sally pulled out a small slip of paper from her handbag. "I've written my details on here." She stood up and handed the paper over to Richard. "Don't feel you have to call. I understand all of this is a lot to take in."

Richard and Alice stood too.

They went to the front door, said their goodbyes, and Sally left.

Richard closed the front door and let out a huge sigh. "Jeeeesus."

Alice didn't respond. She went back into the lounge, where Sally's perfume still lingered, opened a window, then put the three empty cups back on the tray and carried them out to the kitchen. Richard followed her but didn't say anything. He hovered in the doorway, obviously trying to gauge her mood.

The dishwasher was full, so she turned the hot water

on and began rinsing the cups. One of them had pink lipstick on the rim. Sally hadn't seemed to be wearing any lipstick, but there it was: a half circle of colour on Alice's nice white cup. It was a little mark left in their house. A little reminder of an intrusion into their lives. Alice picked up the small sponge in the sink and forcefully scrubbed the lipstick off.

"Are we still going to lunch?" Richard asked behind her.

"Sure." She paused, unable to turn and look at him. "But you're driving. I need a drink."

———

THE WHITE HORSE in Hambrook was busy, which was usual for a Saturday afternoon. It had been there for years, but a new owner had recently taken it over and transformed what was an old man's pub into a gastro delight. The whole place now resembled a five-star Scottish hotel, with old tartan armchairs and stag heads on the walls. The food was superb, as was the wine.

Alice had booked them a garden table, and they were shown through to a nice corner table in the July sun. Jan and Freddie were already there.

"We were getting worried about you," Freddie greeted them. He was wearing a white shirt, which bulged against his large stomach.

"Sorry, something came up," Richard replied, shaking Freddie's hand.

Alice kissed them both on the cheeks. "Sorry we're late," she said. "So lovely to see you both."

Jan looked divine in a pink dress with a graphic red pattern on it, and as usual, she was by far and away the best-dressed person in the place. The sun glistened from her gold bracelets and necklace.

The waiter who had shown them to their table put some menus in front of them. "Can I get you any drinks?"

"Large red wine, please. Merlot," Alice said straight away.

"Oh, well, I'll join you in that," Jan added with a smile, "a red wine, please, although make mine a small."

Richard and Freddie both ordered a pint of craft ale, and the waiter walked off to get their drinks.

"Nice table," Freddie said, looking around at the busy pub garden.

"It's so nice to be out in the sun," Jan agreed. They'd been friends for years, and Alice liked that Jan was her age. As Richard was ten years older than Alice, he had some older friends whom she sometimes found boring and a chore being with, but Jan and Freddie were always great company.

"So how long is it until you disappear from our lives?" Freddie grinned.

"Just over a week, I think, depending on the weather," Richard replied.

"I still can't believe you're doing it." Jan held Alice's hand across the table, a warm and comforting gesture. "Sailing around the Mediterranean in a boat. You know we'll be coming out to visit loads, of course?"

"We hope you do," Richard replied.

"What a way to spend your retirements!" Freddie said. "And knowing you, Alice, I guess you're all packed?"

"Almost," was all she could say, her eyes on the table.

Jan and Freddie looked at each other.

"How have you guys been?" Richard asked.

Freddie was an engineer working at Airbus in Bristol, and he began telling them about his latest project, the new design of a plane engine. Normally Richard liked to discuss jet engines with him, but today he didn't say much. Jan updated them on the refurbishment of her restaurant in the city centre; again her news was met with silence.

The waiter arrived with the drinks. While he was there, he also took their food orders, two steak and ale pies for the men and a steak, cooked rare, for Jan. Alice couldn't face eating, but she ordered a vegetable risotto for appearances.

"Cheers, all!" Freddie said.

"Cheers." Alice took a long sip of her drink. The wine was dry and packed a punch; just what she needed.

Richard was also taking big gulps of his ale.

"Are you two alright? You look like you've just had some bad news. The boat hasn't sunk, has it?" Freddie gave a loud laugh at his attempt at a joke.

Richard and Alice looked at each other.

"You should tell them, Richard."

He nodded.

"We had a visitor this morning," he said, taking another sip of his ale, blinking a few times. "A young woman called Sally. It seems like she might be my daughter."

"What?!" Jan exclaimed for the both of them.

"Your daughter? I thought you didn't have any kids?" Freddie asked.

Alice was glad to see they were so shocked, glad it wasn't just her who had been so floored by the story of Richard having a daughter. She drank her wine, wishing she could feel its effects quicker.

"I don't, or at least, I didn't," he said with a shrug. "I knew that my girlfriend, twenty-five-odd years ago, became pregnant. I thought she'd had an abortion, but it turns out she had the baby and gave it up for adoption."

It was Jan and Freddie's turn to gulp at their drinks.

"That's crazy! How do you feel about it?" Jan asked. "What was she like? Sorry, say if you don't want to talk about it."

Richard put his pint down. "I'm not sure how I feel about it." He looked to Alice. "It was a shock for both of us."

"Oh, Alice, of course," Jan said, and held her hand again.

They all knew what *of course* meant.

It meant *of course, this must be difficult because you've lost babies in the womb.*

It meant *of course, this must be difficult for you because you could never have children, and now Richard is a father, but you're not a mother.*

Jan squeezed her hand, and it felt so comforting that Alice had to stop herself from crying.

Of course, this must be hard; you've always wanted a family of your own more than anything in the world.

"It's fine," Alice said, although her voice wobbled.

She sipped her wine. Wine wasn't the answer to anything, she knew, but right then she couldn't drink it quick enough.

Richard put his hand on her back. She wanted to bat it away but also didn't want to cause an argument in front of their friends.

"What did your daughter want?" Freddie asked Richard.

It was strange to hear "your daughter" spoken aloud, and Alice and Richard both looked at him.

"Want? Nothing. I think she just wanted to meet her biological father. Her own father, her adopted father, had died recently, she said. Which meant she wanted to meet me. We swapped emails, but I don't think we'll see much of her again."

"Not unless she suddenly appears off the coast of Italy," Freddie said.

Richard snorted. "Exactly." He sighed. "I guess she didn't think how disruptive it would be, coming to our house. I suppose it's never an easy situation."

Richard's hand was feeling hot and uncomfortable on Alice's back. She didn't want him touching her.

"Just need the ladies'," Alice murmured.

She got up and left them sitting at the table. In the toilets she locked herself in a cubicle, and the tears came; they flooded out of her in anguish, and she couldn't stop them. Her mind flittered through old memories: the joy at the positive pregnancy tests, the nervous excitement at buying baby clothes, the mental and physical pain of the miscarriages, the pain at the loss. The heartbreak at what was lost from her life. It was always there, just hidden away from the world.

Alice grabbed some tissue and dabbed at her eyes, hoping her mascara wouldn't run too much. It had been a horribly difficult day, and she was struggling to keep hold of the emotions coursing through her.

Eventually, she came out of the cubicle with a handful of tissue and went to the sink and mirror. She ran the water, but it was too hot and burned to the touch. She managed to wet some tissue without burning herself and used it to dab at the mascara streaks on her cheeks.

She thought about Richard. They'd been together for twenty years, and in that time her heart had always belonged to him; she'd been completely in love with him. Could she say the same about Richard's feelings for her? Had there always been a nagging doubt that he wasn't a hundred percent committed to their relationship as she was? For the first time in her life, she started to question who Richard really was.

Alice looked at herself in the mirror. A crack ran up the middle of the glass and crossed through her reflection; it was a thin crack, but it was enough to distort her face.

There were still signs that she'd been crying. Luckily, she had a pair of sunglasses in the pocket of her dress. She sniffed, took a deep breath and put them on. She forced a smile and walked out into the sunshine.

3

SEVEN DAYS TO GO

Alice parked her battered, old green Mini Cooper in the harbour car park and walked down towards the sailing club building. It was a bright morning, and the water glistened in the harbour. She recognised a few people in wetsuits, and they gave her a cheery good morning.

"Morning," she replied, her throat hoarse with hangover.

Alice was also in a wetsuit, a few months ago she had felt an idiot putting it on, but now she felt comfortable wearing it.

"Sorry I'm late," Roger, the sailing instructor, called behind them.

Alice turned to watch him arrive. Roger was tall and well-built with salt-and-pepper hair. She tried to guess his age, as she often did; he had the strong physique of a young man with big arms and broad shoulders, but then the grey in his hair and beard aged him. No, it refined him. She suspected he was a year or two older than her.

She watched as he unlocked the large, caged door that

held the small boats. "Okay, grab yourself a boat and take it down to the water."

Alice let the others in the sailing class go ahead of her, and she was the last to pull out a boat. The bright red Laser Pico was housed on a small trailer. It was easy enough to pick up the front of the trailer and wheel the little plastic boat to the slipway. She had done this over a dozen times now, and her movements were assured as she wheeled it down to the water. She unclipped the boat with her right hand and held its rope with her left. The boat came loose, and she controlled its smooth slide into the water.

"Nice day for it today, about eight knots of wind," Roger said beside her.

"I hope I feel okay on the water. I had a few drinks last night."

He grinned at her. "If pirates can do it, I'm sure you'll be fine."

She laughed, and their eyes met.

"Seriously though, you're one of my best pupils, so don't let me down out there." It was said with warmth, and Alice couldn't help but beam at the praise.

Splashing water sounded, and Roger looked behind her.

"Better go," he said as he went off to help one of the younger pupils, who was struggling with their boat and trailer.

Alice watched him walk away, tall and confident. When she had started her sailing lessons a few months ago, it had been a daunting experience, but having Roger support and teach her had made everything so much easier. He looked tough, but in reality, he was a patient and calm man.

She tore her eyes away from Roger and focused on her boat. Alice gave herself more slack on the rope and then wheeled the trailer over to the side of the slipway. Excited chatter rose around the harbour as the others did the same. The boats soon lined the water, and the pupils began to get into their little vessels. The Pico was nearly twelve feet long with a main sail and a jib; designed as a training boat, it was ideal for children and could be sailed by one person easily, although two could also fit in.

Alice got into her boat and pushed off from the shore with her foot. She looked at the surface of the water for signs of the wind; the key was to be able to recognise the ripple patterns on the surface for the direction and strength of the wind. She took the sail's rope in her right hand and the rudder in her left, and as the wind hit the open sail, the little boat glided across the harbour.

Bristol harbour was a channel of water from Hotwells on one side to Baltic Wharf on the other. Alice's boat cut through the dark water and in less than a minute had reached the far side of the harbour; now, she looked set to crash into the wall. At the last moment she let go of the sail rope, pushed the rudder hard to the left and jumped over to the other side of the boat. She span 180 degrees in the water and in an instant sped off back towards Baltic Wharf.

"Nice moves!" Roger called out to her.

Alice grinned at the pure joy of sailing. She looked over to see Roger in his motorboat, the engine slowly chugging amongst the students' Picos as he kept an eye on them. The other students were having mixed success, some were struggling to get going, others were tick-tacking across the harbour like her, but nobody was as fast as Alice, her dark hair flying in the wind as she led the pack.

Richard had pushed her to learn to sail, and initially she'd envisaged herself taking a huge ship out across the sea.

But instead, every Sunday morning Alice had joined Roger's lessons.

"Become an expert with a Pico; then you can think about taking the big boat out," Richard had told her.

She hadn't even known what a Pico was four months ago, but now she knew. It was a toy, a tough little piece of fun, and Richard had been right; she now understood the principles of sailing thanks to mastering it. Last month Alice had graduated to a larger twenty-foot sailboat, but she'd enjoyed sailing the Pico so much that she'd kept attending the lessons. It helped that Roger was such a good instructor.

Further along the harbour was HB Ship Builders, where Alice and Richard's boat, *Seas the Day*, was being kept. They had bought her at the beginning of the year with their savings, and she'd needed plenty of work to make her seaworthy. Although the cost of the boat had used up a lot of their savings, Alice was due to receive her mum's inheritance soon, and that would give them more than enough to live on for years to come. It was exciting to think *Seas the Day* was almost ready and that Alice would soon be sailing around the Mediterranean in her.

The sound of Roger's whistle interrupted her thoughts, and Alice span around to see why he'd blown it. Her eyes scanned the surface of the water, and she could see a big ripple of wind thundering down the harbour. As the wind hit each little Pico, they were being tipped over into the water, all being pulled down.

She quickly let go of the sail rope so her sail went slack, and she pulled hard on the rudder, her boat facing into the wind. Other students near her were doing the same with their boats, but one by one the freak wind hit them, and they all capsized. Roger was already darting across the harbour, helping the capsized students. Alice couldn't help but grin with nerves, knowing she was going over and glad she was wearing her wetsuit. It wasn't the first time she'd gone into the harbour water and probably wouldn't be the last.

The wind hit, and for half a second she thought she would be the only one to stay upright, but then the Pico mast span down like a clock being wound backwards. She was tossed into the water and sank downwards.

It was a summer's day, but the water was shockingly cold. Alice felt herself falling downwards for a moment, and then she kicked her legs and began to push back to the surface, helped by her lifejacket. She was about to break the surface when something stopped her from coming out of the water. One of the boat's ropes had become wrapped around her neck. Panic flooded through her.

She kicked harder. The rope pulled tighter on her neck, but she managed to break the surface. To her horror she immediately felt a pressure pushing her back under. The bright yellow sail was right above her, covering the surface. She couldn't get a breath of air.

The rope pulled her back into the water, and the life-jacket fought to push her up, which caused the rope to tighten further. Her hands pulled frantically at the rope, trying to relieve the tightness on her throat. Oh, God, she was going to drown? *You can drown in an inch of water* popped into her head. She struggled and fought under the water. Her lungs started to burn. She needed air.

Roger, she thought, with an urgent clarity. Would he come and save her? She needed his big arms to come and pull her out of the blackness.

Alice kicked her legs hard, trying to break free, but each time the rope tightened. She was close to blacking out. She hadn't had time to get a proper lungful of air. Stars peppered her eyes, shut tight in fear. She tried to calm down, tried to think. Her body was shaking with the cold and adrenaline coursing through her.

Swimming upwards was choking her. So she needed to go down. It was strange how silent the world underwater was, when inside she was full of screaming panic.

Alice stopped kicking. Instead, she used her arms to swim downwards against the force of the lifejacket. Let herself sink. She had a few seconds before everything went black. As her body sank, the rope loosened. She had to battle against the instinct to rush and yank at the rope, which was killing her; instead she worked methodically and with jittering hands untied the knots.

The rope came free, and she looped it off her throat.

Alice broke the surface again and used both her hands to push upwards, forcefully making some space for her head under the sail. The sail moved, caught in a breath of wind, and she was free. She gasped and gasped, sucking in air and feeling the warm relief of the sun on her face. As the oxygen filled her body, Alice realised just how close she'd just come to drowning.

A calm mind and a careful movement had kept her alive.

Across the harbour Roger had righted about half of the boats; as she had been the furthest ahead, she was going to be the last to be rescued. Her arms splashed and pulled through the water as she swam around to the other side of the boat. Alice reached up out of the water and took hold of the edge of the boat and began to pull it down. The adrenaline she was filled with made it light work, and her arms felt powerful. The boat creaked and pulled upwards. With the last of her strength, Alice heaved herself up, collapsing into the boat.

She took the rope, the rope that had almost killed her, in her right hand and the tiller in her left hand. The strong gust of wind had passed, and now she took control of the boat so that it shot off across the harbour again. After a few minutes she heard Roger's boat chug up alongside her.

"All okay?" he called over.

She grinned at him. "Yes."

"Freak gust of wind, pretty rare, but they do happen."

She gave him a thumbs-up and turned back to watch her sail, glad he hadn't noticed the tears in her eyes.

ALICE AND RICHARD had developed two Sunday traditions over the last few months. One was Alice's morning sailing lesson. The other was going for a nice roast lunch in the local pub, where they would talk through what she had learned and their plans for sailing south on their own boat.

As she drove along the M32 in her Mini Cooper, the engine sounded like it was in pain, but the plan was for the car to be scrapped when they left Bristol the following week, so she was driving it with her fingers crossed that it wouldn't break down before then. Her hair was still wet, and she couldn't wait to take off her wetsuit from under her big beach coat and get into a hot shower. She'd also worked up a proper appetite and had already decided she was going to have the beef for lunch. She was debating whether she could face talking to Richard over lunch or if she'd be eating in silence. They needed to talk, but since Sally's visit yesterday, they hadn't really had the chance.

Alice arrived back in Winterbourne and parked on the drive.

She walked through the front door. "I'm home."

"Hi," Richard called from the kitchen.

"I got wet," she told him, walking into the kitchen.

"Is that my cue to get the kettle on?" he asked, with his back to her.

"You wouldn't believe what happened; this freak gust of wind hit the harbour and..."

He turned to face her, and she immediately stopped talking.

She gasped.

"What happened?"

His face was a mess. He had a large plaster covering his nose, and blood had seeped through it. His eyes were puffed up and half closed; they looked ready to turn into two big black eyes.

"Oh, right. My face. I fell down the stairs."

"The stairs?"

"Yes, I wasn't concentrating when I got up this morning and flew head first down them."

"No...the stairs? You look like you've been mugged."

He coloured at this and turned back to the kettle.

"I'm fine. Do you want tea or coffee?"

"You should go to the hospital, Richard. It looks really painful," she said as she stepped towards him. "Are you okay?"

"Yes, yes, I'm fine. There's no need for a hospital. What will they do, anyway? I've taken some painkillers, tidied myself up."

"Check for concussion. God, your nose looks broken; they could scan that too?"

"Don't fuss. It looks worse than it is." He turned back to the kettle. "Well, at least I don't have to go to work in the morning," he joked.

She studied his back.

"The stairs? How did you manage that?"

"Still drunk from all those beers with Freddie at the White Horse last night. Do you mind if we don't go out for lunch? I think I need a lazy day around the house."

"You need a day in the hospital."

He shrugged, obviously not up for discussing it. Alice didn't believe him, but she didn't want to call him a liar either. She hovered in the doorway, for a moment unsure what to do.

"We don't need to go out," she said after a moment's silence. "I'll make us some lunch instead. Just need a shower first."

"So, what happened at the harbour? Freak gust of wind?"

She would like to have told him, she needed to share the experience with someone, but the moment had passed.

"I'll tell you later."

She left him and went upstairs. It felt good to pull off the wetsuit and get into the shower. The warmth was magical after her unplanned swim in the harbour. As she let the hot water cascade over her head, she thought about Richard. She thought about the state of his face, then the boat and their plan to sail south. Tears started again, and she turned her face into the spray, letting it wash them away.

After the shower, Alice dressed and dried her hair. There was leftover cottage pie in the freezer, and she put it in the microwave to heat up. Through the kitchen she could see into the lounge; Richard's feet were visible from the end of the sofa where he lay. There was a hole in his sock, and she could hear him snoring.

When they had first met, Alice had been twenty-six years old, working as a lab assistant at Bristol University. She'd been there for four years but had never intended to work at the university. Alice had graduated from Bath Spa with a degree in biology and had gotten a job at a florist's. She loved that job, it was a nice place to work, and it fed her obsession with flowers, but she always had a nagging sense of guilt at not using her degree to build herself a career. When she'd seen the job advertised to work in floral biology, she'd jumped at the chance, and after several interviews, she'd secured the job. She had rightly assumed it would be more demanding than being at the florist's, but it was also more rewarding and better paid.

Alice had enjoyed the work, although it had always seemed like a steppingstone role to move into something else. Until October 2000. Until Professor Richard Barnes had arrived in her life.

She'd been in the midst of a demonstration with a small group of students. As the lab technician, she supported the lecturers and the department as a whole, but she also did some teaching, which she didn't mind, as the groups were always small in number and the students very attentive.

They were in one of the laboratories, and Alice had half a dozen students around her bench as she was dissecting a flower.

"As you know, with the plant's reproductive part, a flower contains a pistil, which is the female part and" – the door opened and in he walked; tall, dark haired and handsome, so hot he looked like he could set the room on fire – "and the stamen," she continued, trying to ignore him, "which is the male part."

He hung around at the back of the lab, leaning on a workbench, politely listening to her. Even from across the room she could see his green eyes, which seemed luminous in the gloomy space.

"So today we will look in more detail at the process of pollination. In the male organ, the stamen, there is the pollen," Alice said as she pointed to the dissected flower in front of her, "and the pollen needs to be moved to the female pistil, to the stigma part. Once pollen reaches here, it travels to the ovary and...and..." Her mind went blank! She had delivered this little demonstration over a dozen times, but in the moment her mind was completely dark.

"It travels to the ovary..."

The students looked at her, patient and attentive. She could feel the heat rising up her neck and face.

"It fertilises the egg," Richard called over.

Alice and the students all looked at him, and he gave them a big bright smile.

"Sorry to interrupt." He winked at her.

Alice felt her knees go weak. No! Was that a thing? Did that really happen? But as he smiled at her, she felt the need to lean on the workbench.

"Sorry, my mind went blank."

The students looked back to her.

"You're doing a great job," he added with a smile, "just perfect."

After that, the lesson was a struggle. She rushed through the topics, and the students had to work quickly to keep up with her as she blurted out the facts they needed to know.

Finally, she finished and sent them on their way with some further reading and homework.

"I'm Richard Barnes; nice to meet you," he introduced himself once the last student had left the laboratory.

"Oh, you're Professor Barnes? I was expecting someone older...I mean someone not so young...not so..."

He didn't seem to notice her swooning.

"You have a great way with the students; no wonder the grades are so good."

"Oh, I'm just the teaching technician. Dr Lewis is the lecturer for this module."

He leaned in closer, and she would later tell her friends that she could actually feel heat radiating from him. He smelled of eau de toilet, which Alice had always thought was vain on a man, but in that moment, she thought how well it suited him.

"It's a team effort though, isn't it? We each have our part to play."

"Yes," was all she could manage.

The following few weeks were a blur as Richard took over the department. Flowers were her passion, and it was amazing to discover Richard had the same love for the world of plants and flowers as she did. What a time it had been! They had started working together and became closer and closer. And, although the thought made her feel unsteady, made the world tip off balance, she realised she loved him.

And then it happened.

One evening they were finishing off the preparation of some lessons on bees when he turned to her.

"Alice," he said, giving her a coy look as he closed the laptop, "I was wondering if I could take you to dinner?"

"Oh..." she replied.

His face fell, like a sad puppy. "But if you have plans..."

"No!" she yelled, at a volume that startled both of them. She swallowed, embarrassed. "I mean, no, I don't have any plans, and yes, it would be nice to go for dinner."

That night was the best of her life. It rained, and they had to try two restaurants before they could find a table, but eventually they managed to track down an Italian bistro that was quiet. They ate pasta and salad and drank white wine, they shared a dark chocolate torte, and their eyes never left each other. At the end of the evening, he took her in his arms and kissed her. Alice hadn't realised that life could be so amazing, so utterly magical!

The frozen cottage pie pinged in the microwave, breaking her reverie, and she laid the dining table with cutlery and glasses of water.

"Lunch is ready," she called into the lounge.

Richard got up and lumbered into the dining room with his eyes half closed and his hair a mess. He was unsteady on his feet and sat heavily onto one of the chairs. They both began eating, and Alice found that she couldn't stop staring at his face. It looked battered. What had really happened? she wondered. She knew he would never tell her, and she didn't have the energy to question him.

Despite the bad view across the dining table, the hot food was delicious and just what she needed after her morning dunk.

"As I was saying earlier," Alice said, trying to carry on as normal, "a freak wind came down the harbour and capsized all the boats. I ended up in the water with the rope caught around my neck, and I was trapped under the sail. I couldn't breathe."

"Sounds rough."

He looked unenthused, as usual. It was at moments like this that she really missed her mum, who would always be very sympathetic to Alice. She wanted to share the terror that she'd felt, explain to Richard how scary it had been, but she knew he wouldn't care. Instead, Alice pictured herself leaning across and flicking his plastered nose to see what sort of reaction that would get. She couldn't help but smile at the thought.

He caught her strange smile. "What?" he asked.

Her face dropped. "Nothing."

He cleared his throat.

"I was thinking of seeing Sally tomorrow."

"Your daughter?"

"Yes, I've been thinking about it. We'll be off on our boat soon, so I might try to see her a few times before we leave."

She watched him closely as he spoke.

"Obviously you should come with me. It would be good for us to get to know her a little."

"Sure." Alice nodded. "So you think she's right, she really is your daughter, then?"

He seemed surprised by the question. "Yes. But I've ordered a DNA test online, and I'm going to take it tomorrow."

"What about the mum...your ex-partner, Julie." Alice's thumbs pushed into the cutlery so hard her fingers turned white. "Maybe you should try to contact her, even if she's in America. I'm sure you could email her."

Richard seemed pleased by this suggestion, and for the first time that day he visibly perked up.

"That's a great idea. We should check with Sally first, but there must be a way to contact her."

"I still don't think it's sunk in," Alice said, watching his face for a reaction. "You have a daughter."

"I know. But having a hangover and banging my head on the stairs isn't the best state to try to think things through. Think it's going to take me a while to digest."

"And to think," Alice said lightly, "you were never sure about having kids."

He looked up from his plate and met her eyes.

"Well, if I'm her dad, then you're her stepmum. Maybe we could get to know her a bit more. There's no reason why she couldn't become part of our lives."

Instead of flicking his nose, Alice wondered how he would react if she leaned over and punched it instead. He would shout in pain, no doubt. She had never hit anyone before, but in that moment the urge to do it was huge. It was so strong, Alice had to put her cutlery down and clasp her hands together in her lap. She took a deep breath.

"Yes, dear, that sounds nice."

4

TWO YEARS AGO

*A*lice drove down Coronation Road in Southville, Bristol, and turned right and then right again until she arrived in Raleigh Road, where she managed to find a parking space near to her mum's house.

Having parked, she got out and grabbed a bag of gifts, locked the car and walked to her childhood home. Alice rang the doorbell, and in an instant her mum was there to greet her with a big hug and smile.

"The great traveller returns!"

"Hi, Mum."

Her mum ushered her inside. "Come in, come in."

Alice went into the lounge and was flooded with a dozen memories; it was always the same when she went back home. The family had moved there when she was only three years old, and until she left for university, it was the only home Alice had known. There was the same striped sofa and matching armchair, the same oak bookcase holding the same old cookbooks and the same chipped oak coffee table. Fortunately, her mum had managed to get a new flat-screen TV, and the curtains around the big bay window were new too, but otherwise the lounge was the same as when Alice was a child.

"Tell me all about it, then; did you eat kangaroo?"

Alice laughed. "No, Mum, the food in Australia was lovely, a lot of fish, no kangaroos."

Her mum was short with curly grey hair. She was wearing her favourite burgundy jumper, grey skirt and fluffy slippers. Even now, Alice marvelled at how happy and warm her smiles were, and how she was always smiling. People always commented on the warmth of Alice's smile; she had definitely inherited it from her mum.

"Crocodile, then, was it?"

Alice laughed again. "Tuna, Mum, and a lot of big prawns. Here," Alice said as she opened the bag she was carrying, "I brought you some bits back."

From the bag she pulled out a plush brown koala bear and gave it to her mum.

"Oh, he's lovely." Her mum took the toy and gave it a cuddle. "Very cute."

"And this," Alice added as she pulled out a wooden boomerang from the bag.

"What am I going to do with that?"

"Take it to the local park and throw it!" They both laughed, and Alice's mum gave her another hug.

"You are daft," her mum said, full of love. "Well, maybe it will make a nice ornament."

Her mum took the boomerang and placed it on the bookshelf. "There, see, that's lovely."

"And, of course, I got you a flower." Alice brought out a paperback book and opened it. Inside there was a single pressed pink flower with a dark red centre. "Gossypium sturtianum. You can only really find them in Australia."

Her mum carefully took the book and admired the desert rose held inside the pages. "Oh, it's lovely, thank you, Alice."

Alice watched her mum admire the flower and give it a little sniff.

"You need to crush it to really get the scent from it, unfortunately."

"Well, it's too pretty to crush!"

"I know."

Her mum gently closed the book and placed it on the bookshelf. Alice brought her mum pressed flowers from every trip she'd ever taken. It was a tradition going back years, and dozens of the books on the bookshelf contained rare and sometimes exotic flowers that Alice had brought back. Of course, she'd had to fill in some import paperwork on each flower, but she didn't like to bore her mum with the tedious details.

"Did the teaching go okay?"

Alice sat on the striped sofa. "Really well. Richard was great as usual, and out of the four weeks we were there, he was only guest lecturer for a dozen lessons, so it gave us loads of free time." Alice took her phone from her pocket and opened a few photos. "You should see Sydney University, Mum; it's stunning."

Her mum had a pair of glasses on a cord around her neck, and she put them on to look at the phone. "Oh, that is nice," she said. "It looks like Clifton College. How strange, the other side of the world and it looks like here."

"It's a totally different place though, and the people were so great."

"And did you get to do any teaching there?"

"Mum, I've told you a thousand times, I'm a lab technician, not a lecturer. I was there to help and support Richard. Although I did do a few demonstrations, which were fun."

"With your brains, you could teach them all about flowers and plants."

Alice just smiled, it was a conversation they'd had a hundred times over the years, and she knew her mum was just thinking of her. But the truth was, Alice was happy enough being a lab technician and didn't want to be a lecturer, however much her mum tried to push her into it. Besides, she did take lessons and do student demonstrations. For some reason, her mum thought that until Alice had the job title of lecturer, she wasn't doing any teaching.

"Anyway, we had loads of free time, so we managed to see a lot of Sydney. One day we did a boat trip around the coast; it was so magical."

"Oh, I'm pleased for you."

"How about a cuppa, Mum?"

"Of course, sorry."

They went into the kitchen, and Alice sat at the small dining table, which was set against one wall. It was the same table where she'd eaten a thousand meals. Her mum filled the kettle and set out two cups on the counter. One of the cups said "World's Best Mum" in pink letters. Alice had bought it for her mum when she was a child.

"Some of the restaurants there are just unbelievable; we went to one that overlooked the harbour; it's just so...bright, blue and sunny."

"Hmmm."

"And the tuna, Mum, it's not like here, out of a little tin. I had a huge slab of it; it was so delicious."

The kettle boiled, and her mum stared at it.

"And we saw the Opera House, I've taken loads of photos of it, but I'll probably only get a few of them developed. Richard said *we should get one of the two of us blown up and put in the lounge, as a memento..."*

Alice stared at her mum's back. She was statue still.

"You okay, Mum?"

"Yes, dear, I'm just..."

"Do you want a hand with the tea?"

"Ummm..."

Looking back, it was at that moment, in that silence, that Alice sensed something was wrong. Neither of them spoke or moved. It was a silence she would dream about for months to come. In reality it was a sunny day, but in her dreams it would always be raining, the rain tap-tapping against the kitchen window.

Alice got up and went to her mum.

The kettle was boiled, the cups were laid out, but her mum had forgotten how to make the tea.

"The teabags are right here," Alice said, opening the box on the counter and putting a teabag in each cup. She looked at her mum, who seemed flustered. There was no smile from her mum now, just a confused frown.

A sinking feeling hit Alice's stomach.

Alice carefully poured the boiling water from the kettle into each cup, took a spoon, drained and binned the teabags and stirred the tea.

"See, all done."

Her mum's face was flushed with embarrassment.

They sat at the dining table. Her mum held on tightly to her "World's Best Mum" cup. Alice continued to talk about her Australian trip, and her mum's smile returned. As they chatted and drank their tea, Alice watched her mum closely. Mostly she was attentive, but there was a moment when the confusion came back, and for several seconds she stared at Alice blankly, as if she didn't recognise her, although that sensation quickly passed. After an hour of talking, Alice got up.

"Well, I've got to go, Mum. I'll pop back in during the week."

"Okay, dear, thanks again for the gifts."

They hugged, and Alice left. She walked back to the car and sat in the driver's seat. She put the key in the ignition but didn't turn the engine on. She sat there feeling unnerved by her mum's confusion and what it could mean.

As she finally drove away, Alice felt the tears streaming silently down her face.

5

SIX DAYS TO GO

The head was huge, the teeth vicious, and the eye sockets deep black holes. Alice stared up into the dinosaur skull and thought of the power of the bite, the force to take something and rip it to shreds.

"The café is downstairs," Richard said behind her.

She turned to him. "Okay."

"Let's go now; we can get a table and a drink."

She followed him through Cardiff museum's wide corridors. They passed artworks and various exhibitions, from glowing replica volcanoes to hundreds of models of fish. The old building was in the city centre, near Cardiff University. The university where Richard had worked and where he and Sally's mother had met.

They took the stairs down to the basement and found the museum café. It was completely empty apart from a young woman at the counter. Alice took a tray, picked up a plate of Welsh cakes and ordered a tea for herself and a coffee for Richard. They sat at a table with four chairs, set against one of the walls. The walls were a deep red, which was in keeping with the Welsh theme, but as there was no natural light in the basement, it made the café feel closed in, even with the various spotlights around the place.

Richard took some painkillers from his pocket and swallowed two tablets with his coffee. His face still looked terrible, the bruising had started to come out, and the skin around both eyes was now turning a deep purple, although he'd put on some of Alice's makeup to hide the worst of it. But there was nothing he could do to hide the nose; he had put on a fresh plaster, which looked better, but the cut over his nose was still very red and swollen.

"Before Sally arrives, there's something I want to tell you," Richard said.

Alice sat up. "Yes?"

"I managed to find Julie Long, Sally's mother. She's lecturing in America now, and I found an email address for her online."

Alice sat back and folded her arms across her chest. "Okay."

"I emailed her. Asked her to explain about Sally and asked her why she hadn't gone through with the abortion."

"Did she reply?"

Richard nodded.

"What did she say?"

He pulled his phone from his jeans pocket, tapped the screen and handed it over to Alice. "Have a read."

Alice took the phone and studied the email from Julie. She read it, her finger scrolling steadily downwards. The email was lengthy and apologetic. Julie explained that she had felt unable to go through with the abortion and instead had decided to leave Cardiff and have the baby. But as the pregnancy advanced, Julie realised she really wasn't ready to be a mum, so had given Sally up for adoption. Julie had planned to tell Richard, but after he'd left for Bristol, she'd struggled to bring herself to talk to him. It was a hugely sad story to read on a small phone screen.

Alice wasn't sure what to say.

"Sorry, I should have told you I'd been in touch with Julie," he said.

Alice nibbled at a Welsh cake, eyes down.

The café door opened, and they both turned to see Sally walk in, dressed in a blue nurse's uniform. She waved to them before heading to the counter to order a drink, her blonde hair bouncing around her as she walked. She brought her cup of coffee over to their table and sat down.

"Hiya," she said. Her Welsh accent felt at home with the red dragon painted on the far wall.

"Hi, Sally," Richard said, awkwardly shaking her hand.

She looked shocked at Richard's bruised face. "Are you okay?"

"Fine, just fell down the stairs after too many beers."

"Hi," Alice said, also taking Sally's hand to shake.

It was hot to the touch.

Sally smiled at Alice before turning back to Richard with a frown of concern. "Have you had it looked at?"

"No, but it's fine, really. How was work?" Richard asked.

"Oh, fine, I was on the night shift, just finished. We had three babies delivered on the ward."

"That must be an amazing experience. I can't imagine delivering a baby, let alone doing it every day." Richard looked from Sally to Alice and smiled to Alice, as if to encourage her to join in with his admiration.

Alice smiled politely but didn't speak. She didn't know what a midwife did during the birth of a baby because she'd never been in a maternity ward. She'd never had the need to.

"Yes, it's a privilege to be a part of people's lives in that way. I've even had a few babies named after me," Sally replied. "If you don't mind, I would love to know what you do and a bit about your life. I suppose I had a lot to tell you when we met a few days ago, but afterwards I was kicking myself for not asking more about you."

Alice saw Richard smile and knew he would be happy to talk about himself all afternoon.

"Funnily enough, I've just retired. I was a professor at Bristol University, the head of the biology department. I've been working there for almost twenty years."

Sally tilted her head at him. "I guess biology and nursing are related."

He laughed, and she laughed back. Alice watched them both together; unable to fake a laugh to join in, her smile was starting to hurt.

Alice remembered watching a documentary about prisons once, where young men would put sugar into their boiling hot drinks to use them as weapons by throwing them at one another's faces. Something about the sugar in the water caused terrible damage, perhaps by sticking to the skin. On the table there was a little pot of sugar sachets, Alice never had sugar in her drinks, but at that moment she thought about pouring the sachet into her hot tea.

"Well, I'm originally from Dorset, but moved around a lot for work. A few years in Birmingham, a few in Cardiff" – he paused – "where I met your mother, and I've been living in Bristol for over twenty years now."

"Do you, ummm, do we still have family in Dorset?"

The word *we* made Alice blink several times.

"Both my parents passed away a few years ago. I have a brother, Stephen, who's a solicitor in Bristol, although I don't see him much." He shrugged. "We're not that close."

"I see."

"My dad was called Eric," he continued. "I guess that would be your grandfather; he was a scientist too."

Alice could see how Sally was hanging on every word.

"I have a few cousins still living down in Dorset, but I haven't spoken to them in a while. Otherwise not much family," he said as he turned to Alice with a smile. "Just me and Alice."

But Sally ignored Alice and kept her attention on Richard.

"What about your mum, what was she like?"

"Oh lovely, she was a real homemaker like much of that generation. Baked amazing cakes, always singing in the kitchen. She loved my dad, would do anything for her family."

Sally's eyes began to fill up with tears. "It's so nice to hear about them. To know I had real grandparents."

Richard reached across to put a hand tentatively on her shoulder. "Sorry, I didn't mean to upset you."

Alice almost flinched. When was the last time Richard had comforted her? He hadn't even reacted when she told him she'd nearly drowned at the harbour the day before. Alice picked up the sachet of sugar from the edge of her cup and squeezed it between her fingers.

"Don't worry, they're happy tears." Sally beamed at him.

"Listen, while we're talking about family..." He hesitated. "This is a bit awkward, but would you mind doing a DNA test?" Richard pulled out a small blue box from his pocket and placed it on the table.

Alice watched Sally like a hawk, her eyes glued to her to see how she would react.

Sally smiled and nodded. "Of course. To be honest, I was going to suggest it myself, for peace of mind."

Was she really? wondered Alice.

Alice watched as Richard reached into a bag at his feet and took out some cleaning cloths and wiped the table. Then he squeezed some sanitiser into his and Sally's hands, and they simultaneously rubbed their hands. Next Richard brought out two pairs of medical gloves; he handed one pair to Sally and pulled the others on himself. Finally, he pulled out the box that contained the DNA test.

Richard opened the box and pulled out two wrapped swabs. He handed one to Sally. "You need to swab the inside of your mouth and then seal it in this envelope."

Sally took the swab and did as she was instructed; it was opened; she swabbed her mouth and placed the used swab in a thin envelope. Richard did the same.

"I will get these posted," Richard said, putting both envelopes back into the box, "and the result should come back in a few days."

They both pulled off their blue medical gloves.

"Oh, the swab's left a funny taste in my mouth," Sally said.

Richard ate some Welsh cake and sipped his coffee. "Welsh cakes might help," he suggested as he pushed the plate to Sally.

"Well, I don't need an excuse to eat a Welsh cake," she said.

He laughed, and she beamed at him again, still pretty even with a mouthful of cake. Alice watched them acting like a happy family. A happy little family. The plate was empty now, and there were no more Welsh cakes for Alice.

"You should tell Sally about our trip," Alice said.

"Yes, right." Richard wiped his mouth with a napkin. "We wanted to let you know that we are actually leaving Bristol and England in a week's time. We're going to be sailing the Mediterranean for the next few years." He turned to Alice. "Just the two of us."

"That sounds incredible; what a great way to spend your retirement! I'd love to do something like that."

Sally seemed genuinely pleased for them, but all Alice wanted to do was slap her and tell her to shove her support up her arse. The force of the thought sent a shudder down her; she'd never felt so aggressive towards someone before. If there was a spider in the house, Alice would gently collect it in a cup and set it free in the garden. She'd never physically hurt anyone or anything in her life, yet here she was, fantasising about hitting Sally.

"We have a boat, *Seas the Day*, that's being repaired down in Bristol harbour. It's almost ready, and then we're off."

Alice could suddenly imagine sailing into Barcelona on a hot summer's day; she could almost taste the salt in the air and feel the momentum of the boat rushing forwards. She wished she were there now.

"You must be good sailors to be able to do that."

"I love sailing. I've been sailing since I was a child," Richard told Sally. "I could sail any boat with my eyes closed. And Alice has been having lessons too; she's quite the little sailor now."

As Sally looked at her, Alice could sense Sally's smile dropping a little as their eyes met. Alice was certain Sally's eyes were colder when looking at her, or was her mind playing tricks?

"Although she had a close call yesterday, didn't you, darling?"

They both looked at Alice expectantly.

"I had my final sailing lesson yesterday, and we got caught in some wind; all the boats capsized. Luckily it was a warm day, so at least the water didn't feel too cold. Although, I was looking forward to a hot shower afterwards. That said, it was a bit of a shock to come home and see Richard so badly beaten up."

He blushed. "I wasn't beaten up..."

"Oh, I know, darling, it's just a turn of phrase. I meant your face looks so beaten."

Sally looked at Richard. "Well, I think you still look distinguished."

He smiled at her. "Thank you."

Alice opened the sachet of sugar and poured it into her hot tea.

"But I still think you should have it looked at," Sally said. "With a broken nose you want to make sure it's set correctly; otherwise it might heal out of shape."

Richard grinned. "And I certainly don't want that! Okay, I'll swing by the hospital this afternoon."

Alice laughed; the sound was eerie in the empty basement café. She had been advising Richard to go to the hospital since yesterday, but one word from Sally and he had agreed to go. Alice stood up.

"I just need to stretch my legs."

Alice walked out of the café, up the stairs, through the huge lobby and out the revolving doors at the museum's front entrance. The sun hit her face, and she took in long, shaky breaths of fresh air. Slowly, ever so slowly, she thought she was going mad.

SEAS THE DAY was a thirty-three-foot single-sail boat. Her sleek white hull had been built by the prestigious Nimbus boat builders in Sweden; her engine was a Volvo. As Alice and Richard walked down the harbour slipway, they couldn't help but admire her beauty. She was floating alongside several smaller boats, which only emphasised her elegance and style.

"She's coming along nicely," Alan called to them as his head popped up from the interior.

"Are we okay to come aboard?" Richard asked.

Alan grinned at them, showing nicotine-stained teeth. "Of course, mate, she's your boat."

Richard walked up the small steps and onto the hull before turning to watch Alice walk unsteadily up the small steps behind him. She stepped aboard and felt a gentle rocking under her feet. Despite the last few days, she felt a thrill at being there. Richard had been into sailing for years, while it had held little interest for her, but since he'd told her of his idea of them both sailing away together, she had grown more and more interested.

As well as her lessons with Roger on the Pico, she'd also had several lessons with a company who took out thirty-foot sailboats. In addition, she'd done a one-day CB radio course and a two-day sea safety course down in Devon. Putting all that together, Alice was now excited to take their boat out of the harbour and onto the sea. The only part of the journey that still worried her was crossing the English Channel and heading into the Atlantic. In total, it was over sixty miles of open sea, not for the faint-hearted.

"Plumber has finished the new bathroom, if you want to have a look," Alan said.

He was wearing tattered blue overalls and a baseball cap. The cap said "Damn Seagulls" on it and had a white stain across the side. Alice was never sure if the stain was part of the design, or if a seagull really had managed to hit it with its droppings.

"Great," Richard replied as he and Alan went down into the body of the boat.

Alice stayed on the deck. Her hands rested on the wheel, and she could just imagine steering through the waves, letting the huge sail pull the boat along in the wind. Could she do it? Could she leave her home and sail out into the world? Her whole life had been safe, an organised routine. She had spent twenty-six years working Monday to Friday. Friday after work she had a bottle of white wine; weekends were for meals with friends and day trips with Richard. They had their favourite restaurants, favourite dishes served there. She liked making lists. Loved her garden and flowers. Gym twice a week. Bed by ten every night. Two holidays a year. Routine. There was safety and comfort in routine. Was she ready to give it all up and sail around Europe? At this stage, did she have any choice?

From below her feet came the muffled sound of Richard opening and closing doors as he checked the boat.

Alice looked around the harbour. There were plenty of people walking along the pathways, enjoying the views across the water. Further down from the boatyard was the sailing school. Just as she was wondering if Roger was working today, he suddenly appeared. Alice could see him in the distance; she could make out his tall frame as he started to unload a boat.

She couldn't help but lean on the steering wheel and sigh as she watched him. Even from here, she could see that he was moving with a relaxed confidence that was mesmerising to watch.

"Roger's a nice guy," Alan said quietly behind her.

Alice jumped in shock; she'd thought she was alone on the deck. She turned to Alan, who was busy rolling a cigarette.

"Oh?" was all she could manage, her face turning a bright red.

"Really nice chap; he's a widower, you know."

"I didn't...I'm not..." she stuttered like a flustered schoolgirl.

Alan seemed to sense her discomfort and gave her a little wink before he went back down to join Richard in the cabin of the boat. She exhaled deeply before she followed Alan below deck. It was darker out of the sun, and it took her eyes a moment to adjust.

"When does the new cooker arrive?" Richard asked Alan.

"Tomorrow, supposed to be."

"And then the kitchen is finished?"

"All done, same as the bathroom. Last thing is to get the GPS system installed; fitter should be here in the next few days. Are you still planning to leave in about a week's time?"

"Yes, obviously weather dependent," Richard said.

"Forecast is looking good all week, so you should be fine. And the boat will be done in four or five days, I reckon." Alan grinned at them. "Exciting times! Got to say it's brave of you to sail off like that."

Alice listened to them talk, her heart still beating fast after Alan's comments about Roger.

"It's been my dream for years," Richard said.

"I'm jealous; will be lovely down along the south coast. Bet you've been saving your money for a long while to do it?"

"Actually," Alice said, "my mum passed away six months ago, and we're using the inheritance money to fund the trip. Plus, our savings."

"Oh," Alan said kindly, "I'm sorry to hear about your mum."

Richard turned to Alice. "Not long now. The boat's looking great, isn't it?"

He was right, Alan and his team had done an amazing job. Alice loved how everything was so neat. Every glossy walnut surface served a purpose, whether it was a hidden cupboard, or a curved edge to stop things rolling away as they were sailing.

"A great job, Alan, thank you so much; it's all looking wonderful."

"Well, glad you're pleased. You've got yourselves a beauty here; should last for many years. Now we're done, I'll get the office to send you the bill."

Richard turned to him with a big smile. "Yes, please, Alan."

6

FIVE DAYS TO GO

"**A**ggh!"

Richard jumped back and banged his elbow on the shed doorframe. He frantically waved his hand, and the spider flew off, scuttling away to the back of the shed. He stamped downwards and squashed it, creating a little ball of yellow goo on the floor.

"Bloody spiders," he said for the fifth time that morning.

He rubbed his elbow and willed the pain away. God, he felt awful. It was so hot, and his eyes stung with hay fever, even though he'd taken his medication. He couldn't wait to be on the boat and away from all the chores and stress that seemed to be following him around recently. With one arm he yanked the lawn mower free and wheeled it to one side of the shed. If all went to plan, he would never need to mow a lawn again; it was a nice thought.

Finally, from the back of the shed, he pulled out two old blue deckchairs and threw them into the rubbish pile that he'd been building up on the side of the house. It was stuff he needed to take to the local tip: old garden furniture, a cheap inflatable paddling pool they'd never used, bits of wood and scraps of old carpet.

Richard picked up his broom and swept dirt, dust and cobwebs into the corner of the shed; there was no dustpan and brush handy, and he couldn't be bothered to search for one, so he left the pile where it was.

"Hello?"

He groaned.

"Hello?"

Richard stepped out from the now empty shed and spied the old lady peering through the broken fence panel. He could just make out her wrinkled face and grey eyes through the gap.

Richard sneezed and wondered how many antihistamines you could take before you overdosed.

"Hello, Mrs Mabel," he greeted her.

"Any news on the new fencing being put up?"

He sighed again.

"Because it's on your side where the tree hit it. You're responsible for getting it fixed."

"Well, as I've told you before..."

"The longer you leave it, the worse the damage will get."

She had one of those voices that seemed to drill into his skull. In all the years Mrs Mabel had lived next door, he couldn't remember her ever saying anything nice to them.

"It's the landlord's responsibility to –" he began.

"Oh, no, no. You live here; it's you who should get it fixed."

Her gnarled old face was a terrifying sight through the broken fence panel; she was like an old witch haunting them.

If he owned the house, he would of course spend money

on it and invest in the property. But it was only a rental, and there was no way Richard would waste his money on repairs. At the back of his mind there was bitterness; he didn't own his own house. This bloody old woman always seemed to remind him of that, and it intensified his natural dislike of her.

For a moment, he was tempted to swing his fist into the gap in the fence and give her something to really moan about. The problem was Mrs Mabel must have been over ninety years old and probably couldn't take a good punch. Richard chuckled at the thought.

"Fencing is no laughing matter, young man."

This made him laugh harder until he was in fits of deep laughter that echoed around the small garden. Mrs Mabel continued to talk, but he couldn't hear her. It was a baking hot day, and Richard decided he'd had enough, so he dropped the broom, ignored Mrs Mabel's ranting and walked back into the house.

In the kitchen, Alice was clearing out bottles of cleaning equipment from under the sink.

"It's too hot out there. I'm going to check my emails," he told her as he walked up the stairs to his office.

"Okay," she called to him from the cupboard.

ALICE FINISHED EMPTYING the cupboard under the sink and went out to the now peaceful garden. She peered at the pile of things by the side of the house, which were due to go to the rubbish tip. Other items were scattered on the lawn: the mower, a pair of large shears, a table and chairs and a barbecue set. Over the next day or two, their friends were coming to collect them all. Richard had wanted to try to sell everything, but Alice didn't think they would get any money for old, second-hand garden items, so she had offered everything to their friends for free.

Lined up neatly against the back wall were her flower pots, her babies.

She'd already given a lot of her flowers away, but there were still a dozen pots with various flowers and flowering plants in them. There were white and pink roses. Alice stroked the white dahlias she'd managed to grow. Next to them was her gardenia plant; usually found in Asia and hot countries, it had needed so much of her attention. But it had been worth it, not just for the beauty of the flowers, which reminded her of white silken sheets, but the scent was amazing, so unique and not something she'd ever experienced before.

There was her delphinium. The stems were taller than Alice at six feet high, and each stem contained over a hundred florets of the brightest violet and blue tones. This plant was going to her friend Elaine, who she knew would take care of it. Still, it broke her heart to leave so many of her beautiful flowers behind.

"Alice!" Richard called from the upstairs window.

She tore her eyes away from her violet delphiniums and went back into the house.

"You okay?" she called up the stairs.

"Alice!" he called again.

She walked up the stairs, wondering what he wanted; with Richard it could be anything. Alice went into the second bedroom that they used as an office. It was stuffy and hot in the small space, and without thinking about it, she opened the window. The room was full of Richard's stuff:

research papers, copies of his books, his certificates hanging on the walls. Against the far wall was the desk, where Richard was sitting.

She saw he looked pale and worried, his bruised face a sorry sight.

"You won't believe what I've just found online!"

"What?"

He motioned to the laptop on his desk.

"It's about Sally."

"As in your new daughter, that Sally?" It was an effort to keep her voice level.

He nodded, his eyes fixed on the screen.

Alice walked around to the other side of the desk to look at the screen. Being so close to him, she could smell his sweaty body, but she thought it wasn't the right moment to suggest he have a shower. Richard clicked his mouse, and a news article came up.

"Have a look," he said.

"That's Sally," Alice said before reading the title of the article on the news website: "'Hero nurse needs operation for autoimmune hepatitis disease'. Oh, how awful."

"I know. It's shocking," he said, his voice distraught. "You should read the whole thing."

Alice leant her left hand on the desk and took control of the mouse with her right hand as she read. The article told of a maternity nurse at Cardiff hospital who had autoimmune hepatitis, an illness that causes liver inflammation when the body's immune system turns against liver cells. It said Sally needed a liver transplant, but it wasn't a normal procedure because she'd had issues with anti-rejection medications. The only option for Sally was to have the operation in

America, as it wasn't offered in the UK. Alice kept reading.

"It says here Sally has delivered over five hundred babies in her job as a midwife."

"I know! Crazy, isn't it?"

"And she's only got a few years to live if she can't get the transplant!"

"It's so awful."

Alice scrolled up and down the article. It showed several photos of Sally in her nurse's uniform. Alice could see why this might make a good story: a pretty nurse with a rare disease who looked good in her uniform. Although Alice thought the title "Hero Nurse" was a bit much.

"How did you find this? Did she email it to you?"

"God no, I was just doing a little online snooping. She hadn't mentioned it."

"Why wouldn't she tell us?"

Richard shrugged.

Alice could see that Richard had several pages open, and she clicked through each one. He had been searching for further information on autoimmune hepatitis.

"It says here it's not life threatening if treated, which can be done in the UK?"

Richard nodded. "I read that, but the article says she's reacting to the medication. Her body has been rejecting it, so it suddenly becomes a much more complicated procedure."

Alice flicked back to the original news article and reread it. Richard was right; it looked like Sally didn't have long to live unless she was able to have the procedure. Alice tried to decide how she felt about this news; her emotions were more jumbled and messier than a teenager's bedroom floor.

At the bottom of the news story was a paragraph about

Sally's Just Giving page. It explained how she was asking for donations to enable her to have the lifesaving operation abroad. Alice stood up and turned to Richard.

"Will you talk to her about it?"

"Not sure." He hesitated, his face almost crumpling in devastation. "I could, but then we're leaving Bristol and England soon, so I can't be much support to her. Besides, what would I say? I was looking you up online and noticed you're" – his voice wobbled – "noticed you're dying."

"I don't think she wants you to support her necessarily, but maybe you should acknowledge it. I'm sure she would appreciate you talking to her about it."

He looked shaken to the core. He was a man steeped in pain, now not just the battered face, but inside she sensed he was broken. The news had clearly had an impact on him. She found it a pitiful sight and also a little surprising, as he was normally a self-centred person and not one for sentimentality. Clearly, he already felt he had a connection to Sally.

"Maybe you're right."

Richard turned back to the laptop and scanned through the article again, hunched over the screen, deep in thought.

"It's typical, isn't it? I find out I have a daughter and then within a few days learn she could be dead in a year or two. It's all just so sad. She seems like such a nice person."

"She has a Just Giving page there; maybe you should make a donation."

Richard looked up at her, a thoughtful frown on his face as he clicked on the charity's website link.

"Could do, but I bet she's got most of the money she needs. A maternity nurse must have loads of people happy to donate to her."

"Here it is, her donations page." He paused. "Oh no, she still has such a long way to go. Huh, look at this."

Once again, Alice leaned down to read what was on the screen. At the top of the Just Giving page was a picture of Sally, and below was the story from the article about her autoimmune hepatitis. To the right of the screen, it showed she needed £120,000 for the operation. Below that figure it indicated that the total raised so far was only £48,000.

"She still needs so much money, so much help," he said.

Alice put a hand on his shoulder. "That's terrible. I'm sorry she has so far to go."

Richard leaned his head against her; his tears dropped onto her hand as she rubbed his back. He sniffed.

"When I get my big pension pay-out in a few years, I'll be able to give her all the money she needs. But that's still a few years away yet."

"Oh Richard, that's so kind of you. But don't worry, I'm sure she will be okay." She gave his shoulders a squeeze.

"Poor Sally," he whimpered.

"Well, maybe we can make a donation?" she suggested.

He nodded.

"Yes, maybe," was all he said.

Richard stood up and headed for the door. He looked like a man ready to collapse from the weight of the world on his shoulders.

"I need a tissue. Do you want a drink? Tea?"

"I can make it. I'll put the kettle on."

"It's not like we can afford to give her that much anyway," he said, almost to himself, as he left the room.

But Alice could, in the next few days. Alice could afford it, if she wanted to, because she was about to get her mum's inheritance money.

7

FOUR DAYS TO GO

R ichard ran as fast as he could, which for a fifty-six-year-old man wasn't that fast. His legs pumped, and his hands clawed at the air. Despite his heavy breaths, he felt as though he just couldn't get enough air into his lungs. Behind him, the car revved as it got closer.

This was a city! Why was there no one around to help him?

His eyes frantically scanned the street ahead of him, but it was deserted. Richard had been on his way to the university to have lunch with a few old colleagues and collect a couple of books when he had spotted them, the two menacing men who were now chasing him in a black Land Rover.

He was running along the pavement, with a row of parked cars between him and the road. Driving parallel to him was the Land Rover. One of the men was hanging out the passenger window.

"Stop running, you bastard," the man called in a strong Russian accent.

Richard knew he was only making the situation worse, he knew the sensible thing to do was to stop and talk to them, but he couldn't help it. When he had seen them waiting for him, fear had taken over, and he couldn't help but run. He felt like he was running for his life.

He was coming to the end of the street and was about to run out of pavement. Up ahead he could turn left, but because he knew the area well, he knew the next street was marked with double yellow lines, so there would be no cars parked on that street, which meant the black Land Rover chasing him could get close, close enough to smash into him. God, his lungs were in agony.

Richard stopped suddenly, skidding in his slip-on brogues.

He turned and ran in the opposite direction.

The huge car braked heavily, making a loud screeching sound and throwing up a jet of smoke. He heard it coming back down the street after him, only this time in a high-pitched reverse gear.

Sweat covered Richard's face. His legs and back burned. But still he ran onwards. His brown brogues slapped down loudly on the paving stones. Behind him the man called again, but this time the words were lost in the noise of the car's engine.

Now, Richard was heading back towards the restaurant where he had parked his car. It was late morning, and the restaurant was closed, but he could get into his Ford Focus and get the hell out of there.

"Stop," he heard behind him. "STOP!"

No way, he thought.

And then he fell.

The pavement, a classic Bristol one, had been built hundreds of years ago, before tarmac was invented, and it was laid with huge, flat paving stones. Over the years those stones had moved and buckled. As Richard's foot caught the edge of one, it sent him flying through the air. He landed badly, heavily, with his knees and elbows taking the brunt of the fall.

He yelped in pain and shock. And then gasped for air.

Despite the shooting pain in his knees, Richard forced himself to stand up. He could feel fresh blood on his legs and arms. Tears of agony and fear filled his eyes, and he blinked to clear them so he could see where he was going. His car was only twenty metres away.

A heavy hand clamped down on his shoulder, and he turned into the face of the man behind him.

"Why you make me chase you?" Igor said slowly, his Russian accent more pronounced with the quiet tone.

"Well, I was just..." But Richard didn't finish the sentence.

Pain exploded across his midriff as a fist flew into his stomach. He doubled over. He couldn't breathe. Was ready to pass out with the agony drilling into his body.

Igor simply pulled him upright and dragged him into the waiting car.

For a brief moment, Richard was glad to lie down on the Land Rover's back seat and take the weight off his legs. But then Igor got in beside him and whispered in his ear.

"You are so fucked now."

IGOR OWNED a laundrette in the south of the city; he smelled of clean clothes and had a strong scent of fabric softener. His smile was friendly, but his eyes were dark. He was wearing a grey suit with a purple shirt that was unbuttoned around the neck to reveal a hairy chest and a gold chain. It was his hands that would make you realise he wasn't a normal businessman. His hands were huge; they were balls of flesh and bone covered in scars. He wore a ring on every finger, each one different, each one gold.

It was those battered hands that held onto Richard in the back of the car.

The car stopped, and Richard could see they were in the empty car park of an industrial estate. To his left was an old brown building that looked abandoned; to his right stood a row of overgrown evergreen hedges. The car doors were opened, and Richard was dragged out. His legs were throbbing in agony from the fall, and he was struggling to stand.

"This is Josef," Igor said by way of introducing the man who was dragging Richard out of the car.

"Hello," Richard croaked.

"Shut up, idiot," Josef snapped, his accent with the same Eastern European intonation as Igor's.

Richard listened to Igor's footsteps as he came around the car, their sound terrifying him as he grew closer. Igor's shadow fell over Richard, who opened his mouth to speak, but was pushed against the car bonnet before he had a chance. It was hot to the touch, and Richard squirmed against it. He was drenched with sweat, but fear made his teeth chatter, as if he were freezing cold.

"What do we need to do to get through to you?" Igor demanded.

"I'm...I'm close to getting the money –"

Igor grabbed him with his huge hands, pulled him forward and then threw him back onto the bonnet of the black Land Rover.

"Idiot," Josef confirmed.

"The money has nearly come through...my partner, Alice, said it should be any day now."

"My partner Alice, my partner Alice..." Igor imitated Richard.

Josef laughed at the impression, and Igor looked at him, pleased with himself. An instant later they remembered Richard and turned back to him with evil glares. Igor grabbed Richard and pulled him close to his face. Richard could smell minty breath and the scent of washing powder.

"I'm sick of hearing about this fucking *partner* Alice. Maybe I should go and see her? I could show her a good time" – the way he said it made Richard think Alice would not have a good time in the slightest – "then she'd give me the money herself."

"I'm sorry. Please. I just need a few more days."

Igor's face turned dark, and anger sparked in his eyes. Richard's knees quivered in fear, and his legs threatened to buckle beneath him.

"You said that two days ago, and what happened then?" Igor's meaty thumb and forefinger grabbed Richard's nose and squeezed. Richard screamed as bolts of agony shot from his nose and into his skull.

"Please...!"

He'd never known pain like it and screamed again. In that moment he would rather they killed him than suffer any more of this torture.

"We gave you a little taste of pain then, yes? But it didn't work. Because I don't have my money. I don't have the sixty thousand pounds you owe me."

The pain grew so intense Richard's scream was cut off as he vomited.

For a big man, Igor was nimble with quick reflexes. He deftly managed to swerve his body out of the path of the vomit, although he had to let go of Richard's nose.

"Dirty man," he grumbled, clearly unwilling to acknowledge that he had caused the old professor to vomit in the first place.

Then Igor nodded to Josef, who walked around to the boot of the car. He opened the boot, took something out and closed it again. He walked back to Igor and Richard at the front of the car. In his hands was a claw hammer, which he held up with a certain sense of pride.

"Oh God, please don't," Richard begged, a pitiful sight with vomit down his chin and all over his shirt.

"I break your nose and you don't listen," Igor said softly. "So now we must break your legs."

"Please, no, please." Tears rolled down Richard's cheeks. "I swear I'll get you the money. I'm so close to getting it."

"Richard, Richard." Igor's accent took on a terrifying edge when he spoke so softly. "You are out of time."

Then Igor suddenly switched into a boiling, terrifying rage. He grabbed the hammer and roughly shoved Richard to Josef, who took hold of Richard's arms.

The sun bounced off the hammer as Igor lifted it above his head. "You bastard, maybe this will make you pay your debts."

"No, please...I can get you the...my car. I can give you my car."

Igor paused. "I already told you I don't want that piece of

shit. I get cars given to me for debts before. Then next week you call police and report it stolen. I get a load of trouble then."

"Idiot," Josef snarled in his ear.

Richard couldn't move; he was locked in Josef's iron grip.

"Hold him still. I need to get the kneecaps square on to break them."

Richard struggled and screamed.

Igor lifted the hammer again.

"Boat...My boat. I have a boat."

Igor tutted.

"What the fuck are you talking about now?"

"I have a boat. We bought it for twenty thousand, but we've had a lot of work done...should be worth twice that now."

Igor stared at him, his dark eyes seeming to crawl into Richard's soul.

"Hmmm." He lowered the hammer, tapping the head of it into his free hand.

"She's over thirty feet. A sailboat. You can keep her. Or sell her. She's yours."

Igor stayed silent for a moment.

Richard wasn't a religious man, but in that moment he prayed to the universe, and whatever gods it held, for Igor to leave his kneecaps intact. He felt his mind whirring as the panic and fear scrambled his brain.

"Okay. I'll take your boat. But it had better be worth what you say it is. Let's go now; where is it? The harbour?"

"It's being sailed into Bristol from up north." The lie came quickly to Richard, so fast that he blurted it out before he could think of the consequences of being caught in the lie. "It should arrive in four days. Tuesday."

Igor frowned at him. "How convenient."

"Tuesday, come to the marina Tuesday afternoon, and I'll meet you there. Opposite the Grain Barge pub. I'll give you the keys…and all the paperwork."

Richard prayed again. Prayed for his kneecaps that his lie would be believed.

"Okay, Professor Barnes. I will be there. Tuesday at one o'clock. But if there is no boat, then it won't be your kneecaps you need to worry about." He leaned into Richard's face, his minty breath fighting against the stench of vomit. "It will be your life."

———

THE DINING ROOM was almost cleared. Alice took another flat cardboard box off the stack, pushed it into shape, taped the bottom closed and turned it over so it was ready to be filled. She took the last of the books from the bookshelf and stacked them neatly in the new box. The final book to go in was *The Evolution of Flowers*.

Alice held it in her hands as she flicked through it. It was a heavy book: a hardback with over four hundred pages, a little bigger than A4. The front cover featured a beautiful photograph of white magnolias, and Alice traced her thumb over the name on the spine: Professor Richard Barnes.

It had been a revolutionary book when it had been published five years ago. Of course, the reality was Alice and Richard had done the research together; they had both worked on the theories within the book. They'd spent years researching the evolution of flowers. Both of them. When it had come to writing the text, Richard had done the initial manuscript, which had been raw and unpolished. Alice had spent weeks rewriting and reworking it.

She thought back to that time when they had been studying the evolution of flowers; the research had been so interesting and fun. Flowers first appeared 134 million years ago; within a few million years they had become the dominant species of plant. Fascinating when you thought about it. Which Alice and Richard had.

Alice had loved the time they spent together on the project; it was such a happy memory for her. They would lecture in the mornings and work on the project in the afternoon. As they'd had outside funding for the research, guest lecturers would come and work with them. At one stage the project had involved eight people in total, although Richard and Alice had been the driving force behind it all.

But towards the end of the project, the shine began to come off their relationship. Not a lot, but enough for Alice to realise that perhaps Richard wasn't the perfect man she had thought he was.

After years of working on the project together, and making some amazing new discoveries together, when Richard approached the publisher with the completed manuscript, only his name was on it. He hadn't given her a writing credit.

"It's dedicated to you!" he'd argued. "What more could you ask for?"

"Equal recognition," she said as calmly as she could. "We worked on the project together; we wrote it together..."

Richard had sulked after that. Looking back, Alice remembered how they had argued for a few days, but in the end, he'd got his own way. Like he always did. So when the book was published, it was his name on the cover, and hers was nowhere to be seen. He took all the credit for their work.

Alice had been upset, but it felt like there was nothing she could do. And there was something else that bothered her about the book.

It was during the rewriting process that Alice started to realise that she and Richard were different people. She had gone into biology for her love of flowers, but Richard went into it for his love of data and science. It was strange how people could look at a flower and see such different things. For Alice, when she looked at a rose, she saw its colour and beauty, how it was both delicate and strong; she appreciated its short lifespan and how amazing it was that it could be cut at the stem and still remain so beautiful. She would never get tired of looking at flowers or of admiring their beauty. Of course, she knew that other people just saw a flower, but she'd always assumed that Richard's approach was the same as hers.

It was a little disappointing, after all these years, to realise that Richard didn't love flowers like she did; he just loved the science, the numbers and theories. He was appreciating them in his own way, she supposed, but he didn't love or admire them like her. He'd always given her the impression that his obsession was the same as hers, but now she knew it wasn't.

Alice threw the book into the box and taped it shut.

That was it; she had packed the last of the dining room things. Alice got up off the floor and looked around the room. It felt so strange now that it was empty.

"Look at that dust," she murmured to herself. "Those shelves need a wipe."

But first she needed a coffee, so she went in the kitchen to switch the coffee machine on.

When the machine was ready, she poured herself a cup and sipped it. On the kitchen counter there were some of the maps Richard had been looking at that morning. So this was it, then; soon she would leave the house. Soon she would be sailing around the southern seas of Europe. She traced a finger along the map; the boat would pass Portugal, then Spain, France and Monaco, Italy, Greece and Croatia. And then away from the coasts, there were thousands of little islands to explore, some inhabited, some deserted. The idea of it sent a thrill of excitement through her.

For a moment she pictured the bright blue seas and being in control of *Seas the Day*. She pictured herself steering the boat to catch the wind, the prow cutting through the water, the sun on her face. Despite everything, she couldn't help but grin at the thought of it.

Behind her the front door opened.

She turned to see Richard walk into the house.

"Did they cancel the lunch?" she asked him.

"No, I did."

As he walked in, she noticed something on his shirt. Then she caught a whiff of vomit.

"Is that sick?" she asked, thinking how awful he looked.

His hair was dishevelled; his face was pale and clammy.

"Yes, I was on my way there when I suddenly came over all sweaty and horrible. It must have been something I ate."

He looked like he'd aged ten years in a morning. She watched as he took a glass from the cupboard and filled it with water from the sink. His trousers had black marks down them, and his tweed jacket was pulled out of shape.

"Oh, Richard, you're shaking."

He swilled his mouth out and spat in the sink; then he gulped more water down.

"Are you okay? What happened?"

He swallowed the water and gasped. "I was walking along and then came over all hot. I suddenly felt terrible and fainted. Straight down onto the pavement. When I came around, I was sick."

"Oh God, that sounds terrible. Can I get you anything? Should we call the doctor?"

"I'm fine now. Maybe it was something I ate; maybe I've been overdoing it recently, what with clearing my office out, sorting the house, packing for the boat..."

"I've never seen you look so white."

She watched him as he gulped down another glass of water. His face was still a mess, and coupled with the effects of his latest accident, he looked truly dreadful. He couldn't stand straight and was hunched at the sink, gasping and spluttering as he drank. It was almost comical, but she didn't laugh.

"Let me drive you to A and E now. You should really get checked out."

But Richard only waved the idea away. It was just like him, he knew best, and he wouldn't go. Instead, he hobbled over to the medicine cabinet. Alice watched him as he took two painkillers. Why was he so stubborn? she wondered.

"The washing machine is empty," Alice told him. "You should get your shirt and trousers in there."

He put the glass in the sink and walked into the utility room. She watched as he pulled off his clothes and put them in the washing machine.

"Your elbow is bleeding."

"What?"

"You've got a scrape on your elbow."

"Really? It must have been when I fell."

"You poor thing."

He walked back into the kitchen.

"Sit here." Alice motioned to the breakfast bar. "I'll put some antiseptic cream on it."

He did as he was told and sat heavily on one of the stools. Alice went to the cupboard and found some cream. There were two tubes in the medicine box; one was new; one was old. She saw that the old one was out of date and needed throwing away. She put the new tube back in the medicine box and uncapped the old tube. The white antiseptic cream had turned a dirty grey colour.

"Hold still." She lathered the grey cream into his bloody elbow.

Richard gasped in pain.

"Shouldn't I wash it first?" he asked.

Alice felt bits of gravel under her finger as she rubbed in the cream. "No, it looks clean enough."

"Have you managed to do much packing?" he asked, making conversation through gritted teeth.

"Yes," she replied, "I've finally done all the books in the dining room."

"Hmmm. I don't suppose you've heard from the solicitors? About your mum's money?"

"Actually, they called earlier. The money should be transferred in the next day or two."

She sensed him tense. Alice stared at his back. His grey hair was neatly trimmed; a smart line cut across the neck. Across his back the skin was wrinkled and sagging where it was once firm and tight.

"That's good news, I suppose."

"I suppose, although I don't really think of it like that."

Alice continued to rub the cream over his bloody wounds. "You've got a hair on your back."

"It was only waxed last week." His vanity made his voice sound annoyed.

"Well, she missed a bit."

"Bloody girl is useless."

"Hold on, I'll get it." She tried to pull the grey hair out, but she couldn't get a grip on it. Alice reached over to the counter and picked up a knife she'd used to make her lunch. It was small and razor sharp.

She held the hair in the fingers of her left hand, the knife in her right.

"Don't stab me in the back," he joked.

Alice didn't reply.

She cut the hair, carried it to the bin and dropped it in. "All done."

"Thanks," he said as he stood up. "I'm going to have a wash and get changed."

"You should have a lie-down."

"I need to go out. Still a few bits to do. Make sure you keep packing everything up. We leave in a few days!" he called from the stairs. His voice had perked up.

Alice listened to him walk upstairs and into the bathroom. She realised she was still holding the knife and was surprised to see her hand gripping it so tightly.

8

ONE YEAR AGO

Alice rang the doorbell to her mum's house and waited with Richard's supportive hand on her shoulder. After a moment, a woman opened the front door to greet them.

"Hello?" she said with a big smile and a Jamaican accent.

"You must be Irene?"

"Yes, yes. And you are Alice and Richard?"

Richard stepped forward. "We are indeed!" He held out his hand and smiled. "Pleased to meet you."

Irene seemed dazzled by him; she shook his hand with her eyes wide and a huge smile on her face, as if she'd just won the lottery. Irene was a big woman, and she had to move backwards to let them into the house.

"How's Mum?" Alice asked.

"Oh, she's fine; she's just had a nap and a shower."

As they walked into the lounge, Alice studied Irene. She seemed relaxed but capable, and Alice was already feeling a little better about her mum's situation. Since the Alzheimer's had become worse, Alice and Richard had been looking at care homes, but the thought of her mum in one of those places had been so upsetting. The doctor had also informed them that her mum going into a care home and leaving her own house forever had the potential to make the Alzheimer's worse. This had made Alice determined to try to keep her mum at the house. For the past month her mum had been in the hospital, as her condition had deteriorated so quickly, and this was the first time they'd come to visit her with her new carer in place. The company they'd employed to look after her mum had a great reputation, and actually meeting Irene was already making Alice feel a million times better.

"Can I get you something to drink? Cup of tea?" Irene offered.

Alice's heart sank, and tears threatened to come; Irene was offering because her mum couldn't even make a drink anymore.

"It's okay, let me make them," Richard said as he set off for the kitchen.

Alice went to the old oak bookcase and put a hand on the books there. She'd bought most of them for her parents and knew they were filled with pressed flowers. Each book, with its hidden flower, was a different memory. Her mum had loved taking the books down and admiring the hidden pieces of floral colour held within. Did her mum even know they were still there? Did she just see a bookcase now, unaware of the memories hidden within it?

Footsteps could be heard on the stairs, and then her mum appeared. She was wearing a floor-length pink dressing gown, and her grey hair was tied back. As she slowly entered the room, she looked at Alice, her face unsure.

"Hi, Mum." Alice hugged her.

Her mum felt so frail in Alice's arms, and she didn't return the embrace. But at least she let Alice hug her, which was something.

"Is it nice to be out of hospital and back home?" Alice asked.

Her mum didn't reply; she didn't even register that Alice was talking to her, and was instead gazing around the lounge with a look of curiosity on her face.

"Now, what would you ladies like to do?" Irene said. "There are some good things on the telly?"

Her mum's face perked up at this, so Alice led her to the sofa, where they sat together, holding hands. Irene put a gardening show on. Part of Alice wanted to cry; part of her was glad to be able to sit on the sofa so close to her mum and hold her hand. It was a strange mix of emotions that she never thought she'd feel, emotions that she battled with even as she sat there.

Richard appeared with a tray of four teas.

"Here you go. I made everyone a cuppa." He placed the tray on the coffee table, took one of the teas and then sat in the armchair by the window.

"Thank you, Richard," Irene said. "Mrs Walker doesn't like tea anymore; let me get her a drink." Irene picked up one of the cups and disappeared into the kitchen. She quickly returned with a child's spill-proof cup of orange squash.

Alice couldn't look at the cup, couldn't face looking at her mum as she drank out of it, sucking on it like a toddler. Instead, she focused on Richard, who gave her a smile of support. Alice was glad he was there.

"Thanks, Irene," Alice said, her wobbling voice threatening to break.

Irene smiled and took the empty tray back into the kitchen.

They sat and watched the gardening programme, Richard in the armchair with his tea. Alice sat with her mum holding hands. It was peaceful, and although her mum wasn't well, Alice found it comforting. On the wall there was an old photo of her mum and dad walking along a beach. Her dad had been a bricklayer but had died from a heart attack over ten years ago now. Alice wondered what he would have made of her mum's condition; he'd loved her so much it would have probably ruined him seeing her like this.

"John wants me to work tomorrow," her mum said.

"John? At the newsagent's?"

"Wants me to work tomorrow."

Her mum had worked at the newsagent shop around the corner for almost thirty years, and all the locals knew her as "Sue on the counter". Over the decades, Sue had seen all sorts, met thousands of people and was always a warm welcome behind the counter with a smile and a ready bit of chat. As adults, people would come and say hello to the woman who had served them as kids. When her mum finished the job a few years ago, all the locals had come out on their doorsteps and clapped her as she walked home. It had been an amazing day, the local paper came to interview her, she'd received gifts and flowers, and she had cried at everyone's generosity. Did the fact she now thought she was due into work mean she'd forgotten one of the happiest days of her life?

"You don't work there anymore, Mum, remember? You retired."

Her mum nodded. "Wants me to do the late shift."

"Okay, Mum."

Alice turned her glistening eyes back to the television and gripped her mum's hand tighter. From the kitchen they could hear Irene doing the dishes.

Richard got up and nodded towards the downstairs bathroom. Alice gave him a little nod back. He disappeared for a moment and then returned. He stood in the doorway to the lounge, and Alice looked over her mum's head to him. Richard was trying to show her something.

Alice could see Richard was holding a necklace that was dripping wet. She recognised it as one of her mum's, one her dad had given to her as an anniversary present one year.

"Found this in the toilet," he said quietly.

Alice just nodded mutely, unsure what else to do or say.

9

THREE DAYS TO GO

Richard was woken by the pain in his face and knees. He felt old and, quite literally, battered. His legs and back were stiff, and his head pounded from the damaged nose and the several whiskeys he'd consumed the night before.

He rolled over in the bed and was startled to see Alice lying next to him, watching him.

"Morning," he croaked at her.

"Morning," she replied.

She seemed wide awake, and he wondered how long she'd been watching him.

"You were up late."

"Stayed up watching a film," he said, "and had a few whiskeys."

She smiled at him. "Perfect combination."

"Hmm. Are you making some coffee?" he asked.

"I can do. I should be up anyway; there's so much more packing to do."

"Let's have a coffee, and then we can see what needs doing."

Alice got up, put on her dressing gown and walked quietly downstairs. Richard heard her put the kettle on and start breakfast. He then rolled over and went back to sleep.

AN HOUR LATER, Richard joined Alice in the kitchen and sipped his coffee.

"Tastes funny."

"Sorry, it's a new brand; the shop was out of our usual one."

"What's the plan today, then? I was thinking I could finish packing my office?"

"Yes, dear, if you like. The dining room is all done, so I was going to do the lounge next."

He drank his coffee, ate his fruit and watched her do the dishes. She looked so drab and old. The dressing gown took away any shape her body had, not that there was much shape left; but he decided from behind she looked like an eighty-year-old woman.

"There are more empty boxes in the garage, although we're running low on parcel tape."

Even her voice grated on him. How odd, he thought, that it was once something he found so attractive about her, and now he just wanted her to shut up and stop talking to him.

"Okay."

Richard went into the garage and grabbed three flat-packed boxes and the brown parcel tape and carried them with his coffee upstairs to his office and closed the door. He set the coffee down on his desk and assembled one of the boxes. Once he'd done that, he quickly flung a few things in it and then sat at his desk and switched on his laptop.

He entered his pin number, which was his date of birth, and then loaded up his accounts. First of all, he looked through the football matches, but there was nothing much on because the season had ended; there was a friendly match in Australia with interesting odds, but he didn't know much about the teams. Despite that, he warmed up with a £50 bet on one of the teams at 4-1 to win.

The Tour de France was underway, and he spent a little while researching some of the front-runners. He read through different articles about the racers and the trainers, and then the pundits' views. After a while he put a £150 bet on one of the racers to win the next stage of the race with odds of 18-1.

Then on to the big one, the Wimbledon final. It was only a few days away, and things were heating up. It was looking like a Djokovic and Anderson final. Of course, Djokovic was the favourite, but the odds were so poor. Richard took his time; he read the articles, watched the highlights of previous games, tried to find an angle or nugget of information that would help him make a decision. Eventually he decided on Anderson, he was strong enough to win, and the odds were much better at 3-1.

Richard put a £500 bet on Anderson.

Next he looked at the golf. He already had several bets placed on next week's Open in Scotland, but that didn't stop him from looking through the odds. Spieth had actually dropped down to 12-1, which was good for him. Surely that was worth £100? Richard went to make the bet, but the screen flashed up *Insufficient Funds*. He looked at his account, which showed £12 credit.

"Bloody website."

Hadn't he had some wins the other day? There should have been a lot more in the account than that. But then, it was hard to keep track. Normally, he would simply top up his online gambling account, but there was nothing in his current account to do that with. And he knew his credit card was at its limit because it had been declined when he'd tried to buy something in a shop last week.

It was so annoying!

Anger bubbled up inside him. He tried to control himself; the last thing he needed to do was smash his hand on the desk again; it was about the only part of his body that wasn't aching.

There was a knock on his office door. Alice popped her head into the room.

"How are you getting on?"

"Fine." It was an effort to keep the frustration from his voice.

She looked down at the one half-filled box but didn't comment.

"Would you like another coffee?"

"Yes."

Alice left, and he unclenched his fists. Why was she always bothering him? He slammed the laptop shut and got up to pace around his office.

Maybe his account hadn't updated with some of his winnings? Wasn't there a boxing match he had done well on the previous week? He could email the site's admin to make sure they were putting his winnings back into his account, but he knew it was pointless; he'd done it too many times before and had too many email replies showing the website was correct and he was wrong.

Pushing the betting out of his mind, he looked around the office, as if seeing it for the first time that day.

What did he want to take with him on the boat? Nothing. There were shelves of books, pictures, photos, drawers full of stationery and worthless junk. It could all burn as far as he was concerned. He was sick of it, sick of it all; he'd had enough of staring at it for all these years. The plan was for the majority of their possessions to go into storage, and a few cases were to go with them on the boat. But he suddenly had the urge to pour petrol on everything and throw in a match.

His mind wandered back to six months ago when he'd met his brother, Stephen, for lunch at a restaurant in Bristol city centre. Stephen had been five minutes early, Richard five minutes late. They were both wearing grey suits, Stephen in an impeccable three-piece, Richard in misshapen old jacket and trousers. They weren't close as brothers, but it had still been nice to see him.

They'd both ordered the catch of the day, which was bream; Stephen had a water, Richard a glass of white wine.

Richard remembered tasting his fish. "Just like Mum used to make."

Stephen had laughed; their mum used to overcook everything.

It had been pleasant small talk for a while until they finished their food and ordered coffees.

"Go on then, ask me," Stephen said.

"What?"

"The last few times we've spoken, you've asked me for money, so I'm guessing this lunch is about you needing money?"

Richard shook his head. "No, actually, I was after some advice."

Stephen seemed a little surprised by this. "Legal advice?"

"I'm thinking of leaving Alice."

"Ah."

"And you're a lawyer."

"Employment law though, it's different."

"But you must know stuff, like where I stand?"

"Where you stand?"

"Financially."

A waiter arrived with two coffees on a tray. Richard watched Stephen as he slowly poured milk into his cup, stirring it with a little silver spoon. He took his time, deep in thought.

"I'm not an expert, although I did a little bit of family law as part of my degree and training. We have a few guys in the firm who are divorce experts, so I can talk to them." He sipped his drink. "That said, I know it's highly likely she wouldn't be entitled to anything of yours, if that's what you're worried about?"

Richard picked up his coffee cup but put it down again without drinking. Stephen watched him silently.

"And what about me? What am I entitled to of hers? Do we split everything fifty-fifty?"

Stephen shook his head. "You'd both keep what's yours and wouldn't have to share with the other."

"But we've been together twenty years, just because we're not married...we're common-law partners."

Stephen winced. "It's a myth. Common-law partners is just a grown-up name for boyfriend and girlfriend. You don't have the same separation rights as a married couple. Doesn't matter if you've been together two weeks or twenty years; if you split up, you're not entitled to each other's money or assets."

Richard slumped back in his chair. This was shocking news to him. He couldn't believe what he was hearing.

"Nothing?"

"If you were a millionaire and she were penniless and she would end up on the streets, maybe you'd have to give her a little bit. But in your situation" – Stephen waved his silver spoon at Richard – "forget it."

"But common-law partners..."

Stephen shrugged. "What can I say, you're not alone. Most people think they have the same rights as married couples, but they don't. It's like you're roommates."

Richard had been devastated by the news.

"I'm assuming by the look on your face that this isn't good news. You weren't worried about protecting your bank balance, you were interested in hers?"

It was tempting to lie, but it seemed like that was all he'd done for a while. Instead, Richard told him how he was feeling.

"I want to leave her. I've had enough. If I'm honest, I can't stand to be around her anymore. She drives me bloody mad!"

"Why?"

Where to begin? He couldn't even articulate how sick of Alice he was.

"So many things, her voice, she's always nagging, moaning about stuff." He paused. "And she's boring; we don't have anything in common anymore..." He stopped himself from saying she'd put on some weight recently too; even he knew that would sound harsh.

"Sounds a bit vague. I always liked her; she seems really sweet."

"You should try living with her."

Stephen smiled at this.

"Maybe it is all a bit vague, as you say, but really what it comes down to is that I don't love her, and it's driving me crazy living with her. I don't want to be with this woman anymore, in any capacity."

Saying the words aloud felt like a bit of the weight from his shoulders easing off him. It was something he'd been thinking about for a long time but had never told anyone. When had he started to feel like this? It wasn't an overnight thing. It had taken years, really. Ever so slowly, he'd become bored with their relationship, bored of Alice. He had stopped loving her and, for a while, was just indifferent to her. But then that indifference had turned to annoyance and eventually hatred. Why? He'd often asked himself that, and there was no particular reason. It had just happened. And judging by the divorce rates in the western world, he wasn't the only person to feel like this.

"So, are you going to leave her? You'll be okay anyway; work seems to be going well."

"Actually, I think my days there are numbered."

Stephen raised an eyebrow but refrained from probing further.

"Why don't you live on your savings for a while, then get another job."

Richard couldn't bring himself to explain to Stephen that it was only a matter of time before the university found out that he'd been fiddling his expenses and siphoning money from them in other ways too. Once they did, he wouldn't be able to work in any university again. He'd be lucky to get a private tutoring job for £10 an hour. If he was honest with himself, he wasn't even sure how he'd gotten into this mess. Of course, he liked to gamble, and he'd had a run of bad bets for a while, but he'd always assumed the wins and losses would even out in the end. But they didn't. He quickly pushed the thought from his mind.

"The savings are a bit light at the moment."

"And you rent that place, don't you? You never bought? There's no equity in it? Jeez."

Richard nodded. Why had he seemed so certain that renting was better than buying a property? Years ago, he'd been a big rising star with papers published in highly respectable journals and several textbooks published, all in the field of biology. Women had thrown themselves at him, he was very young to be a head of a department, and he had money in the bank. He had even done a few TV interviews for science shows, his name was known, and he had the chance to be a star. He was moving up in the world, building a great life for himself. The idea of getting married and buying a house had seemed so final, too settled and rigid. He wanted to be free; he was too busy moving forward to stop.

He had a few years of success, and then a few years of living off that success, and then slowly, a soupon of decline until one day, a few years ago, he woke up and looked at his life in despair. He had no house equity; he'd always invested the bare minimum in his pension, which wasn't going to give him much of a payout, always assumed he would be very wealthy when he retired. Cash savings had never quite stuck. Ironically, he wanted to leave Alice, but he would be better off if they were married. What an utter balls-up of a life. He was now facing retirement as a pauper unless he could think of a way to get his hands on a large sum of money.

"Now it all makes sense," Stephen said. "Well, I'm not sure what to tell you."

Richard sighed. He was screwed. Fifty-six years old,

broke and soon to be jobless. He had no choice but to stay with Alice. Unless he could think of something else.

"The good news is, in ten years you'll get your state pension," Stephen joked. "I think it's £180 a week now!"

The waiter had brought over the bill and laid it on the table. Richard and Stephen had looked at each other in silence for a moment before Stephen snorted and picked it up.

"I'll get it."

"Thanks."

Richard blinked away the memory and looked around his home office. There were years' worth of possessions, but now they were all just a reminder of how he'd messed his life up. He just wanted to leave it all behind him.

He just wanted to get on the boat and leave everything behind.

10

THREE DAYS TO GO

By the afternoon a heatwave was underway, which in Britain was a rare and uncomfortable experience. Alice was driving her and Richard to Jan and Freddie's house in her Mini Cooper, as Richard had encouraged her to drive so he could have a drink. He kept playing with the dials on the console.

"I've told you, the air conditioning doesn't work," Alice said patiently.

"Christ, it's so hot. Surely the fan must work?"

He could feel sweat rolling down his back and knew he'd look an idiot turning up with a wet shirt. If she'd told him her car would be so hot, they could have taken his.

Typical bloody Alice not thinking things through.

He pushed another button, and a pop song blasted out at them.

"That's the radio!" she yelled over the noise.

He switched it off quickly, his heart hammering from the shock of it coming on so loudly and so suddenly.

"Okay, okay," he said.

He left the dials alone and sat back. Traffic was slow, so there was no fresh air coming in through the windows. Jan and Freddie lived in Redland, an affluent neighbourhood, and it meant driving through the city centre to get to their house.

"Do we have to do this?" he asked.

"They are our friends, and they're throwing us a going-away party; of course we have to go."

Richard sighed. He had tried several times to get out of attending, but he'd struggled to find an excuse good enough; Alice had been like a dog with a bone, insisting they both go.

Alice looked over to him. "We really should have brought something though, maybe a bottle of wine?"

Richard just snorted and didn't reply; he wasn't going to waste his money. He would have folded his arms, but he was already too hot in that damn car.

Finally, they pulled into Jan and Freddie's road, and Alice managed to find a parking space near to the house. The tree-lined street was full of parked cars. The houses were old, Victorian-style buildings, many had been converted into apartments, but Jan and Freddie had managed to buy a whole house.

Alice rang the bell, and Jan opened the door.

"The guests of honour!" Jan greeted them with a huge smile. She was wearing a yellow dress and holding a pink cocktail in a martini glass.

"Oh, Richard, what happened to you?"

He hadn't even stepped into the house, and already he could feel himself blushing. "I fell down the stairs."

"He's fine," Alice said, "just a little accident."

They walked through the house, and Jan showed them out into the garden, where a dozen of their friends were standing and sitting with drinks in hand. In the corner of the large garden, two men dressed in white chef's outfits were attending to an impressive barbeque. As Alice and Richard walked into the garden, everyone called out greetings to them, although Richard noticed most were directed at Alice. He could see them clock his bruised face, and he felt himself blush again.

A waiter appeared at Richard's shoulder. "Can I get you a..."

"White wine. Large."

"And a sparkling water for me, please," Alice said and smiled to the waiter.

"Water!" Jan exclaimed behind her.

Alice turned to Jan. "I'm driving."

"Don't be silly, dear; give me your car keys. I'll get Freddie and one of the boys to drop the car over to you in the morning. Just get a taxi home tonight."

"Well..."

Jan turned to her waiter. "Make those two large wines, please, Jack."

And who's paying for the taxi? Richard wondered. Late night taxis always cost more; he didn't even have any cash on him. Well, if Alice wanted to drink alcohol, then she could pay for the taxi.

Alice hugged Jan. "Thank you."

ALICE HAD A WONDERFUL TIME. Jan and Freddie's garden had been redone by a garden designer the year before, and it was a beautiful, simple space with purple, green and silver plants and flowers. It was so nice to see their friends gathered together to wish them well on their travels. The food was delicious and the wine superb. Jan owned one of the best restaurants in the city, and she was always the most amazing host. Afternoon turned to evening and evening to night, and at one point Alice realised she was drunk.

"You're the best," Lucy was saying. "I can't believe you're going!"

Alice laughed, pleased at the kind words. "Make sure you come and visit us."

Lucy was one of the administrators at the university, and she and Alice had been friends for years. They'd already had a teary night out together the previous month when Alice had left her job.

"I've told Pete to take a week off in September. Where are you going to be in September?" Lucy asked, tipsily slurring her words.

"September? Maybe Italy. Why don't we meet in Sicily?"

"Oh, that would be amazing!" Lucy said.

"I can't believe you're going," Sarah said.

Sarah was another friend from the university, although she had retired the year before. Alice, Lucy and Sarah stood in the middle of the garden, all three of them clutching wine glasses to their breast and swaying unsteadily in the candlelight.

"I know, it still doesn't feel real."

"You're honestly the last person I would imagine sailing off on a boat," Sarah said.

Alice and Lucy laughed.

Jack, the waiter, appeared from the darkness and topped

up their wine glasses. Alice hardly noticed, although she took another sip from her glass.

"I know, it's such a crazy thing to do."

"No, for a normal person it's crazy." Sarah waved her wine glass. "But for you, I mean..."

Alice laughed.

"Don't get me wrong, we all love how prim and proper you are, you're so sweet and lovely, but it's just so unlike you." Sarah stroked Alice's hair in a burst of drunken affection.

"I know what you mean; at first I couldn't imagine living on a boat. I mean, sailing around on the sea? It's so not me."

Lucy giggled.

"We're going to miss you so much," Sarah said, her eyes glistening.

Alice found herself welling up with emotion too. It was just so lovely that her friends cared about her so much.

"I'm going to miss you too." Her voice wobbled.

"It's so sad that you're leaving..." Lucy sniffed.

Before Alice knew it, they were crying and hugging, and even though there were three of them in an embrace, she felt unsteady on her feet. Over Sarah's shoulder, Alice could see that Richard was sat on his own, scrolling through his phone. Nearby, a few of the men were chatting and laughing, but they had their backs to him.

MORE CANDLES WERE LIT, and the garden took on a warm glow despite the dark night. It was late but still warm, and Alice felt lucky they'd had such nice weather for the evening. At some point she had switched to water, although she couldn't remember asking for the water she was now sipping.

"We've got six bedrooms here," Jan was telling her.

Alice looked around, the garden spinning in her drunken vision. She and Jan were sitting on a low wall near the kitchen.

"Show off!" she slurred.

Jan laughed. "I mean, if ever you feel like a break from the boat, you're always welcome to stay here."

"A break? From the boat?"

"Just come here to stay."

"Well, Richard and I have already said we'll stop off in some hotels for sightseeing as we harbour in different places."

"Hmmm..." Jan said.

"What?"

"Sometimes it's nice to have your own space; you might want to...ummm...have a little break from everything."

Alice frowned. Jan was trying to hint at something, but Alice was too drunk to work out what. Instead, she sipped her water.

"The food was lovely. Thank you so much for this."

"It's my pleasure, honey. Pierre did the cooking. I borrowed him from the restaurant for the night."

"The guy's a genius. Those lobster tails were so good."

"That's why I hired him." Jan laughed. "But, Alice, you're always –"

"Oi...You...How dare you –"

From the end of the garden, angry shouting erupted. In the shadows Alice could just make out several men pushing and grabbing each other.

"Pack it in!" Freddie's voice boomed.

"...you still owe me..." another voice was shouting.

Alice tried to stand to see what was happening, but she was too unsteady on her feet. Jan put her hand gently on her shoulder, then went over to see what the fuss was.

From her position on the wall, Alice could see Freddie pulling someone back by the arms. She squinted and saw it was Graham being restrained. Graham? He was such a gentle man; it seemed so unlike him to cause any trouble.

Alice looked beyond Freddie and the struggling Graham and tried to see who Graham was being pulled away from. Beyond them, stepping out from the darkness with a ripped shirt, was Richard.

IT WAS LATE when the taxi pulled up at their house in Winterbourne. Alice was still drunk, but her head had cleared a little, and she felt more stable on her feet. It was clear they needed to leave after the altercation, so Alice had no real idea what had happened. Richard had refused to discuss it except to say that Graham was an "absolute arse-hole". The shirt would need to go in the bin.

Alice paid the driver, and they got out of the taxi.

As they walked to the front door, a figure appeared out of the shadows.

Alice jumped in fright. "Shit!"

"Who's there?" Richard slurred.

"Well, there is no need for that language," said a voice that Alice recognised, but for a moment was struggling to place.

Then an old woman stepped forward into the light of the

street lamp, the orange light doing nothing for her miserable face and grey complexion.

"Mrs Mabel?" Alice asked.

The woman looked like a ghost, and Alice kept blinking to focus on her; she seemed unreal in Alice's drunken vision. Despite the warm night, Mrs Mabel was wearing a long coat and a look on her face that would make children scream in terror.

"I'm not a post office."

Richard sniggered. "What the hell is she talking about?" he muttered.

"Post office?" was all Alice could manage.

Mrs Mabel held up a brown envelope.

"A courier delivered this letter this afternoon, and I had to sign for it! I told the young man it wasn't addressed to me, but he was very insistent."

Alice had to concentrate on not stumbling as she stepped forward.

"Look at the state of you!"

Richard laughed and continued ambling to their front door, jangling his keys as he tried to find the right one.

Alice took the letter and refrained from telling Mrs Mabel she was a grown adult and could have a drink if she liked. But at that moment she really thought she might be sick, so she just managed a "thank you" and a hiccup.

"Next time, tell the delivery company that I should not be expected to sign for your correspondence."

Alice squinted at the envelope and saw it had their address on, but no name.

"Could this not have waited until the morning?" she said.

"Oh, no! Not when I've signed for something. The

responsibility has been put on me, and I can't relax until I've passed this letter on to you."

In the darkness the old woman's eyes looked black. Alice wondered what had made her so bitter, as she was always ready with a complaint about something. For a moment she thought about asking her, but then decided she didn't have the energy.

"Goodnight, Mrs Mabel."

Alice turned and made her way up the pathway as Richard opened their front door. He stumbled in and switched on the hallway light. Maybe she should have driven instead of drinking so much? There was a terrible hangover heading her way in the morning. Although it had been such a great night, saying goodbye to their dear friends. She was going to miss them so much.

"What was it?" he asked her.

"Huh?"

Alice closed the front door and slid the bolt across it.

"The letter?" Richard insisted.

"Oh yes." She had already forgotten she was holding the brown envelope. She looked at it closely; it had their address on, but no name.

"She's a nightmare," Richard said. "Any normal person would wait until the morning. I mean, what the hell time is it? Crazy cow."

Alice needed more water. And to lie down.

"Well?" he said.

"What?"

He tutted. "What is it?"

God, she was drunk. With a great effort she tore the envelope open and pulled out the letter inside. Alice had to work hard at focusing on the words.

Her heart hammered, but then she perked up as she read it.

"It's the results of the DNA test," she said, looking him in the eye.

"Oh." His face fell. "And?" he snapped.

"It's a match. Sally is your daughter."

11

EIGHT MONTHS AGO

R ichard smiled at Irene as she opened the front door. It was his widest, most charming smile, and it had the desired effect as she beamed back at him.

"Oh, Richard, I wasn't expecting you."

He held up a box of chocolate biscuits. "Thought I would drop a little treat in for Sue," he said with a wink, "and for you."

"How lovely, please come in." She opened the door wider for him.

"And how is she today?" Richard asked with concern on his face as he stepped into the hallway.

"She's okay; we've just been getting some gentle exercise, doing our arm and back stretches."

"Sounds great." He gave Irene's shoulder a little squeeze. "Well done."

Irene's face lit up as if she'd been touched by the hand of God. She couldn't contain her pride and delight at Richard's praise, which was what he had been hoping for; he was on a charm offensive, and he was an expert at it.

They went into the lounge. Sue was sitting on the sofa and was once again wearing her pink floor-length dressing gown.

"Hi there, Sue, and how are you today?"

Sue looked at him blankly. She had a string of snot hanging from her nose, which she seemed oblivious to. Richard tried not to look at it. The smile plastered on his face threatened to falter before Irene appeared with a tissue.

"Here, Mrs Walker, let me get that for you," Irene said as she wiped Sue's nose clean.

"I brought you some biscuits."

Richard took up his usual seat in the armchair opposite Sue. He noticed a faint smell of urine, which he also forced himself to ignore.

"Shall I make some tea?"

"It's a yes from me," he said with an easy smile, and Irene swooned off to the kitchen.

The smile faded from Richard's face as he stared at Sue on the sofa. She stared blankly back at him. He should make a show of talking to her, but he knew she wouldn't understand anything he said, so he saved his breath.

Sue leaned forward, her eyes never leaving him. "It went woosh," she whispered.

"Yes," he replied.

He also leaned forward and looked deep into her eyes, searching for any sign of the woman she once was, but there was nothing there. It was as if they were strangers meeting for the first time.

Irene returned with the drinks: two teas and Sue's child's cup of orange cordial. They sat with their drinks and talked about nothing in particular, the weather, the traffic, the fact that Christmas was approaching fast. Richard opened the biscuits, and he and Irene ate a few each before Irene helped Sue to eat one.

Richard told himself to remain patient and wait for his opportunity.

"Need the toilet," Sue suddenly announced.

"No problem," Irene said pleasantly as she got up.

"I'll stay here and look after the biscuits," Richard joked.

Irene dutifully laughed as she gently guided Sue to the downstairs bathroom. Richard listened as they slowly walked down the hallway and went into the downstairs loo.

As soon as he heard the door close, he jumped up, tiptoed down the hallway and silently ran up the stairs. He went through the second door on the left into Sue's room. As soon as he entered, a strong smell of urine stung his nostrils.

"Jeez," he muttered and held his breath as best he could.

The walls were plain cream and the bedding a light pink. There was a built-in wardrobe, a chest of drawers and a chair in the corner with a cushion on it.

He went to the chest of drawers and softly opened the top drawer. It was full of tissues; he grimaced as he rooted amongst them and realised they were wet with mucus. Sue must have been storing them in there without Irene knowing. His hand brushed a particularly wet one, and he gagged.

"Fuuuuuck," he mouthed silently.

He closed the drawer and tried another. There was a jewellery box inside, and he grinned in delight. "Gotcha!" he said under his breath. Richard took the jewellery box out, gently placed it on top of the chest of drawers and opened it. Inside was a jumble of earrings, necklaces and rings. He picked up several rings and held them to the light; they were obviously cheap trinkets. However, there was a green jade ring that caught the light magnificently. He slipped it into his pocket. There was also a pair of pearl earrings, which he took. There were a lot of necklaces; he picked a few solid gold ones and slid those into his pocket too.

Finally, Richard picked up a cheap-looking ring that was clearly a fake diamond and kept it in his hand. Quickly, he snapped the jewellery box shut and put it back in the drawer exactly as he had found it. He checked that he'd not disturbed anything and left the room, glad to be away from its foul stench.

Richard went into the upstairs bathroom and tossed the fake diamond ring into the toilet. He had done the same thing several times now, and they must suspect Sue was flushing, or trying to flush, her jewellery away. It was a cruel ploy, but it acted as a cover for Richard's activities.

He was back downstairs sipping his tea by the time Irene finally led Sue back into the lounge. Richard barely registered their return, as he was trying to calculate how much the stolen jewellery in his pocket was worth. Maybe £500? There was a pawnshop on Gloucester Road that had given him a good price on the last batch. It was helpful having the cash, but what he really needed was a big lump sum. There was an idea bubbling away in his mind, but he still needed to work out all the details.

"Sorry about that," Irene said.

"Listen, I've got to head off," Richard said as he stood up. "It's been lovely to see you both." He gave Irene another winning smile, which he could tell she loved.

"I don't know what we'd do without you. You're a saint," he told her. "Keep up the good work."

"Thank you, Richard. You come back anytime now; Mrs Walker loves to see you."

He walked to the front door, the jewellery digging into his thigh through his trouser pocket, and he called back to her.

"Don't worry, Irene. I'll be back real soon."

12

TWO DAYS AGO

Richard walked past the Winterbourne duck pond that overlooked the fields of the Frome Valley. It was another hot day, and the heatwave was forecast to continue for another week. His hangover from the night before was mild, he'd certainly had worse, and the morning air was refreshing.

Up ahead an old lady was out litter picking along the street; locals often volunteered for the task to make sure the village was kept as clean as possible.

"Hello." She smiled at him as he passed her.

"Good morning!" he replied.

A large village located on the edge of Bristol, Winterbourne is peaceful and surrounded by greenery, yet because of its proximity to the vibrant city of Bristol and its amazing transport links, the village forms an affluent part of the southwest, and its residents, for the most part, are known to be warm and friendly.

Richard continued along Flaxpits Lane, past the small

library and the fish and chip shop until he reached the barber's.

"Morning, Neil," Richard said as he entered.

"Morning," Neil replied, gesturing for Richard to take a seat. "Wow, what happened to you?" he asked as he took in Richard's battered reflection in the mirror.

"The face? Oh, I fell down the stairs."

"Looks nasty."

"It looks worse than it feels."

Neil wrapped a barber's sheet around Richard. "The usual?"

"Yes, please," Richard replied.

Richard had been frequenting the barber's for many years, and Neil had always given him a great haircut. They both chatted, and Richard felt himself relaxing in the comfortable chair and easy conversation.

Once Neil had finished, Richard stood up and stepped to the counter.

"Oh, bugger," he said as he patted his pockets. "I've forgotten my wallet!"

Neil smiled at him. "Don't worry about it, mate; just drop the money in next time you're passing."

"Are you sure? It might not be for a few days."

"Sure, no worries," Neil said as he waved Richard out of the barber's.

"Thank you, I'll see you in a few days."

Richard left and walked next door to the bakery. There was a young team working there, and they sold the most amazing pastries.

"Morning," he said as he entered. "Sausage roll and a scotch egg, please."

The young blonde woman behind the counter placed the

food in a paper bag and handed it over. He took out the warm, freshly made sausage roll and took a bite of it as she typed his order into the till.

"That will be six pounds, please."

Richard swallowed the food in his mouth. "Oh, I don't believe it. I've forgotten my wallet!"

The shop assistant's face fell. "Oh."

"Let me go home and get it."

"Ummm..."

"You know me. I come in here all the time," he said as he flashed her a wide smile.

"Okay," she agreed reluctantly. "It will be six pounds to pay when you return."

"Back soon," Richard called as he walked out.

He made his way back along the high street and headed home. He took his time and thoroughly enjoyed his free lunch. Once he'd finished eating, he screwed up the paper bag and threw it in a hedge. He then felt his pocket, making sure his wallet was still safely there.

RICHARD DROVE through the city of Bristol and towards Stokes Croft. Many of the walls at the corners of streets or of old buildings were covered in vibrant spray-painted images and murals that years ago might have kept people away, but were now seen as an attraction to the area. He wished he'd had the foresight to invest in Stokes Croft before it had become popular; those old apartments that had once cost nothing were now worth a small fortune.

He reached North Road and parked. As he got out of the car and locked it, he couldn't help but look up and

down the road to check no one was around who might
recognise him. Only then did he knock on the door of
number 49.

The door opened, and there she stood.

She wore only a pink towel wrapped around her torso.
Her blonde hair dripped onto the tiled floor, and he
assumed she had just come out of the shower. Her eyes were
bright, her smile dazzling.

Richard stepped into the hallway, closing the door
behind him.

He took her in his arms and kissed her, a passionate kiss
full on the lips.

"Hello, young lady."

She giggled with joy.

They kissed again, Richard's hands gripping her bare
shoulders tightly. He could feel the towel wrapped around
her naked body coming loose.

"How is the old bitch?" she said.

"Miserable as ever. God, it's a nightmare being in that
house. All I do is think about you."

Her face glowed at this. "Well, no flatmates here today.
This house is empty right now..."

They kissed again, this time slower and more intensely.
He marvelled at how soft yet forceful her tongue was and
how firm her body felt to the touch. Every inch of her flesh
gave him huge delight. His hands slid from her shoulders to
the towel. He eased it open, and his heart hammered with
pleasure as it dropped to the floor.

Richard took a step back and gazed at her.

"You look like a goddess," he said breathlessly.

She gave him a knowing grin, basking in the attention
and the compliment.

He stepped back to her and wrapped her in his arms. His hands were all over her body as they kissed again.

"Oh, Professor," she murmured, playfully gasping in delight as he touched her.

Her hands dropped down and fumbled with his belt until it came loose, and his trousers dropped to his ankles. She wriggled from his hug and dropped to her knees in front of him.

He groaned. "God, I love you, Sally."

LATER, they lay in her bed together, their naked bodies wrapped around each other. Her bedroom was small with pink walls and purple bedding.

"You are a wonder." He sighed. "You played your part so well."

"I told you I was the top student in my drama class! Remember, I got a first in my degree."

He kissed the top of her head. "You were amazing."

"I know." She giggled. "But Alice really is so drab and boring, isn't she? Just like you said."

"It's a nightmare being there with her," he said, feeling her nestle further into his arms, "but you really were great. At one point I actually believed I had a long-lost daughter."

Sally laughed.

"I was adopted as a baby. By two lovely people, Jeff and Deidre," she said in a singsong voice, repeating her lines from the first time she'd met Alice.

For weeks they had practised what Sally would say. Richard had written their scripts, and they had spent time in her bed, often naked and usually with a bottle of wine, rehearsing their lines together. Sally had loved it, and he had been amazed at how well she'd taken on the role; she really was an excellent actor. Her three-year drama degree hadn't been a waste.

As well as her acting skills, Richard had been impressed that she'd never questioned what they had planned. He had spent weeks telling Sally how horrible Alice was, most of it fabricated, but when he had finally presented the idea of Sally pretending to be his long-lost terminally ill daughter, she had been completely on board from the beginning.

Richard laughed. "You turned in an Oscar-winning performance. She believes in you completely."

He squeezed her tightly to him, the feeling of her naked body against his making him shudder in delight. They were hot and sweaty, and he loved it.

"Everything is going to plan," Richard told her. "We just need to speed things along a little."

"So, now we leave in two days? And not next week? I can finally quit working in that crappy café?"

"Yes, the money is nearly here, so there is no need to wait to put our plan into action. We'll be together forever, just the two of us."

Sally squeezed him, and they kissed her again. "I can't wait. Tell me again about our trip."

"Well," he began, "we'll leave Bristol when the tide is high, get out of the harbour and set a course for the south-west. We'll hug the coast of North Devon for a day and spend our first night in Cornwall. Then we head south. From there it should only take us a day to reach France. For a week we'll let the winds carry us along the French coast, stopping every evening in little ports for wine and food."

"About the French food..." Sally nestled her head into his chest. "Do they really serve frogs' legs?"

"Actually yes, they do, although it's rare. You won't need to eat them..."

"Good."

"You'll be too busy eating all the snails they like to serve up."

"Richard!" She tilted her head to look up at him with a big grin, her eyes filled with amusement and love. She knew he was only teasing her, and she soaked it up.

He kissed the top of her head. "Once we reach Portugal, we turn east, into the Mediterranean. We'll sail along until Spain, and then we can leave the coast, start exploring all the little islands there." In his mind he was already there, as he described to her the blue water, the white sandy beaches, the heat and the freedom. "We can anchor the boat and swim in the sea; it's so warm this time of year it's like being in a bath. A big, beautiful bath."

"Tell me again about the fish."

"In the afternoons we'll fish; you only need to drop your line in and you'll pull up all sorts of delicious delights. We can eat fresh fish and drink cold white wine every night."

"It sounds wonderful."

He was so close now, so near to making it all happen. Sod Alfred at the university, sod Igor the crazy Russian bastard, sod all of his so-called friends chasing him for the money he owed them, but most of all, sod Alice, the miserable, boring old bitch. Richard was leaving in two days. He was going and never coming back, leaving this hell hole and going to find his heaven.

"It will be. And it's only two days away." He held her

tightly. "It's almost time; before you know it, we'll be leaving."

Richard imagined himself in a few days, out on the boat, sailing with Sally by his side. She was so young and firm. She adored him, and he couldn't wait to get her on the boat, just the two of them. His plan was so close to working: rid himself of Alice, money in the bank, a hot young woman by his side as he sailed his own boat around the Med. Of course, Alice would be left at home. Well, not at home, because they were giving the keys back to the landlord in a few days, and all of their things would be in storage.

Alice would be asked to leave the house with nowhere to go, but he didn't care; if he was really honest with himself, he just didn't care that he would be leaving his partner of twenty years homeless and alone.

"I can't wait until we can be together all of the time," Sally said.

"Me neither. Have you started packing yet? You'll need to now that we only have two days."

"Sort of, well, not really. But I don't have much; it shouldn't take very long. I only have what's in this room. Everything around the house belongs to my housemates."

"Oh, I see," he declared as he jumped up off the bed dramatically. "Leaving it till the last minute, eh?"

Richard opened her wardrobe and found a suitcase. He pulled it out and tossed it on the floor at the foot of the bed. With Sally giggling behind him, he reached into the wardrobe, grabbed a bunch of hangers with dresses on and turned to drop them into the suitcase.

"There, now you have started packing."

"Oi, stop that! I need to fold them." She laughed.

He jumped back into the bed.

"No time for that; it's too late."

They kissed passionately, his arms wrapped around her. Richard could feel her hands over his body, and he loved it.

"Are you sure we have to pack now? Surely, there are better things we could do..."

He rolled on top of her and kissed her neck, his hands pinning her arms down.

"The packing can wait."

"Okay, Professor."

13

ONE DAY TO GO

Alice sauntered around the house, marvelling at how empty it seemed. The evening sun still lit the rooms, casting long shadows on the polished floors. There were boxes in every room, all taped up, neatly stacked and ready for the removal men to collect in the morning. These boxes would go to the storage warehouse in Filton. On each one she had written in black pen what the contents were: *Alice – shoes, Alice – paperwork, Richard – books, Richard – coats* and so on.

They'd been in the house for six years, and she would miss it. There was so much of her old life she would miss, and, for a moment, Alice had to fight back the tears at the thought of leaving that life behind. No, she stopped herself. She had done too much crying lately, and it was time to look to the future. Alice knew she needed to embrace leaving England and sail headfirst into her new life.

Alice stepped through the back door and stood in the garden, the air refreshing after being in the stuffy house. Her flowerpots were gone now; everything had been collected by her friends over the past few days. A pang of sadness hit her; already she was missing the flowers more than she thought she would. *It's because I've cared for them,* she thought; anything you invest time and love in will always be missed.

In the quiet gloom she spied a lone plant pot in the corner of the garden. She walked over and bent down to inspect it. It was a small purple hyacinth. A vague memory of planting it came to her. It must have been missed, and she wondered what to do with it now.

Behind her, she heard Richard step out of the house and into the garden.

"We should go out for dinner," he said.

"Okay. Where do you fancy?"

"Don't mind."

Alice stroked the hyacinth's small purple petals and tried to remember if you gave hyacinths for sorrow or regret. She could smell it now, it had a beautiful scent, but she decided she would leave it for the house's new tenants. Alice stood up and turned to face Richard.

"How about the White Horse?" she suggested.

"You live in that place," he replied, but he acquiesced with a smile.

"I'll get changed."

She went upstairs and showered. Most of her clothes were packed, but she found a red dress in one of her suitcases. Alice normally wore it with tights, but her legs actually had some colour to them, so she kept them bare. The sun dipped away, and she switched on the bathroom mirror to do her makeup. When she was done, Alice stood back and observed herself; she looked good.

Richard was waiting for her downstairs.

"You look great," he said. He seemed a little surprised, as if he'd forgotten just how beautiful she was.

"Let's get a taxi; then we can have a drink."

"Good idea," he replied.

THE PUB GARDEN was mostly full of people eating and drinking, but they managed to secure a corner table. String lights lined the walls, and their soft glow lit the faces of the happy customers.

They ordered food and drinks from the waiter, and despite how busy the pub was, the service was quick, and they enjoyed their food.

"How was your fish risotto?" he asked her after they'd eaten.

"Oh, delicious. I'll miss this place."

Alice looked youthful in the soft, evening light, and Richard decided he liked her dressed in red. Her new blonde highlights suited her too. But it didn't matter how good she scrubbed up; Richard was finished with her now. He watched Alice dab gently at her lips with a napkin and take a tiny sip of her drink. All being well, this would be their last night together.

He smiled. "Don't worry, I'll be catching you a fresh fish every day on the boat."

"I can't wait."

He sipped his ale and looked around the pub garden. Richard had been planning this evening for a long time, and he took a moment to gather his thoughts.

"So, this is our last night in Blighty," he said.

"It's come around so quick." She paused, eyes on him. "I

always thought I would hate leaving, but now the time has come, I can't wait for a new change."

"It will be great to get away from here," he said. "We've worked hard for years; it's only right that we start to enjoy our lives."

She smiled.

Richard made sure his face looked right, a little sad and wistful. It was time to give her a nudge.

He sighed.

"Are you okay? How are you feeling about leaving?" she asked with a concerned face.

"About leaving? Oh, I'm excited. It's just..." He paused for effect. "I've been thinking a lot about Sally. She's been on my mind so much recently."

Alice nodded. "We haven't really spoken about the letter from last night, the DNA results."

"It sounds odd, but I think I always knew she was my daughter, from the day we met her. Although, it was important to get the DNA test to confirm it."

But, of course, the DNA test was a fake; Richard had bought a real one and used it to forge Sally's results. He'd then had the fake document, showing him and Sally were related, delivered to their house for Alice's benefit.

"I owe you an apology."

Alice was surprised by these words. "Why?"

"I've been insensitive, really; I should have considered you and the miscarriages."

Her face fell. "We don't need to talk about that."

Richard could see her getting upset, which suited him perfectly. He knew exactly how to pull her strings.

He looked at her intensely. "When Sally arrived out of the blue like that, it was such a shock, but now I've come around to the idea of having a daughter. It's been such a happy thing that she's come into our lives. But I should have spent time thinking about you..."

Her eyes welled up. "Don't..."

"What you went through with those miscarriages..."

The tears came then, the mascara leaving black lines down her cheeks. He wanted her blinded with emotions; he didn't care that it was a painful subject for her, didn't care at all; he simply wanted her fucking money.

"To have a daughter! It's an amazing feeling, but I really should have been more considerate about what you've been through."

Then he changed his face, made it sad. A little frown. He tried to cry; a few tears would be a dream for him now. *Cry, damn it!* he willed himself. Richard could feel his eyes getting wet; that would have to do.

"And then to find out she's dying," he murmured as he dropped his voice, made it crack, like he was on the edge. "It's strange, but I already feel so protective over Sally. Like any parent, I would do anything to keep her safe and well."

His tears were coming now; a little one rolled down his face. *Yes!*

Alice was in floods of tears, a look of devastation on her face. And this was why he'd chosen a strategy based on him having a fake daughter; because he knew Alice was so emotionally sensitive around the subject of babies and family. He knew it was a weakness of hers and one that he could exploit. He knew that once he got into her head, she would donate a big chunk of her inheritance money to Sally, to help her with her terrible illness. It was a crazy plan, but also simple and potentially effective. Richard had been so pleased with himself when he thought of it.

Alice used her napkin to wipe her cheek, a strange look on her face. "I don't think I've ever seen you cry."

"I've tried not to bother you with it, because we've been so busy packing, but I'm really worried about Sally."

Alice nodded sympathetically. "I'm sure it will work out okay for her."

"Did you mean what you said before?" he asked. *Go lightly,* he told himself.

"What?"

"That we should think about making a donation? I have my big pension pay-out coming in a few years, but I'm just worried that it may come too late."

He kept the sad look on his face and tried to push out a few more tears. It was so hard. But it seemed as though Alice was always bloody crying; how did she manage it? He frowned, letting the silence linger, letting the idea percolate.

"Well, I have Mum's money due tomorrow."

"Right."

"I mean, we could give her some from that?"

"Listen, that's your mum's money. That's money that she's left to you. I mean, of course we're in a relationship, but I see it as your money, and it wouldn't be right for you to give it all away."

"Hmmm..."

"But anything we can donate from your inheritance, I will pay back to you when I get my pension."

Alice sat up a little straighter as she wiped away her tears. "We should help her. She's family. How much were you thinking?"

He shrugged, like he hadn't thought that far ahead. But, of course, it was all he had thought about for six months.

"Fifty thousand?"

He watched her like a hawk, trying to gauge her reaction. She gave a little frown, her lips pursed. What did that mean? He leaned back, inhaled slowly to relax himself. He was desperate to wipe his tear away, as it was annoying him, but he left it there.

"That's an awful lot of money," Alice said.

Bugger.

"But then, will that be enough for her?"

Bingo!

"Well, I think she needs another seventy thousand to secure the operation, but I thought that would be too much."

His heart pounded, and his palms felt wet with sweat. Months of planning and preparation all came down to this moment, and he had to stop himself from gulping at his beer as the nerves coursed through him.

"Seventy thousand?"

"Like I said, I'd pay you back every penny." He paused, as if considering everything. "But it's up to you; let's just give her what you're comfortable with. I'm probably not the best person to decide..." He made his voice wobble, then looked away from her as if trying to hide his pain. "Because I'm just too emotional about it all."

His tears welled up again. *Yes! Come on, you beautiful tears, make me look pathetic*, he thought.

"We should make a donation," she said, and her voice was small. "I just need to think about how much. Do you mind if we sleep on it?"

That's okay, he thought; he could live with that. The ideal scenario would be to get a firm commitment now, but he sensed she would in fact go along with making a donation. He'd pushed it as far as he could for now.

Richard took her hand. "Thank you."

She smiled, wiped her tears away and raised her wine glass. "Let's have a toast."

"Sure." He raised his pint glass, giving her a warm smile with his eyes.

"To the future," she said.

"Cheers!" And their glasses clinked.

14

LEAVING DAY

Richard woke with a headache. The cause was a combination of his damaged nose and the previous night's drinking. He lay in the empty bed for a while, yawning and scratching himself.

"The money has come through," a voice said.

It startled him; he hadn't realised Alice was in the room.

He sat up in the bed and saw her at her dressing table. The table was bare, as everything had been packed away, and Alice was just sitting there watching him, her phone in her hands.

"Can you believe we're leaving today?" she asked with a smile. "Are you feeling nervous?"

He tried to clear his head and focus on her.

"Today's the day." He was desperate for a coffee. "Glad we haven't packed the coffee machine." But she didn't react to his hint.

"It will be high tide in a few hours, so tonight we'll be having dinner together on the boat."

"Yes." He looked away. "Did you say your mum's money

has gone into your account? The full two hundred thousand pounds?"

"The full two hundred," she replied.

"Oh."

"I've been busy this morning. I made the last payment on the boat to Alan and paid the last of the rent on this place."

"Well done," he whispered, trying to stay calm. He felt hot and resisted the urge to kick off the duvet.

"And yes, before you ask, I've made the donation to Sally's account."

He dared not speak, unsure what sound would come out of him. Their eyes met; he hoped she couldn't somehow see that his heart was hammering. Sweat suddenly peppered his forehead.

All he could manage in response was to raise his eyebrows.

"The full seventy thousand, like we discussed. Are you sure you'll be able to pay it back when your pension comes through?"

Richard didn't trust his voice; he just nodded.

He couldn't help but exhale loudly. It had worked! His plan had worked. The blood seemed to course through his veins quicker, and he felt a surge of freedom, like a great weight being lifted from him.

Seventy grand wasn't a fortune, but he could live off it. Plus, he had Stephen ready to sell his car for him, which would be worth another three grand. If he had been staying in Bristol, then £73,000 wouldn't last long with rent and bills. But he wasn't staying; he was leaving. The boat was powered by wind, which was free. And thanks to Alan, the boat was now in perfect condition, so it wouldn't need any money spending on it. All he needed was money for food and wine. He could make it last for years. Obviously, he wanted more; you always wanted more. But he could live off it comfortably. Maybe in a few years he could get a little part-time job if he needed, so could Sally, if she was still with him at that point. Then of course, his real pension would start coming through...

"Richard?"

"Sorry, dear, I was just thinking how generous it is of you. Thank you."

"Well, she is your daughter, after all."

He got up, dressed into a pair of navy shorts and a cream polo top, and tried to remain calm. Which wasn't an easy task, with Alice's eyes never leaving him.

"We'd better get the cars loaded up," he suggested, "and start taking things down to the boat."

"I can't believe it's actually happening; we're leaving today. After all the planning and talking about it." She looked up at him expectantly, wanting something, maybe reassurance or a hug.

"I know."

He gave her shoulder a little squeeze as he passed her. Downstairs, he switched on the coffee machine and turned on his phone. As soon as the screen lit up, it started to ring. The screen told him it was Igor calling.

Damn it. He'd managed to completely forget about the crazy Russian debt collector.

Richard ignored the call and saw that he had several voicemails, probably also from Igor. They weren't supposed to be meeting until that afternoon, so why was he calling him so early? It was only 9 a.m.

Instead of responding to Igor, Richard quickly typed out a text:

> We are all go for today! Pick you up in an hour. Xxx

"Are you making coffee?"

Richard jumped. He hadn't heard Alice come into the kitchen. He shoved the phone into his pocket.

"Yes, would you like one?"

"Please."

He set two cups clattering onto the worktop, grabbed the coffee pot and poured them both a drink. His hand shook as he poured, and dark liquid spilled onto the counter. Alice didn't seem to notice. He handed her a cup, and she smiled at him.

"Thanks. I chopped some fruit; it's in the fridge."

He took the bowl from the almost empty fridge and sat at the breakfast bar. The last thing he wanted was to eat, but he needed to stay calm and act normal. Alice joined him with her cereal, and they ate together. Richard tried to ignore the thought that this would be their last meal together, that soon they would never see each other again.

He wolfed down his food.

"Hungry?"

"Just want to get started, you know, loading the boat. I think we'll need to do a few trips."

She nodded. "Yes, and I've marked everything we're taking with a *B* for boat and *S* for storage."

"Well done, you've done a great job on the packing."

He got up, put his empty bowl in the sink and drained the last of his coffee.

"Why don't I take the first load down whilst you have a final sort out and clean up here?" Before she could reply,

Richard walked out into the hallway, picked up his keys and opened the front door.

His car was on the driveway, near to the door. He unlocked it and opened the boot. Trying to slow himself, he went back into the house and walked upstairs to the bedroom. He had two large cases already packed, and with a gasp, he picked them up and carried them down the stairs. He could hear Alice clattering away in the kitchen as he passed through the hallway and outside to the car. One by one he hefted the cases into the boot. They filled the entire space, and he slammed the door shut on them.

He went back into the house and up the stairs to his office. Amongst the dozen boxes there was just one he wanted: it held a few files, a few books and his certificates. Richard took that one box down the stairs and placed it on the back seat of the car. His breathing was becoming heavy, and he was struggling to contain his excitement; he was going to be free! Free from his debts, free from Alice.

"Richard," Alice called out.

He went into the kitchen.

"Please make sure you take these two boxes on the first trip down to the boat." Alice pointed to two large boxes of crockery and utensils. "I need them out of the way so I can clean the kitchen for the landlord."

He thought about telling her he would get them on the next load, but he just wanted to get going. And, as he thought about it, the stuff would be useful on the boat.

Richard bent down and lifted one of the boxes. His phone started to ring in his pocket.

"Shall I get it for you?" Alice asked, stepping towards him.

"No, no," he gasped as he span away from her. "I've got it."

Struggling under the weight of the box, he made his way down the hall and out to his car, the sound of the phone ringing all the way. He managed to get the heavy box onto the back seat just as his phone stopped ringing. He dug it out of his pocket and saw that it was Igor who had called. There was also a text:

> Yay babe! See you soon. Can't wait. Xxx

He put his phone on silent and went back into the house for the second box from the kitchen. Alice was already spraying the cupboard doors with cleaning liquid and giving them a good wipe. He put the second box in the car and shut the door.

Back in the house, he stepped into each room and looked at the piles of boxes. A lot of the stuff was his, but he didn't want it. He didn't care that he would never see it again. Should it make him sad that all he was taking was a few suitcases and one or two boxes? Perhaps. But, on the contrary, it made him happy. He couldn't wait to leave it all behind.

Alice walked into the lounge with their vacuum cleaner.

"Car's full with the first load," he told her. "So I'm off. I'll be back in an hour."

"Okay, dear." She put the vacuum down and leaned up to him for a kiss.

He pecked her coldly on the forehead and shuffled around her to the lounge door. This would be the last time he ever saw her. The last image he would have of Alice was of her standing in an empty room, yellow Marigold gloves on, unwrapping the cord of the vacuum cleaner. After twenty years, this was it.

"Bye," he said.

"Bye. See you soon."

Richard left the house and had to stop himself from running to the car. For a moment a wave of guilt enveloped him, but he quickly shook it off. He was leaving their house, leaving Bristol and leaving Alice for good. He put the key in the ignition.

His phone vibrated in his pocket. Richard took it out and saw that it was Igor calling again. Was he down at the harbour, waiting for him? That would be a nightmare. Reluctantly, Richard answered.

"Hello?"

"Why you ignoring me?" The man's Russian accent seemed even more pronounced on the phone.

"Sorry, Igor, I've been busy."

"I don't like you ignoring me."

"Sorry." Richard was tempted to tell him to sod off, but he consoled himself that he would soon be having the last laugh.

"I'm going to the docks," Igor said. "You will meet us there. Come now."

Oh God, this was a disaster! Richard felt sick. His plan, so close to being complete, was at risk of unravelling. God damn Igor, the Russian bastard.

"I can't...It's not time yet."

"You think I am stupid? You want to meet after boat is in docks? No, we meet before boat arrives; that way you won't be escaping on it."

"I wouldn't..."

"We meet now."

Richard's mind raced.

"Why don't we meet at my house? I have some things to do here. Then we can all go to the harbour together. Besides, I have the papers for the boat here, so I can sign it over to you officially."

The phone line went silent.

Richard couldn't breathe. He was so close.

"Alright, Professor. I am coming to your house now."

"Okay." Richard exhaled. "The address is three-twelve Borough Way, Winterbourne."

"Borough Way," Igor repeated slowly, as if he was writing it down.

From the car seat Richard could see into the lounge. Alice was in there, yellow gloves flashing back and forth as she pushed the vacuum around the carpet. She looked happy.

"I will be there. And Richard." He paused. "You'd better be there too."

Richard peeled his eyes away from Alice and swallowed the rising feeling of dread. Igor would be at the house soon, and Alice would be there to greet him and his sidekick, Josef. How would she react to that? More importantly, how would they react when they found out Richard had screwed them over?

"Don't worry, I'm here all day."

Richard cut the call and threw the phone onto the car seat.

He turned the key, and the engine clicked to life. Richard reversed off the driveway, put the car into gear and slammed his foot onto the accelerator. The car shot off, heading towards the city.

RICHARD PUSHED THE DOORBELL, and Sally appeared, looking absolutely radiant. She wore skintight jeans and a Breton stripe top.

"It's finally happening!" she squealed at him.

He couldn't stop himself from grabbing her and giving her a big, wet kiss. She returned the kiss, her tongue pushing into his mouth. His hands were all over her, and she groaned.

For a moment he wondered if they had time to go to her room, but instead he pulled back.

"We'd better get going," he said.

"I'm all packed. Just two cases, right?"

"That's it, just two cases." He grinned at her.

"It was a struggle to squash everything in, but my room-mates are pleased to have inherited a lot of my old dresses. Do you want a drink before we leave?"

"There's no time, sorry, babe." He tried to keep the impatience from his voice. "Now, where's the stuff you want to take?"

"In the lounge."

Richard went into the lounge and found two pink cases waiting for him. He picked them up, and pain shot up his arms. He put them down and decided to take one at a time.

"What the hell have you got in here?"

He gasped and struggled with the suitcase but managed to get it out of the house and into his car. He piled the boxes on the back seat onto each other, making room for Sally's case, which he then wrestled onto the back seat.

"My big strong man," Sally called to him from the hallway as he wiped the sweat from his brow.

He smiled and waved at her, trying to ignore the pain in his back. Thank goodness he'd told her only two cases; any more and she was in danger of sinking the boat.

"It's only a small cabin, you know."

"I know, babe, but didn't you say there are two rooms on there? I could use one of the rooms as a dressing room?"

This was the first he'd heard about it. But right now, he didn't care. In fact, he grinned at her as he struggled to get the second case out of the house. If anything, this one was even heavier.

"Okay, you can have the second room."

"Yay!"

He finally managed to get the second case into the car and shut the door. He stepped back, noticing how low his Ford Focus was now. The bottom bumper was so close to the road, any bumps and it would be scraping the tarmac. He would have to keep his fingers crossed that the police didn't stop him.

"Right, let's go."

Sally locked the front door, and they got into the car. The car's suspension sank even further, but Richard didn't care. His eyes drank in the sight of Sally and her long legs as she clipped on her seatbelt. He leaned over and kissed her again. It was ridiculous how sexy she looked. And she was all his.

He put the key into the ignition and started the engine.

"Next stop, the boat."

He set off, this time driving slowly owing to the extra weight in the car. Richard's mind was racing, trying to think through all the angles. Had he forgotten anything? His heart was pounding, and he had to take some deep breaths to calm himself down. It would not be good to have a heart attack now! He smirked at the thought, knowing he was physically fit and strong for his age.

As they drove down Cheltenham Road and through the city centre, Richard's eyes were scanning all around him, just in case Igor suddenly made an appearance. But there was no sign of him. It was a quiet day on the roads, even in the city. People were out walking and cycling in the morning sun, and there was very little traffic on the road.

They reached the harbour, and Richard pulled into the small car park. He got out and looked around; there was no one around. The place was empty. Perfect. He checked his watch. High tide was scheduled for 10 a.m. It was 10:35 a.m. Great timing.

All he had to do was get the cases and boxes from the car and into the boat and then cast off. The plan was for his brother, Stephen, who had a spare car key, to pick his car up later that afternoon and sell it over the coming weeks. He'd happily agreed to do it and would give Richard the full amount from the sale, which was very kind of him. Although Richard knew his brother didn't need the money himself.

Richard started to unload the cases.

"What a lovely day!" Sally exclaimed. "Just look at that sunshine!"

She was right. From across the harbour, Richard could see that the tide was high, and the weather was perfect for sailing out of Bristol and into the main channel. He watched as Sally pulled out a large sun hat and put it on.

"You look stunning. I hope you've packed your bikinis?"

Sally laughed. "I've got a few, but there's not much to them."

The thought of Sally in her bikini on the boat sent his pulse racing. "Sounds amazing."

His phone pinged in his pocket, and he took it out.

It was a message from Igor: *Will be at your house in 10 minutes.*

"All okay?" Sally asked.

Richard put the phone back in his pocket and gave her a huge grin. He'd made it. The plan had worked. He had the money, the boat and the girl. It was time to leave.

"Just perfect," he told her.

PART II

15

FOURTEEN DAYS TO GO

"We all miss you so much," Emily said.

The university café was busy that morning, and they had been lucky to find a quiet corner to sit for a drink.

"Thanks, I miss you guys too. How are things here?" Alice asked.

"All good; nothing ever changes in the biology department." Emily pushed her spectacles up. "Your replacement seems nice. Isla. She moved here from London."

Alice felt a little jealous at the thought of someone else doing her job. Still, Richard was due to leave the university in a few days, so she assumed Isla and Richard wouldn't be working together much.

"That's good," Alice managed.

"I'm thinking of having highlights," Alice said, to change the subject. "What do you reckon?" She flicked her hair in a playful gesture.

"Oh yes, they'd really suit you. I love your hair."

Emily nibbled at a biscuit. Alice always thought how she

was like a little songbird, dainty and precise. It was a warm day, but she was still wearing a cardigan. It didn't matter what the weather was like; Emily always wore a cardigan. It was one of the things Alice loved about her.

"So, how's retired life?"

Alice sipped her green tea and looked around the café. It was mid-morning, and there were a lot of bleary-eyed students drifting in and out, ordering coffees and bacon rolls. How was retired life?

"I'm too young to be retired. I'm looking at it like a sabbatical." Alice smiled. "But it's okay, I suppose. I've been enjoying more time in the garden, and it seems like there is always something to do. We only have a few weeks until we leave, and there's a lot to sort out."

"I can't believe you're doing it; it's so exciting."

"I know. I can't believe Richard has convinced me to go and live on a boat."

Emily laughed; it was a small noise lost in the background clamour.

"You guys will have such an adventure, sailing around Spain and France."

"Half of me is excited, the other half really nervous, especially about the thought of sailing across English Channel. Going along the coast is one thing, but the open channel is quite another. Still, it's weeks away yet, so I'm not thinking about it too much."

"The weeks will fly by," Emily said with a smile, "and you'll soon be off."

A young man wearing an American flag around his shoulders walked into the café, and a corner table of students cheered him. The newcomer joined the table of loud students, and they handed him a beer.

"Bit early to be drinking, isn't it?"

Emily turned around to look at the group. "Them? But they're American."

Alice looked at her blankly.

"It's the Fourth of July."

"Oh."

"Don't you remember seeing them every year? Our American students always get together and celebrate around the campus."

Alice shrugged. In reality, she never spent much time in the café or took much notice of the students and their different activities around campus. Her time here had always been spent with her head in a book, or deep in thought about the latest floral project they were working on.

"It's amazing the things you notice when you're not working," Alice mused. "You are coming to Richard's leaving party next week, aren't you?" she asked, the sight of the student's beer having reminded her. "I've booked the Lido and ordered a buffet."

"Yes, Alex and I will be there..." Emily hesitated, as if she was deliberating about saying something.

"What?"

Emily drank her tea, her eyes lowered. Alice waited patiently for her friend to speak.

"Well, are you worried about people saying something?"

"What do you mean?"

"About Richard."

Alice felt confused. "Richard? What about him?"

"Well, the issues he's had here..." Emily paused, and her pretty face turned red with embarrassment. "I'm so sorry. I thought you knew."

"Knew what?" What was Emily talking about?

Emily looked around, but there was no escape. She had well and truly put her foot in it.

"The reason he's leaving...the university...well." She gulped. "Well, Alfred asked Richard to leave."

"No, that's not true." Alice frowned. "Richard's retiring. He's older than me, and he's simply had enough of work."

"Richard?" Emily tilted her head. "He loves this place."

It was true. Richard loved his job: the title, the prestige, the easy hours and the relaxed working environment. If Alice was honest with herself, she had never thought Richard would leave his role as head of the biology department at Bristol University until he was a very old man. But now they were both leaving. Richard had convinced Alice to quit her job, and he was working his notice. They had planned it so that they would both leave within a few weeks of each other. Alice had believed what Richard had told her; she had never considered that he was being asked to leave.

"Why?" was all she could manage.

"I don't really know the details..."

"Are you sure?" Alice folded her arms. "Emily?"

"I heard it was something to do with his expenses."

"Expenses? Something to do with money?"

"Perhaps." Emily seemed genuinely stricken. "I don't know."

"But that doesn't make sense."

"I'm not sure." Emily looked horrified by her role as a gossip. "Maybe you should speak to Alfred."

Alice wouldn't normally dream of bothering the dean, but she suddenly had an urge to track him down and talk to him. She'd had no idea that there was something untoward behind Richard leaving his job. She finished her tea.

"I've got to go." Alice stood up abruptly. "It was great to

see you." She leaned down and hugged Emily. "Make sure you are both at the Lido next week."

Emily smiled awkwardly. "Don't worry, we'll be there."

"Hi, Alfred. Good afternoon."

"Afternoon, Alice. How are you? Enjoying the retirement?"

He got up from behind his old oak desk and walked around to give her a strong handshake and a warm smile. Alfred's grey beard was wilder than normal, although he had on the usual two pairs of spectacles: one on his head, one on a chain around his neck.

She smiled. "Well, it's more of a sabbatical."

"Sure, sure. Please take a seat. Would you like a tea?"

"No, thank you."

"Not long now then, when do you both set sail for the sunny south and leave us poor workers here?"

"Only a few weeks now." Alice hesitated, but then decided to be direct with him. "Listen, Alfred, I appreciate how busy you are. But I just wanted to ask you about Richard."

"Ah. Professor Richard Barnes." Alfred leaned back in his chair, his eyes scanning the desk. "Surely, if there is anything you want to know, you should speak to him."

"Of course." Alice shrugged, not wanting to be put off. "But what I need to know is...Has he been fired?"

Alfred sighed and ran a hand through his beard. He sat forward and fiddled with a paperclip on his desk, clearly trying to decide on what he should say. Alice waited, ready to insist he give her more information if necessary. It was unlike her, and she was surprised at how resolute she felt.

After a moment he spoke. "He hasn't been dismissed from his role, no."

"I heard a rumour that he may have been," Alice fired straight back.

"We simply suggested that his time with Bristol University has come to an end. All of us here are very grateful for his contributions over the years."

"But why?" Alice sat forward in her chair, her eyes fixed on the old dean. "Why ask him to leave?"

"It's really not appropriate to divulge..."

"Alfred," she insisted, her voice sharper than she'd intended, "I've known you for over twenty years. You gave me a job here, and I'll always be grateful," she continued, her voice becoming louder, "but if you don't tell me what's happened, I'm going to get annoyed."

"Alright." He held his hands up. "But I am speaking to you here in the strictest confidence."

She nodded her understanding, and he went on.

"Look, all our department heads have their budgets to manage. We know they're not all accountants, so we give them a bit of leeway on the figures. At the end of the year, we always have to go through things with them, make sure everything ties up with the accounts." He shifted in his chair. "Richard had some issues with his accounts."

"So? Like you said, he's not an accountant. Isn't that why you help them?"

"His situation is a little more complicated."

"How?"

Alfred hesitated again.

Alice lowered her voice. "How is it more complicated, Alfred?"

"When we looked at Richard's spending for the department, there was some money missing. But the issue was, he had deliberately tried to cover up and hide it."

"That's ridiculous!" She couldn't help the outburst.

"Hmmm, that was my first reaction when the accountants raised it with me. I made them check and double-check. Then I got them to talk me through it line by line. We spent hours going through the online expense system and his paperwork. Turns out they were right." He paused, then winced. "I'm sorry, Alice. In total, £12,000 had been taken, and he'd tried to cover it up."

Alice's mouth fell open. Her legs went weak, and she was glad she was sitting down. £12,000? But why? They had money. There was no need for Richard to do anything like this.

"Because of the longevity of his tenure here, because of the published textbooks related to the university, the TV interviews he's done over the years...well, we thought it was best that we did this quietly. Let him hand his notice in and pay the money back bit by bit. We'll throw him a little leaving party, smile and wish him the best. But, from now on, Richard is no longer welcome at the university."

Alice looked up. Her head was spinning with the news, but she could see how kindly Alfred's behaviour was. He was acting with grace and compassion. He would be within his rights to call the police and have Richard arrested. Richard could be in a cell right now awaiting trial if it weren't for Alfred.

"Thank you," she said in a small voice; those were the

only words she could manage. Then she got up and shook his hand again, although this time it felt awkward.

"Talk to him."

"I will," she whispered.

"RICHARD?"

There was no answer; the house was empty. In the hallway there was a large parcel, and Alice knew it was the flat-packed boxes she had ordered online so she could pack up their house because they were supposed to be leaving it in two weeks. Two weeks! And today she had suddenly learned that her partner of all these years was a thief.

Alice kicked off her shoes and hung up her jacket. She went into the kitchen and put the kettle on. Where was he? She needed to talk to him. Maybe even shout at him. Why had he taken that money? It didn't make sense. Alice took her mobile phone out of her pocket and called him, but there was no answer.

The kettle boiled, but she felt sick and couldn't face anything, not even tea.

What would he need £12,000 for? The boat had been paid for. The repairs bill was due, but they had plenty of money to pay for it. Didn't they? And, of course, her mum's inheritance was due to arrive soon. The solicitors had estimated the figure would be in the hundreds of thousands. Between them, Alice and Richard had plenty of money. So why? Why would he steal from the university? She just couldn't make sense of it.

Alice felt awful. Her head was spinning with the news. She dialled again. Still no answer. She typed out a text:

Where are you? Call me.

She went upstairs, just to check he wasn't having an afternoon nap, but the bedroom was empty. Alice walked into his office and opened the door. His laptop was on the desk. Slowly she sat down on his chair. Without thinking about it, she hit the power button.

The screen came on, asking for a PIN.

She knew the PIN. He didn't know that she knew it, but she did. It was his date of birth.

The screen opened, and she put her hand on the mouse. Could she get into his email account and check his mail? She wasn't sure what she would find. Alice clicked onto his email, but it required a password to open it. She tried the same password as his PIN, but it didn't work. She tried different variations of dates, key words and names, but none of them worked; she couldn't access his mail.

Instead, she looked at his search history.

And immediately she saw that there were dozens of gambling sites listed.

"Gambling?" she exclaimed.

He was a gambler?

She clicked onto one of the sites, and this time she didn't even need to log in; the account details had been saved. Alice went into the account and looked at the history of bets made. Her finger rolled the mouse wheel down to scroll through the bets. There were hundreds. No. There were thousands.

He was a gambler.

Richard was a gambler. He had never mentioned it to her. She wasn't aware of him even putting a single bet on. Not one, in all the years they'd known each other.

"Oh, Richard," she whispered.

So was that why he needed the money? He had obviously spent far too much on his gambling and taken the money from the university to fund his habit. Thank God they didn't have a joint account. He hadn't had access to any of her funds. What did she have? Maybe £8,000 across her various accounts? Not much, but it was hers. So, was he penniless? Did Richard have no money?

Alice continued to scroll through the list of bets. There was something noticeable she could see; a year ago he had been placing bets between £2,000 to £5,000 in value, but six months ago those bets had shrunk in size. It looked like Richard had less to gamble with, and the bets were only in the hundreds of pounds. His most recent bet had been for £50. It was a sharp decline.

Alice spent time clicking through some other sites in the search history, and they all told her the same story; her partner was a gambler, and he had spent a small fortune on placing bets.

She slumped back into the chair, her head spinning even more. The house was silent. Where was he? They needed to talk about this. He needed help. Alice needed to get him some support, some counselling for his addiction. This was bad, but it wasn't a complete disaster. They could still have a good time on the boat, they could still sail down south to the hot sun and open seas. In fact, being on the boat would make it easier to keep him away from placing any more bets. This could be a good thing. Things were going to be okay.

She sat up and put her hand on the laptop screen, ready to close it.

But something stopped her.

She took control of the mouse again and clicked through

Richard's documents, which weren't password protected. There were hundreds, and once again, Alice scrolled through them. There were standard files: old work projects, photos organised by years and trips, half-finished manuscripts, research projects. And amongst them all there was a folder simply called 'S'.

What was S?

Alice clicked on the folder.

It contained a few Word documents, and she opened the first one.

Alice read through the document. It was a list of dates and times and plans for different days, starting from six months ago and ending two weeks from now. It was a long document, as there was a lot of detail. Halfway through reading it, tears began to roll down her cheeks.

The second document she opened was a single page. It appeared to show the results of a DNA test, indicating that Richard and someone called Sally were related. The date of the test was for the following week.

Alice blinked away her tears, staring hard at the screen as she opened a third document. This had details on how to make a fake Just Giving website page. There was a link to the website, and Alice clicked on it. It did indeed look just like a legitimate charity site. There was a picture of a young, blonde woman Alice had never seen before. She was pretty, in a sort of obviously sexy way.

Alice's hands were shaking now. The shuddering moved up her arms, and soon her whole body was shivering with shock and anger and anguish.

She braced herself against the desk and forced herself to open the fourth document. It was a news article about a maternity nurse called Sally who was dying and needed funding for an operation to save her life. There was something strange about the layout, and Alice stared at it for a moment before she realised what it was that was so odd; the document had been made to look like a webpage. Alice clicked a few buttons, switched to full-screen mode, and now the text looked just like a website.

The last document was an email with next week's date on it. It was from someone called Julie Long, sent to Richard. It explained how she had been unable go through with an abortion. It was fake. It was all lies.

Alice went back and reread all of the documents again. And again.

Then she knew; *S* stood for Sally.

And she also knew that Richard's sick plan was due to start the following week.

She knew everything.

Alice stood up, clenched her fists and screamed.

16

NINE DAYS TO GO

"Professor Richard Barnes has been a stalwart member of staff at the university for fifteen years." Alfred paused to make sure the crowd was listening to him. "Of course, he's been with us for almost twenty years, but the less said about his early days, the better."

Laughter erupted around the restaurant, and Richard tensed. *What a two-faced arsehole*, he thought.

"Of course, I'm joking," Alfred continued, as he went on to speak about Richard and what a good job he'd done while at the university.

Obviously not a good enough job to overlook some missing money though, was it? Richard had really just borrowed that money; he was planning on paying it all back, every penny! But Alfred hadn't listened; he'd just told Richard to leave, to hand in his notice and pack his things up.

"...So please raise your glasses in a farewell toast to our dear friend and colleague," he said as everyone raised their drinks. "To Richard, wishing you a well-deserved rest in your retirement, cheers."

"Cheers!" the room chorused.

Richard smiled and looked around the restaurant. They were in the Lido in Clifton, near to the university. It was okay, but he'd always thought his retirement party would be grander, a big, huge send-off in recognition of all the great things he'd accomplished as Head of Biology.

He looked at Alice next to him, and she smiled encouragingly. Richard couldn't wait to be rid of her, she looked so boring and drab that night, and he was embarrassed to be seen with her. For a moment he imagined Sally being there with him; she would be in some sort of tight dress with the curves of her firm young body and large breasts looking fabulous. It would be a dream to be seen out with her, and he didn't have to wait much longer for that dream to come true. In just over a week, he would be leaving Bristol, sailing away on his boat with the beautiful Sally.

Alfred moved back into the crowd of lecturers, and Richard took that as his cue to walk forward to the front and address everyone gathered there. A hush fell over the room as his eyes slowly looked around at everyone gathered. *Is this it?* he thought. It was a crap turnout; maybe forty or fifty people at most. His eyes landed on Alfred, who, despite his usual composure, looked nervous.

Richard sipped from his glass of red wine, enjoying the attention.

"I think the food will soon be ready, so I will keep this brief."

Should he tell them to all bugger off? Tell them to shove their university, their department, their reputation up their arse? It was very tempting, but he did have his pension to think about, however far ahead in the future it was.

"The university has been such a great place to work, and I've enjoyed my time working alongside all of you. As you know, my partner Alice and I will be sailing off to the Mediterranean soon."

Richard looked over to where Alice was standing at the bar; *Miserable bitch*, he thought.

"Although after receiving my leaving gifts," Richard said with a wave to a table in the corner, which was littered with lifejackets and various pieces of safety equipment, "I think I need to reassure you that I'm an excellent sailor."

The room reverberated with laughter.

"So please don't worry about me. And if things get too rough, I'm sure Alice could try to pitch in." He waited for more laughter, but none came.

"Well, you've got our email, so if ever you find yourself around the coasts of Spain, France or Italy, let us know, and we may sail over and join you for a glass or two of wine." He gave them one of his biggest smiles, and he could see them smiling back at him.

A waiter appeared in the corner of the room.

"Ah, it looks like the buffet is ready. So I'll just say, once again, thank you for all your support over the years, and I wish you all the best for the future."

The room applauded, and he moved back into the mass of people, taking large sips of his wine as he went. He needed to get drunk. He made it back to Alice, who wittered on at him, but he hardly heard her.

They got some food, and he had to admit the buffet was tasty. Then he made his way to the bar and ordered a large gin and tonic. He talked to his colleagues and drank. They shared funny stories of their times together, and as he chatted, he continued to drink. He had a few more gin and tonics, then a few more glasses of wine. The night continued at the bar with a small crowd of people around him. A few of the guests came up to him before they headed home and wished him well, but from their embarrassed looks, he could tell they knew about the missing money.

At one point he found himself alone and chatting to the barman when Alice appeared beside him.

"It's time to leave; our taxi will be outside in a moment."

Richard looked around and wondered where everyone had gone.

"Just need the toilet," he slurred at her.

He took a mouthful of wine and stumbled off. Just as he went into the men's toilets, there was someone walking out of one of the cubicles. It was Alfred.

As their eyes met, Alfred's face dropped, and he hesitated.

Richard grinned at him. "Go on then, wash your hands."

Alfred slowly moved over to the sink and turned on the tap as he watched Richard through the reflection in the mirror. Richard was stood in the middle of the small room swaying, his eyes boring into Alfred.

"Have you had a nice evening, Richard?" Alfred asked.

"Shut up, dickhead."

Alfred turned to face Richard, his wet hands dripping water on the floor. "Now, Richard, listen..."

Richard stepped forward, a mean look on his face. "No, you listen, you fat old bastard."

"Richard!"

"After everything I've given you and that bloody university, after all I've done, one little error of judgement and you throw me under the bus..."

"One little error? You stole a significant sum of money, Richard."

Richard simply snorted in reply and stepped closer to Alfred, whose face had turned pale in terror. Richard grabbed him by the lapel and pulled him closer so that their noses were touching.

"What are you doing?" Alfred gasped.

"I'm going to beat you up."

Alfred pushed back. They were both older men, and unfit, but Richard's slim frame was no match to Alfred's bulk, and before he knew it, Richard found himself on the floor as his former boss hurried from the toilets.

"You fat..." Richard put his hands down to push himself up and realised the floor was wet. "Ugghhh."

He managed to get up and stumbled towards the sink, where he threw up. The vomit stank of rancid wine and gin. He turned the tap on and splashed some cold water on his face. As he looked up, he saw himself in the mirror. His eyes were bloodshot, and his hair was all out of place.

Richard wet his hands and smoothed his hair down; then he splashed more water on his face and cupped his hands to swill his mouth out.

He stood up straight, wiping his hands on his trousers.

The toilets smelled like sewage.

"Bastard."

"Winterbourne, please, mate."

"No problem," the driver called back to them.

They got into the taxi, Richard clutching bundles of gifts, Alice holding a collection of retirement cards. She clipped on her seatbelt, but Richard was too drunk to bother.

The car set off from the city and began the fifteen-minute drive north to their village on the borders of Bristol. It was late, but the summer sky was still light.

"Did you see that git Alfred?" Richard slurred.

Alice looked across at him as he ran a hand through his hair. She thought how he had looked dashing that evening in his red crushed-velvet jacket.

The previous week, Alice had phoned a gambling addiction hotline and talked through what she'd discovered about Richard. They had been very helpful, and she'd been surprised to learn just how crippling the addiction could be. And, as she'd thought through things, Alice had realised it was Richard's gambling addiction that had made him write out that crazy plan to get his hands on her inheritance money. There was no way he would actually go through with it, she told herself. It was obviously just a way for him to work out how he might get away from his debt, but now that she was aware of the issue, she was going to help him.

She knew that Richard was too proud to admit he had a problem, and he would hate it if Alice knew about his gambling. But, still, she was going to help him. Once they were on that boat and away from Bristol, Alice was determined to stop him gambling.

"You still haven't told me all of the details," Alice said. "Why exactly did they push you out?"

Richard looked out the window, the passing streetlamps flashing orange light on and off his face.

"I told you, Alfred was playing politics, and he made up some rubbish about my admin not being correct."

"Admin?"

He adjusted the pile of gifts on his lap, trying to get comfortable.

"You know, my expenses and stuff."

"Expenses?"

"Don't worry, it was nothing untoward, I'd done a few expenses slips wrong, and he jumped on them as an excuse to have me replaced. The important thing is, it's nothing that's going to interfere with my pension in a few years."

Just tell me, she thought, *just open up and tell me. I won't judge you; we've been together too long for me to judge you.* Her eyes were pleading, but he didn't turn to look at her.

"You sound drunk," she told him and smiled.

He grinned out the window. "Yes, I had a few wines."

"Well, if ever there's a time for it..."

"My bloody retirement party is it."

Alice ran her hand over his shoulder. She'd had a few glasses of wine herself to celebrate an end of an era. What had he done wrong, really? Hidden a gambling addiction from her? That wasn't his fault; it was part of being an addict. He'd stolen money from the university. Again, the addiction had driven him to it. And then he had written out some wild plan to take her money. But he hadn't gone through with it, and she didn't think he would. The start date on his plan was tomorrow. For the past few weeks, Alice had been so loving with Richard, to remind him of what he'd got with her, and in her heart she felt sure he wouldn't go through with his silly little plan.

"I love you, you know," Alice told him.

The taxi driver's eyes flickered to them through the rear-view mirror.

Richard didn't turn from staring out the window as he squeezed her hand.

"Love you too."

EIGHT DAYS TO GO

RICHARD'S SNORING WOKE ALICE. Or maybe it was the stifling Saturday morning heat. They were due a heatwave that weekend, and it felt like it had already started despite it only being 7 a.m.

Alice dragged herself out of bed, went to the toilet and then headed downstairs to put the kettle on. From the fridge she pulled out packets of fresh fruit and cut them up into small pieces ready for his breakfast.

On the kitchen counter were the cards and gifts from last night's retirement party. Alice put the cards up on the mantelpiece in the lounge; as she did so, a photo of her mum looked up at her, and a jolt of pain hit her.

"Miss you, Mum," she whispered to the picture.

Back in the kitchen she sorted through the gifts; there were two slim lifejackets, a yellow waterproof bag, a waterproof torch, a handheld beacon, a first aid kit and a rubber-handled knife. She picked the knife up and couldn't help but smile; there was nothing safe about that.

She poured Richard a cup of coffee from the pot and took it upstairs to him.

"Morning, darling." She put the coffee on the bedside table.

He stirred under the covers.

"Uggh, how much did I drink?"

She laughed. "Enough."

Alice showered and then sat at her dressing table in the bedroom. She studied her hair and admired her new highlights, pleased with how they framed her face. She pulled out all her makeup from its various drawers and got to work putting on her face.

After a while Richard sat up and slurped at his coffee.

"That's good," he said.

He got out of bed and showered whilst Alice dried her hair, before he reappeared looking more alive.

He showered and got dressed, and they went downstairs together. *This is what they mean by domestic bliss*, Alice thought. Richard poured himself more coffee from the pot, and she got his fruit from the fridge for his breakfast. Alice then poured herself some cereal into a bowl.

The front doorbell chimed.

"Why don't they just leave the parcel in the porch?" Richard said through a mouthful of fruit.

They looked at each other, but he didn't seem like he was about to get up.

"I'll get it," she said with a roll of her eyes.

She walked down the hallway to the front door. There was a figure stood on the front porch, blocking out the morning light. Alice opened the door to see a young woman standing there, tall and blonde, nervous and curious. Alice had seen this woman before; her photo was the one on Richard's computer.

"Hello?" Alice croaked.

"Hi, my name is Sally; umm, does Professor Barnes live here?" she asked with a Welsh lilt to her voice.

Sally.

S.

Oh, please God, no.

He was going to do it. He was going to go through with it.
As the world span around her, time seemed to slow for Alice.
She had read the details of Richard's crazy plan two weeks
ago, and since reading it, Alice had convinced herself that he
wasn't actually going to go through with it. Her initial horror
at what she'd read had turned to cynicism, and she'd
become dismissive of the idea he might actually carry it out.
At no point in the last two weeks did she really imagine
Richard could be such a bastard as to do something so devious, so devastating.

The sun was too bright that morning, she suddenly
realised. Had it always been that dazzling?

What should she do? Sally was staring at her
expectantly.

"Richard," Alice called over her shoulder.

She thought she might faint. The sound of Richard's
footsteps came down the hallway to her.

"What's up?"

Alice stepped aside and pulled the front door open
wider.

"There's someone here to see you," Alice said, watching
him, taking in every inch of his face, trying to catch his eye.

Richard arrived and looked at the young woman.

"Can I help you?" he asked cautiously.

For a moment the newcomer seemed speechless and just
stared at him. Her eyes scanned his face, much like Alice was
doing. She put her hand to her own face, as if feeling the
features there for the first time.

"Professor Barnes," she said. It wasn't a question.

He nodded.

"My name is Sally; I think I'm your daughter."

Alice and Richard stared at her, both of them speechless.

"Twenty-five years ago, you and my mum...my mum is Julie Long. She got pregnant and gave me up for adoption."

"I didn't. I'm not..." He tried to talk, but it seemed that he couldn't.

He was acting. Acting this look of surprise and shock. Oh God, it was so convincing, so real. He was lying. She had been living with a lying bastard all these years, and at that moment, all at once, her world was destroyed. This was too much. The complete audacity, the...what was the word...the evilness of what he was doing.

No, her mind wailed. How could he do this to her?

How could he?

She should have said right there and then that she knew this was all fake. An act. She knew. Alice should have slammed the door, slapped Richard's face and run upstairs to pack her things. But she couldn't, somehow the madness of his plan had frozen her to inactivity. Surely, he didn't think he would get away with it. Could he really keep this monumental lie going? She should have run away right then. But she didn't.

Instead, she turned to Sally.

"You'd better come in," Alice said.

17

EIGHT DAYS TO GO

The lounge was a long room that was painted white apart from one wall covered in blue and gold wallpaper. Two sofas faced each other at one end of the room, one on each wall. Richard sat on the left-hand sofa, Sally on the right. Alice sat in the armchair facing the two sofas, watching them both.

Alice cleared her throat. "Shall I make us all a drink?"

Sally looked up, there was a nervous glow to her cheeks, and her eyes kept jumping around the room. "Yes, please."

"What would you like?"

"Coffee with milk would be fantastic, thank you." The word *fantastic* sounded very Welsh.

Alice went to the kitchen and put the kettle on with shaking hands. Richard appeared behind her. He looked shell-shocked.

"Bloody hell," he said.

"A daughter?" was all she could manage.

"If she's telling the truth," he whispered. "How would we know?"

Alice shrugged weakly. "Oh, Richard, at least give her a chance to explain."

"Of course."

Alice should say something. She should speak up and tell Richard she knew this wasn't real, that last week she had found the files about Sally on his computer. But she was in shock, her mind was whirring with what was happening, and the words wouldn't come to her.

They looked at each other as the kettle boiled behind them.

What a bastard!

"She must be about twenty-four years old," he said, "and you know I've never been unfaithful." He was doing the math, they had been together twenty years, so she couldn't have been conceived when they were together.

A small laugh escaped from Alice's mouth. "I know; the thought hadn't even occurred to me."

He seemed relieved by this.

"What do you want to drink?"

"Coffee, please."

She turned to the counter and made the drinks, two coffees and a green tea for her. Richard found a tray in one of the cupboards, and she put the hot drinks on there. They walked back into the lounge. Sally hadn't moved; she was still sat looking around the room.

"Here you go," Alice said as she put the tray of drinks down on the coffee table in between the two sofas.

Richard resumed his seat back on the sofa facing Sally and motioned for Alice to sit next to him. She pretended not to see; instead she took her drink from the tray and sat on the armchair again.

Sally sipped her coffee.

"So," Richard said, "what makes you think I'm your biological dad?"

Alice suddenly wanted to throw her drink at him. Burn his face, burn his lying, evil face.

Sally put her coffee cup down on the table. "I was adopted when I was just born. By two lovely people, Jeff and Deidre. They never tried to hide anything from me, and I've always known I was adopted. Maybe I was six when they first told me." Sally looked from Richard to Alice. "Of course, it didn't really mean anything when I was little, but the older I got, that changed. Anyway, I never thought about finding my real parents until a year ago."

It was all so believable! It sounded so real, but Alice knew it was fabricated. Now. Now was her chance to say, "I know you're lying!" and push them both out of the house. But still she found herself going along with them.

"What changed?" Alice asked.

"My father died. Cancer. They were a lot older when they adopted me, so he was eighty-three."

"Sorry to hear that," Richard said. His voice was dry and cracked.

"Mum's still going strong, although she's in a home now. I guess you get to an age where you think about things differently. So I got in touch with my mum...biological mum... Julie Long. Do you remember her? She was a lab assistant at Cardiff university."

A jolt of shock hit Alice. "A lab assistant?"

Richard looked ashen, but still couldn't speak.

"You were sleeping with your lab assistant at Cardiff?" Alice asked, her voice getting louder and sharper.

"Yes." He wouldn't look at her; his eyes were fixed to the floor.

Sally looked at Alice, her head tilted to the side.

Oh, he was clever! He would know that Alice would be jealous of that little fact, that Richard had supposedly slept with another lab assistant. He'd made it up to throw her off the scent of them lying. The devious bastard.

Alice took a deep breath. "Richard and I have been together for twenty years, after we met at Bristol University. I was his lab assistant."

"Ohh," Sally replied. "I'm so sorry. I didn't mean to make things awkward."

"It's fine, Sally," Richard assured her. "I should have told Alice." He looked up at Alice. "Sorry, it was remiss of me not to mention it."

Alice realised her hands were clenched, and she tried to relax. She took a sip of her green tea, but it was too hot and burned her mouth.

"So, might there be any other lab assistants you've got pregnant?" It was petty, but Alice couldn't help it.

"No," he said to the floor.

"I'm so sorry," Sally murmured. "I didn't think..."

He was really going to do this, was he? He was going to act out this lie? Did her face indicate that she believed them? Alice studied Richard; he thought this was all working, didn't he? He had no idea that Alice knew this was all bullshit.

"It's fine, Sally. Truly," she said with as much grace as she could muster. "It was before Richard and I met, so I shouldn't get worked up about it. Please do continue."

"Well, Julie Long's details, my mother's details, were on the adoption letter, and I managed to get a copy of it."

Sally reached into her bag, took out a folded piece of paper and handed it over to Richard. At first, he seemed reluctant to take it, but Sally didn't retract her arm, so he reached out and took the document from her. Slowly he opened it and scanned the page.

"Julie Long," were the only words he could manage.

"Well?" Alice asked.

He seemed to resign himself to talking, sat up straight and finally lifted his head up to look at them both. "Yes. I was a new lecturer there, though in the end I spent three years at the university. We were both single and started seeing each other. I knew she got pregnant, but we were both so young she decided to have an abortion. It caused things to become strained between us, and we ended our relationship not long after."

He was a good actor. Alice realised he must have practised this little act, rehearsed the phrasing for maximum impact. She turned to Sally. Who was she? They must have been rehearsing this for a long time. Richard and Sally must have spent a lot of time together practising what they'd both say, how they'd behave. There seemed to be a real chemistry between them.

Alice watched them both, her head slowly moving back and forth. They were acting, but Sally really did seem genuinely besotted with Richard. And Richard? He was in full charm mode: the bright eyes, the big smile and the occasional flick of his hair.

She thought about them both alone together. How did he convince Sally to go through with this? Surely she wouldn't do something so mean unless...oh God. The realisation hit Alice like a mule kick to the stomach. They were having an affair. It was so obvious. Richard had been sleeping with this woman. The thought made her want to throw up. Why was she only just realising this now? There was so much to take in.

"Oh, I am so, so sorry. I should have thought this would all be overwhelming." The Welsh accent was already starting to grate on Alice. "As you can see from the birth documents, she did in fact give birth to me, and she put your name as the father. She was listed as a lab technician and you, as my father, was listed as a lecturer. I traced her to the university, and from there it was easy enough to find you. I'm twenty-five, so the dates all match up too."

Richard stared at the paper in his hands.

"Well, that was all a bit uncomfortable." He smiled at her, the full-on Professor Barnes charm oozing out. She had to stop herself from punching him in the face.

"Yes."

"Like I said, I'm sorry," Sally said. "For any upset caused."

"I think you're right, looking at this document, and hearing your story, it does sound like I'm your father." Richard paused. "Although – and I don't mean to be rude – might it be worth thinking about a DNA test?"

"Oh, of course." She smiled brightly at him.

"So I have a daughter? I must say, it's all a bit of a shock."

"Where do you live, Sally?" Alice asked.

"Yes, please tell us about yourself."

"Oh, well. I live in Cardiff with my boyfriend, Ryan. I'm a nurse..."

"A nurse? Good for you."

"Thanks. I'm a midwife at Heath Hospital."

"A midwife! I can't imagine delivering all those babies."

Alice watched them talk, flooded with emotions so strong they clawed like acid in her stomach. Was she really a nurse? Alice doubted it. What did she really do? Where did she really live? It was all false, all lies, lies, lies. Her heart ached; her head was spinning. How could he do this to her?

"We have a dog, Dudley. We spend a lot of time taking him for walks up at the Brecon Beacon's. Ryan has a big family, so we spend a lot of time with them."

They talked for a while, mostly Richard asking questions, Sally answering them and Alice watching them both, not daring herself to speak.

Eventually the conversation ran out of steam.

"Thank you for sharing all of that with us," Richard said. "Perhaps we can swap email addresses and get in touch again once we have processed all of this." He sounded as if he were wrapping up a job interview.

"Of course; honestly, I don't have any expectations from you. I just wanted to make contact. I really appreciate your time and you talking to me."

Sally pulled a slip of paper from her handbag. "I've written my details on here." She stood up and handed the paper over to Richard. "Don't feel like you have to get back in touch. I understand this is a lot to take in."

Richard and Alice stood too.

"I'll show you out."

They went to the front door, said their goodbyes, and Sally left.

Richard closed the door and gave a huge sigh. "Jeeeesus."

Alice didn't reply. She went back into the lounge, put the three empty cups back on the tray and took them out to the kitchen. Richard followed her but didn't say anything. He hovered in the doorway, obviously trying to gauge her mood.

The dishwasher was full, so she turned the hot water tap

on and began rinsing the cups. One of them had pink lipstick on the rim. Sally hadn't seemed to be wearing any lipstick, but there it was, a little half circle of colour on Alice's nice white cup. It was a little mark left in their house. A little reminder of an intrusion into their lives. Alice used the sponge in the sink and forcefully scrubbed the lipstick off.

"Are we still going to lunch?" Richard asked behind her.

Alice wanted to throw the cup at his head. She wanted to scream at him, but she didn't. So he really was determined to screw her over? Most people would just get up and leave, but not this bastard. Alice thought back to the documents she'd read on Richard's computer. What happened next? A few meetings with Sally, and then he would reveal the news about her being ill: terminally ill. And how she needed money and *"oh, do you think we should make a donation?"* and then Alice would donate a lot of money for the terminally ill Sally.

Then they would disappear.

She couldn't think straight, couldn't process what was happening.

How could he do this to her?

And what should she do?

"Sure." She paused, unable to turn and look at him. "But you're driving. I need a drink."

THE WHITE HORSE in Hambrook was busy, which was usual for a Saturday afternoon. Alice had booked them a garden table, and they were shown through the gardens to a nice corner table in the sun. Their friends Jan and Freddie were already there.

It was nice to see Jan and Freddie. Jan looked divine, and they both offered Alice and Richard their usual warm greetings. The four of them ordered food and drinks, and once the drinks arrived, they toasted one another with a "cheers".

They talked for a while as Alice gulped at her red wine. Her mind was such a mess that she struggled to keep up with the conversation.

Their friends seemed to sense the strain hovering around Alice and Richard, and the table became quiet for a moment.

"Are you two alright? You look like you've just had some bad news. The boat hasn't sunk, has it?" Freddie gave a short laugh at his joke.

Richard and Alice looked at each other.

"You should tell them, Richard." *Yes,* she thought, *lie to our friends too. You total bastard.*

He nodded to her.

"We had a visitor this morning. A young woman called Sally. It turns out she's my daughter."

"What?!" Jan exclaimed for the both of them.

"Your daughter. I thought you didn't have any kids?" Freddie asked.

"I don't, or I didn't. My girlfriend twenty-five years ago got pregnant. I thought she'd had an abortion, but it turns out she had the baby and gave it up for adoption."

It was Jan and Freddie's turn to gulp at their drinks.

"That's crazy. How do you feel about it? What was she like? Sorry, just say if you don't want to talk about it."

Richard shrugged. "I'm not sure how I feel about it." He looked to Alice. "It was a shock for both of us."

"Oh, of course," Jan said, and squeezed her hand again.

They all knew what *of course* meant.

It meant *of course, this must be difficult because you've lost babies in the womb.*

It meant *of course, this must be difficult for you because you could never have children, and now Richard is a father, but you're not a mother.*

Jan squeezed her hand, and it was so comforting that Alice had to stop herself from crying.

Of course, this must be hard; you've always wanted a family of your own more than anything in the world.

Richard knew how upsetting those experiences had been. He knew how devastating they were to Alice, and she had honestly thought he'd been upset by the miscarriages too. But here he was, using a story about a fake daughter as an excuse to get his hands on her money. Had he actually cared at all? How could he use such a sad set of experiences from their past to deceive her like this?

But then it suddenly dawned on Alice that he was hoping that she would be upset about the miscarriages. After all, the more she wasn't thinking straight, the easier it would be for him to get away with his plan.

How could he be so horrible? Alice realised that she didn't really know him at all.

He wasn't the man she thought he was.

"It's fine," Alice said, although her voice wobbled.

She sipped her wine. Perhaps she wouldn't be the woman he assumed she was, either.

Freddie looked at Richard. "What did she want?"

"Want? Nothing. I think she just wanted to meet her biological father. Her own dad, well, her adopted dad had died recently, she said. Which meant she wanted to meet me.

We swapped emails, but I don't think we'll see much of her again."

"Not unless she suddenly appears off the coast of Italy."

Richard snorted. "Exactly." He gave Alice a rub on her back. "I guess she didn't think how disruptive it might be, coming to our house. I suppose it's difficult for everyone."

"Just need the ladies'," Alice said, desperate to get away from Richard's touch.

She got up and left them. In the toilets she locked herself in a cubicle, and the tears came; they flooded out of her in anguish. Alice grabbed some tissue and dabbed at her eyes, hoping her mascara wouldn't run too much. It had been a monumentally difficult morning, and she was struggling to keep hold of the emotions coursing through her.

Eventually, she came out of the cubicle with a handful of tissue and went to the sink and mirror. Alice looked at herself. A crack ran up the middle of the mirror and crossed through her reflection, it was a thin crack, but it was enough to distort her face.

Nice Alice. Sweet Alice. *"Oh, that's Alice, she's lovely."* She'd always been polite, nice, friends with everyone. Lovely little Alice. But nice didn't mean weak. Nice didn't mean stupid.

Richard had underestimated her.

So, he wanted to spin this complex, deliberate web of lies to cheat her out of her money? Well, he wasn't the only one who could be devious. He wasn't the only one who could lie. And suddenly the fog in her mind lifted, things became clearer for her, and she decided she wasn't going to let him get away with this.

Alice was going to be like the yellow flowers of the bird's-foot trefoil. Small, pretty and filled with cyanide.

There were still signs that she'd been crying. Luckily, she had a pair of sunglasses in the pocket of her dress. She sniffed, took a deep breath and put them on.

Alice forced a smile and walked out into the sunshine.

18

SEVEN DAYS TO GO

The rope pulled at her neck, and she fought the urge to open her mouth under the water. Panic flooded through her, a panicked horror that one moment she was having a sailing lesson and the next she was about to die. She didn't want to die, yet here she was, underwater in Bristol's harbour, a rope around her neck and the sail of her capsized boat covering the surface above her.

Alice wrestled with the adrenaline pumping through her body and pushed away the panic to try to think. She couldn't go up. She had to go down. Every fibre in her body fought against going further down into the darkness, but she willed herself to stop pushing up and let her terrified body sink downwards. She sank towards the black depths.

As she went down, she could feel the rope around her throat loosening. With calm hands Alice untied the rope and felt it fall away from her skin. As her lungs burned and her vision started to fade, her hands worked calmly.

And then she was free.

She found the energy for one kick, and it was just enough to break the surface. With exhausted arms, Alice pushed the sail towards the sky as she gasped in the open air. It was the single greatest feeling she'd ever had; it wasn't just air, it was life. She gasped and coughed, and for a moment, she couldn't believe how close she had just come to dying.

Alice was suddenly aware of her body shaking uncontrollably. She scanned the area and could see that Roger was way down the harbour, busy helping other students whose boats had also capsized.

With tired arms, Alice swam away from the sail and came around the other side of her boat. There was a trick to righting the boat that she'd been taught but had never done. She grabbed a rope, reached up out of the water and put her body weight on one side of the boat. Surprisingly, it started to move, and despite feeling so drained, Alice pulled backwards on the rope and watched as the boat righted itself. She climbed back in and once again took control.

Behind her she could hear Roger's engine approaching.

"All okay?" he called.

Alice turned and gave him a thumbs-up and a smile. He grinned back at her, but she had to turn her back to him so he didn't see the tears that were forming, or notice that her hands were shaking.

She continued to sail across the harbour, still with the feeling of the rope around her neck; several times her hand went to her throat to check there was nothing there. The lesson continued as normal. After an hour Roger blew his whistle to signal it was finished, and she tacked back to the jetty of the sailing school.

"Good lesson, everyone," Roger called out as he helped

the students hook their boats back to their trailers. The sails were then wrapped around the masts and the rudders pulled into the boats.

As Alice was the last to leave the water, there was no one around to help her, so she gingerly wheeled the trailer down to the water's edge and slipped the boat onto it. Her arms were in agony as she manoeuvred the boat up to the storage area. It was a building with no walls, a huge metal cage with a roof that housed over a hundred boats and kayaks.

A few people waved their goodbyes, and then she was the last student remaining. She wheeled the boat into the open warehouse and dropped it back into place with satisfaction.

"Are you okay?" a voice asked from the shadows.

Alice turned to see Roger stepping towards her. His broad frame seemed to loom large in the tight space, and a line of sunlight caught his eyes, so they glowed in the darkness.

"Yes, I'm fine..." she began, but then her voice caught, and she couldn't speak.

He moved closer and put a hand to her throat, his touch gentle despite the strength of his big arms. "This looks painful," he said.

"When the boat went over, I got a rope caught around my neck."

"Oh shit, you should have told me. Does it hurt still?"

His voice was full of concern, and she realised it was something she wasn't used to. The caring look in Roger's eyes felt so comforting and warm that Alice felt a pang of loss, a feeling that she'd been missing something in her life.

She nodded and blinked as tears filled her eyes.

Then, before she could stop herself, Alice fell into his arms. He didn't speak, just wrapped his big arms around her and held her tightly. The tears came then; tears at Roger's gentle nature, tears at the death she had just avoided and tears for what Richard was planning to do to her.

After a moment Roger stepped back, keeping his hands on her shoulders. "Do you want me to take you to the hospital?"

"No, I'm fine. I'm so sorry for crying on you like that."

He smiled, his teeth white in the darkness of the warehouse.

"Seems like you had a tough session."

"Actually, it's not just the unexpected dunk in the harbour," Alice said as she made a decision. "It's my arsehole partner too."

He chuckled. "Come into the office; let me make you a coffee and get you warmed up."

As Alice followed him, she watched as he locked the caged door, and then she walked with him across the car park to a single glass door. They both stepped inside the small office: one desk, a filing cabinet and two chairs. On the walls were navigational maps of the seas and rivers around Bristol.

"Take a seat." He motioned to one of the chairs.

On the filing cabinet there was a tray with a kettle and a few mugs, plus a jar of coffee and half a pint of milk. He flicked the kettle on.

"Sugar?"

"No, thanks."

He handed her a steaming mug and sat down on the other chair. The warmth of the drink felt good in her hands.

She suddenly felt embarrassed at her tears and lowered her gaze to the mug. It had a photo of a sausage dog on it.

"That's Oscar."

"Sorry?"

"The picture, it's my dog, Oscar."

"Oh, he seems cute."

Roger grinned at her. "He's far too cute. I often think I look like an idiot walking him, me striding along and then him with his tiny legs strutting along beside me."

Alice laughed. "I bet you make quite the pair."

"Yeah, but I wouldn't be without him." He took a drink from his own mug. "I got him a few years ago, after my wife died. A doctor recommended I get a dog to help cope with the loss, which was good advice."

Alice smiled, her eyes tender. "I'm so sorry, though, about your wife."

He shrugged, went to say something but closed his mouth without speaking.

Alice sipped her coffee. The hot drink was helping to calm her.

"Is the coffee –"

"Richard is having an affair," she blurted out. She couldn't help it, it had been bouncing around inside her, and suddenly she just had to tell someone.

"Oh." He leaned back, his soft eyes on her. "How did you find out?"

And so she told him, she explained the whole thing: how she'd discovered Richard was a gambler and how he had devised a plan to take her mum's inheritance money; how a young woman called Sally had turned up on their doorstep and was pretending to be his daughter. Soon Richard would say that Sally was sick, just as Alice was about to get her mum's inheritance. His plan was for Alice to donate a load of money to Sally and then for Richard and Sally to run away on the boat. As Alice spoke, she knew it sounded crazy, but she also appreciated the look of sympathy on Roger's face.

It felt good to tell someone everything, and once she'd finished talking, she sipped again at her coffee.

"That's quite the story. I'm not sure what to say after that!"

"Isn't it." Alice looked at him. "Imagine how I feel."

"You're telling me he's planned to have someone pretend to be his sick daughter so you'll give her your inheritance, and then he's going to run off with her?"

"That's it in a nutshell."

"If you don't mind me saying so, this guy of yours sounds a bit mad."

She snorted. "I know. I'm starting to realise just how mad he actually is."

"You're not married?"

"No, he never wanted to get married."

"What about you?"

She sighed as a feeling of sadness welled within her. Yes, she had wanted to get married, but in their relationship, Richard was always the one who had the say on what they did and didn't do.

Alice shrugged and stared into her coffee.

"Years ago, I had a friend who got hooked on gambling," he said. "He was a smart bloke, had his own roofing firm with ten guys working for him; he had a big house and a great young family. He lost the lot because of his gambling."

"That's awful."

"It is, but that's addictions; they ruin lives. From what I

remember, this guy did some crazy stuff too." He paused. "Although not quite as crazy as what Richard is planning."

"You're right, it is crazy."

"Do you think he'll actually do it? I mean, writing out a plan is one thing; actually going through with it is quite another."

"He's already started. We had his retirement party a few days ago, and the following morning, this Sally turned up on our doorstep. In a few days' time he's going to tell me she's sick and needs a lot of money from us. Well, money from me. In a week they will be gone."

They drank their coffees, and she enjoyed the quiet. She sensed Roger watching her, and she liked the feeling of his eyes on her.

"Do you mind if I ask you something?" he asked.

"Not at all." She nodded at him.

"Now you know this about Richard, what are you going to do about it?"

It was a good question and something she'd been asking herself repeatedly over the last few days.

"When I first found out about his plan, I spent the week trying to convince myself he wouldn't go through with it. I really made the effort to be loving with him, to show him what we have together so he wouldn't do it," she said, and her voice wobbled again. She closed her eyes and took a deep breath before she could continue. "But it didn't make any difference."

"Bless you."

Alice touched her throat, sore from the rope burn. There had been an idea circling in her mind, something she'd been toying with. She wanted to stop Richard and Sally taking her money and leaving with the boat, and suddenly it became clear what she should do.

"He's not going to get away with this." She opened her eyes and looked at Roger. "I'm going to make a little plan of my own. Will you help me with it?"

19

LEAVING DAY

Richard parked the car at Bristol harbour. He got out and unloaded the cases from the boot.

"What a lovely day!" Sally said.

Although it was still early, the sun was shining brightly. Across the harbour, Richard could see that the tide was high, and the conditions were perfect to sail out of Bristol and into the main channel. He watched as Sally pulled out a large sunhat from the car and put it on. He couldn't keep his eyes off her.

"You look amazing. Hope you've packed your bikinis?"

Sally laughed. "I've got a few, but there's not much to them."

The thought of having her on the boat wearing her bikini sent his pulse racing. "Sounds great."

His phone pinged in his pocket, and he took it out.

It was a message from Igor. *Will be at your house in 10 minutes.*

"All okay?" Sally asked.

Richard put the phone back in his pocket and gave her a huge grin. He'd made it. The plan had worked. He had the money, the boat and the girl. Now it was time to leave.

"Just perfect," he told her. "Okay, I'll get a ticket for the car, and then we can load the boat."

Sally was looking at herself reflected in the windscreen, adjusting her hat and pouting. "Okay, babe, I'll be here."

He smiled and walked to the ticket machine at the end of the car park. As he approached, he heard the sudden screech of a car pulling in too fast. Richard span around, his heart pumping hard, adrenaline surging through him. A small silver car veered into the car park.

At the wheel was an old lady. It was just an old lady, one who couldn't drive very well. He squinted for a better look and could see that the passenger seats were empty, no Igor hiding in the back. He exhaled loudly and felt the tension release from his body.

He had to get going.

Richard pulled out his bank card and tapped it against the parking machine. It beeped.

Declined.

He tapped again. "Bloody thing."

Declined.

He took a deep breath. Just what he needed, a broken machine. Well, he would have to leave the car without a ticket. His brother wouldn't be happy at paying a £50 fine, but at that moment he didn't care.

Richard turned to walk back to the car, then stopped dead in his tracks.

He pulled out his phone and unlocked it with his thumbprint. He clicked on his banking app and stared down at the screen in horror. A wave of sickness crashed over him.

His bank account was empty.

There was no money in there.

Nothing.

That wasn't right, surely? But then, it was a large amount of money, and perhaps it would take a while to get to him? He hadn't even thought to check that Alice had done the transfer correctly; she was normally so good at stuff like that. He hesitated. What to do? He'd have to get the boat loaded and then phone the bank to check the money was on its way.

He made his way back to the car.

"Let's crack on and get the boat loaded."

He started wheeling his two cases down to the water's edge. It was a beautiful day, and several seagulls squawked happily overhead. He could smell the water as he neared it, fresh and invigorating. From behind him came the sound of Sally tottering on her heels. Richard turned to see she was carrying just her handbag, and he couldn't help but laugh.

"Shall I bring your cases from the car, madam?"

She laughed too. "Sorry, babe, they're a bit heavy for me."

He stopped, and as she caught up to him, he kissed her, feeling her red lipstick rubbing off onto his lips. "Don't worry about it, sexy."

They kept walking, and then Richard stopped again.

It wasn't there.

Seas the Day was nowhere to be seen. He let go of the cases and looked up and down the water's edge. There were other boats around that he recognised, but his boat wasn't there.

Richard blinked his eyes open and shut, as if hoping that *Seas the Day* might magically reappear.

But still, no boat. Where the hell was the boat? It was time for him and Sally to leave Bristol, to leave England and head south towards the sun. His plan had been perfect, just great, but it was now in danger of exploding at the final hurdle. A rising sense of panic started to build in him.

Sweat rolled down his spine.

"Shall we load the boat, then?" Sally chirped.

"What boat?!" he snapped. "Do you see a fucking boat?"

She recoiled, as if he'd slapped her around the face.

"Sorry. It's just..." He tried to stay calm. "The boat is supposed to be here," he said, uselessly gesturing at the empty docks.

And not only was the boat missing, but the money wasn't in his account yet. That was concerning too, but he was assuming it would take a while for the money to clear into his account. Perhaps Alan would know where *Seas the Day* was? His office was on the marina.

"You wait here with the car," he told Sally. "I'll go and see the guys who've been working on the boat, see what they've done with her."

"Okay." She sniffed, close to tears. "I was just excited, that's all."

God, how young and sensitive could a person be? He took a deep breath.

"Sorry for getting angry, baby." He gave her a hug, fighting his own impatience. "I won't be long."

He strode off, heading to the office. It was going to be a

hot day, the sun was up and blazing, and all he wanted was to feel the spray of the sea on his face. The water in the harbour looked beautiful; he was desperate to get on the boat, to sail her away on the ocean and, finally, make his escape.

As Richard stepped into the boatyard, it took a moment for his eyes to adjust to the gloom after the bright morning sun outside. There was an old twenty-foot wooden boat up on the racks, halfway through having its hull sanded and repainted. The place was deserted. He walked past the boat, up the staircase to the office and knocked on the door. A voice called from within, and Richard pulled open the door.

Alan was sitting at a desk in his usual paint-splattered navy overalls. A landline phone was cradled to his ear as he used his hands to roll a cigarette. He stopped for a moment to wave Richard into the office. The room was small, one desk and one filing cabinet.

With his eyes fixed on Richard, Alan spoke into the phone. "Hey, Burt; listen, I need to go, mate." He looked Richard up and down as he listened to the other end of the phone. "Okay, okay, speak to you soon."

Alan hung up and licked his roll-up to seal the paper.

"Where is the boat?"

"The boat?"

"*Seas the Day*, where is she?"

Alan put the fresh roll-up in his mouth and leaned back on his chair.

"Didn't your wife tell you?"

"She's not my wife, and no, she didn't tell me anything."

"Don't suppose you've got a light, have you?" Alan asked, waving his roll-up towards Richard.

Richard felt like he was being messed with. The room was small and stuffy and stank of sweat and stale cigarettes; he felt like a schoolboy standing at the headmaster's desk.

"No, I don't have a light. I don't smoke." He was desperately trying to stay calm, trying to ignore the rush of panic rising within him. "Alan, where's the bloody boat?"

"I thought Alice would have mentioned –"

"Tell me!" he shouted, his voice loud in the small space. "You tell me; forget what Alice did or didn't tell me. You explain it; where's the boat?"

"Okay, okay." Alan casually held up his hands in defeat. "Roger came last night and moved it…"

"Roger?" He knew the name from somewhere but couldn't think from where. "Roger? Who the fuck is Roger?"

"Roger is the sailing instructor from next door," Alan explained. "And he said Alice had asked him to move the boat up towards Brislington. Said it would make it easier to load up, ready for your trip."

Richard had a sick feeling in his stomach again. A strong and relentless feeling of dread. He was desperate for some fresh air, but there was no window in the small office.

Roger? Richard thought maybe he'd met him once, or had he seen him when he'd picked Alice up from a sailing lesson? A vague memory of a tall, grey-haired man came to mind. Why the hell would Alice ask *him* to move the boat? It didn't make any sense. His mind was whirring.

Richard looked up. "Where?" was all he could manage.

"Huh?"

"Towards Brislington where?"

"Oh, that I don't know. Roger just came down last night, jumped on the boat and shipped her off somewhere."

Alan seemed oblivious to Richard's increasing panic; instead, he simply opened a drawer on the desk and started to root through it.

"So you didn't move *Seas the Day*? Roger the sailing instructor moved her?"

"Yeah."

In a flash, Richard's feeling of dread spread from his stomach to his whole body. Something was terribly wrong here, but he couldn't pinpoint what it was. Why would Alice ask Roger to move the boat? Had she forgotten to tell him?

"Ah, here you go." Alan held up a box of matches at Richard before taking one out and lighting his roll-up. Richard watched as he took a drag and blew out smoke, the blue haze instantly filling the room.

Richard turned and left the office without saying goodbye.

As he walked down the stairs, he stumbled onto the handrail. He felt sick, and his damaged nose had started to ache again. As he reached the bottom of the stairs, he felt so desperate to be outside that he set off through the gloomy boatyard, moving quickly until his knee suddenly struck something hard. He gasped in pain and squinted in the darkness to see a metal toolbox on the floor.

"Bastard thing!" he cursed as he rubbed his knee. He hobbled onwards, squinting his way to the large doors.

Richard stepped out into the sunshine and paused a moment to take a few deep breaths. He was glad to be out of that stinking office. His knee throbbed, but he let go of it and stood up straight. Roger? Why him?

Think, he told himself as he pulled his phone out. Should he phone Alice? There was no reason why he shouldn't. All she knew was that he was taking some boxes down to the boat, nothing else.

Before he called Alice, he checked his banking app again. The phone screen showed him a balance of £2.70, not even enough to pay for the car park. How long would it take? After all, £70,000 was a lot to transfer, and maybe the bank would take a few hours to do it; maybe it wouldn't be instant?

He brought up Alice's number and clicked to call her.

"Hello?"

"Hi, it's me."

"Are you on your way back?" Alice asked him.

"Not quite. I'm at the harbour, but the boat isn't here. Did...did you move it?"

"Oh, I'm so sorry! I totally forgot to tell you; I got it moved up towards Brislington. I thought that would make it easier to load up."

"Why would you do that? Brislington isn't any easier."

"Isn't the ring road better access, saves us going through traffic?"

He pictured the route and supposed she was right. In the long run it wouldn't save too much time, but then Alice had never been the most practical of people.

"I asked Roger to move it, you know, the sailing instructor."

"Why him?"

"He volunteered to help."

Was she messing with him? Did she know what he was planning? He thought about it for a second. She couldn't; there was no way she could know. And he knew Alice; she didn't have the brain capacity to mess with him like this intentionally.

Richard's sense of worry abated for a moment, and he took a deep breath, feeling a weight being lifted; everything was okay. His plan was still on track; it was just that there would just be a little detour.

"So where in Brislington is –"

He could hear their doorbell chime in the background.

"There's someone at the door. I'd better answer it. Let me text you the address of the new mooring –"

"Don't answer it!" he barked into the phone, suddenly remembering that he had given Igor their home address. Not for her sake, but because he knew that in a few moments she would be unable to give him any information.

Too late, she had already hung up.

IGOR WAS a simple but effective man. He liked making money, drinking vodka and having sex with women. Back in Russia, he'd served with the 331st Guards Parachute Regiment, which had a reputation as one of the best. He'd spent time in various conflicts around the globe, fighting and killing for Mother Russia. They had done some raping too, but not as much as he'd hoped.

After the army he got into racketeering for his cousin Dimitry in Moscow.

For a few years he'd enjoyed the work until one night when he'd been beating a shopkeeper for not making his monthly payment and things had gone too far. Maybe Igor had had too many vodkas that day, but he was really enjoying the beating, enjoying the feeling of his old brass knuckle duster going into the soft flesh of the face. Enjoying seeing how much blood he could make pump out. After a while he had stopped and realised the man was dead; in fact, he had probably been dead for a while. Igor had laughed.

Dimitry didn't care about the dead shopkeeper; it was good for business. It sent the right kind of message to all the other shopkeepers and business owners. But he did worry about the Politsiya finding and arresting Igor, so Igor needed to leave Russia. Dimitry had a plan for Igor; he would send him to England.

"England? Why the fuck would I go there?"

"Why do you think? Money. And it will keep you out of a prison cell."

Igor had never been to the UK, but in the end, he was happy enough to go. He texted his girlfriend goodbye, packed a few bags and left his homeland. In Bristol he had set up a laundrette as a cover for his more criminal activities. He soon began lending money out to people, small amounts at first, but steadily getting bigger and bigger. During the past four years, he had lent out hundreds of thousands of pounds.

For a while Igor had been excited by this new job, in this new country. He was looking forward to beating some English businesspeople. But then he noticed that something frustrating tended to happen; the money he lent out was paid back. People came to him for a quick cash loan for all sorts of reasons, with all sorts of stories. And it turned out they were telling the truth!

"*I need £5,000 to help pay the business rent this month. But next month I can pay you back the full amount.*"

And what happens? Next month the little man comes back with the £5,000 plus the five points of interest. In four years, he'd only had two people pay him late, and as soon as he'd gotten nasty and threatened to beat them, they had magically produced the money. Ha! The English were rich.

It had been good, but boring. Which meant that when Professor Richard Barnes had approached him for a quick loan, he was happy to accept. A big professor at the university, of course he would lend to him. First it was £20,000, then the figure went to £45,000, and finally £60,000.

Normally Igor would have stopped at the first £20,000. He had seen gamblers before, and they always struggled to pay the money back. But Igor had a lot of cash, and he was bored of England, and for some reason he really wanted to beat the old professor's face in. Igor was like a shark; he could smell the potential for blood miles away. In his heart he'd known the old professor wouldn't be able to pay. But he was a professional man, right? He would have assets that it would be fun to take. A car, a house...a boat. And Igor had been right. So now it was time to pay up, and Igor was going to take it all.

Then he was going to rub down his brass knuckle duster and beat that old fucker hard.

JOSEF DROVE the Land Rover up the M32 and took junction one. He looped around the roundabout onto the ring road; then he turned left and headed towards Winterbourne. The satnav said they were two miles away.

"Why you so excited?" Josef asked Igor, speaking in Russian.

Igor grinned at him. "I've been bored these last few months," he said as he pulled out his knuckle duster and slipped it onto his huge right hand, "but today we are going to have some fun."

Josef laughed.

They had one mile to go.

———

ALICE WATCHED Richard put the final box into his car and get into the driver's seat. She pushed the vacuum around the lounge carpet, her yellow plastic gloves gripping the handle tightly.

Through the lounge window she could see him take a phone call. Who was he talking to? That bitch, probably. Sally must be excited; after all, she believed they were heading off on a boat together. She had a big bank balance and a handsome man to sail her around the world. Little did she know she wasn't going anywhere.

Alice could see Richard finish the call, start the car and reverse out of the driveway. He sped down the road, and she realised that was the last she would ever see of Professor Richard Barnes, the man who had been her partner of twenty years. A few weeks ago, that thought would have ruined her, but she had hardened her heart now, and there was only a dead, cold feeling in the pit of her stomach.

As soon as the car was out of sight, Alice turned off the vacuum. She pulled off the Marigolds and threw them on the sofa.

What an utter bastard. He'd gone through with it. He had compiled this crazy plan and actually put it into action. What made her blood run cold was the fact that if she hadn't found those files on the laptop, his plan would have worked. He would have fooled her; he would have taken her inheritance money and their boat and left with that two-faced little slut.

But sweet little Alice had a plan of her own. After the gut-wrenching realisation of what Richard was doing to her had really sunk in, and after she had calmed down, Alice had devised a plan of her own. She was taking the boat, and she would be leaving Bristol and England by herself.

Alice unplugged the vacuum, looped the cord around it and put it back under the stairs. She estimated that she only had an hour, so she moved quickly. She went upstairs and brought down her two suitcases from the bedroom. They were heavy, so she took one at a time through the front door and loaded them into her Mini Cooper. The cases filled the boot. Back inside, she went into the kitchen and took hold of a large box of utensils. Like Richard had done moments before her, Alice put the box on the back seat of her car. Finally, there was a small box of papers, which she loaded onto the back seat.

She went back into the house and walked into each room. There were pieces of furniture and some cardboard boxes piled in the lounge that would go into storage, but she planned never to come back to retrieve them. Alice had packed two cases of clothes, a box of papers and a box of crockery. That was all she was planning to take. She had thought about it a lot, and travelling light made sense. She was planning to start a new life in Europe, so she would buy new things as and when she needed them.

Alice did a final check; she switched off the boiler, made sure nothing was left plugged in, checked all the windows were locked. This was it; she was leaving to start her new life. It wasn't exactly a happy ending for her, but it was a situation she was in control of. After the trauma of the last few weeks, that was the best she could hope for.

She picked up her handbag and keys.

"Well, goodbye, Bristol, it's been fun," she whispered.

This was the end; time to leave.

Her phone vibrated in her pocket, and she took it out: Richard.

She was tempted to ignore it, but by now he must know the boat wasn't there, and she was curious to see how he was reacting.

"Hello?"

"Hi, it's me."

"Are you on your way back?" she asked him, knowing full well she would never see him again.

"Not quite. I'm at the harbour, but the boat isn't here. Did...did you move it?" His voice sounded strained; he was definitely worried.

"Oh, I'm so sorry! I totally forgot to tell you. I got it moved up towards Brislington. I thought that would make it easier to load up." Alice tried to keep her voice light and innocent.

"Brislington isn't any easier for us to load the boat."

"Isn't the ring road easier access, saves us going through traffic?" She had a sudden urge to laugh at him. "Fuck you," she wanted to scream. "The boat's gone, and you're screwed!"

But instead she said: "I asked Roger to move it, you know, the sailing instructor."

"Why him?"

"He volunteered to help us."

Richard went quiet on the phone, and Alice could picture him trying to work out if she knew what he was up to. She stayed silent, wondering if he would realise what was happening.

"So where in Brislington is –"

The front doorbell rang, the sound echoing around the now empty house.

"There's someone at the door. I'd better answer it. Let me text you the address of the new mooring."

She hung up as he was still speaking. Sod him. She didn't care what he had to say. Alice put the phone back in her pocket, she would get rid of whoever was at the door, and then it was her time to leave Bristol forever.

20

LEAVING DAY

Who was at the door? As Alice stepped into the hallway, she could see two shapes through the glass of the front door. Could it be the landlord? Something made her hesitate, but she couldn't think of a reason not to answer the door.

Alice opened the front door.

Two large men were standing on her doorstep. Both were broad and had short, cropped hair. The sun was in her face, and she couldn't quite make out their eyes, although she caught their polite smiles. One of them had a flat nose, and he spoke slowly to her.

"Hello, ma'am," he said with a heavy Eastern European accent. "We are here to see Professor Richard."

Alice could smell fresh laundry; it was a pleasant lavender smell, which was incongruous with these two big men.

"I'm afraid you just missed him," she told them.

The men looked at each other, some silent code shared in a stare. Her stomach started to flutter with nerves. For some reason her skin was tingling in the summer sun, and she decided she wanted to close the door on them; she didn't have to be polite or sociable.

"Do you mind if we wait for him?" the man with the flat nose asked.

Before she could reply, they stepped forward as one, somehow gently moving the door open, causing her to unthinkingly step backwards to allow them inside. Before she could speak, they were inside the house. It happened so quickly.

"Now really isn't a good –"

"Don't worry about us," one of them said by way of a loud and jolly reply, cutting her off. "We will be quiet."

They walked down the hallway and into the lounge.

"Really, you can't just –"

"We'll sit here on the sofa, nice and calm."

The word *calm* threw her. Why calm? It was something you said when there was a high risk of someone not being calm. *Let's all remain calm*, people said, because they were close to being the opposite of that.

The two men sat on the grey sofa in the lounge, their large frames filling the room. The scent of fabric softener was strong. Who the hell were they? If they were here for Richard, could he owe them money from his gambling? Would he really be stupid enough to borrow money from these two brutes? Even as she asked herself the question, she knew the answer, knew that Richard was capable of making some very reckless decisions.

"Looks like you are moving?" Mr Flat Nose said.

She could see his eyes clearly now and was taken aback at how dark they were as they scanned the room.

Alice had the urge to lie, but instead she just folded her

arms and stood in the doorway. These men might be big and tough, but it was still her house.

"Why do you want to see Richard?"

Mr Flat Nose tilted his head at her, silently considering. After a long moment he spoke.

"He owes us money, and today is payment day."

Alice nodded. "Well, he won't be back for at least half an hour."

The lie came without thought, spoken by some animal instinct of survival. She turned her hands into fists to hide the shaking. The plan was that Richard would return to take more boxes down to the boat, but the reality was Alice would never see him again. That bastard Richard! He had led his debt collectors to her house to save his own skin. How much did he owe them? Probably a lot. And they didn't look like normal debt collectors. She couldn't picture these two abiding by the law. She had seen a programme on TV once, a show that followed a team of debt collectors. They wore black combats, black polo tops and stab-vests. They had seemed like boys playing soldiers. But the two men sitting on her sofa didn't seem anything like that.

"Hmmm," was the reply.

She had to get out of the house. Would they let her? Mr Flat Nose was playing with something in his pocket. What did he have in there? Oh God! Only a moment ago she had been leaving, but now she felt trapped in her own home.

Alice sensed they wouldn't let her leave.

"Would you like a cup of tea?" she asked.

"Okay," said Mr Flat Nose.

The other one, whose eyes had never left her, just nodded.

She went into the kitchen. There wasn't even a kettle in

there. Panic started to flood through her. This was a disaster; she knew she was in danger. These two men were going to hurt her, and there would be nothing she could do to stop them. What was she going to do? In seconds they would wonder why there was no kettle boiling. Why had she asked if they wanted a drink? Oh God.

Everyone has a plan until they get hit. Was that the saying?

Her eyes scanned the kitchen, wild and desperate.

She needed to leave.

Right now.

Alice turned on the kitchen tap, the sound of the water running loud in the empty space. It was enough. She opened the back door, trying to be as quiet as possible. It gave a little creak, and she glared at the door, her mind screaming at it to not make any noise. She could feel the warm outside air on her face as she gently opened it wider and wider.

As soon as her small frame could fit through, she stepped out into the back garden. Outside, she could still hear the water running from the tap. Alice moved quickly now. She opened the side gate and walked along the length of the house to the front as she dug her car keys out of her pocket. Her car was on the drive, but Alice hesitated.

She would need to walk across the wide lawn and past the lounge window to get to her car; if she ran, would it give her enough time to get in the car and drive off? No.

Instead, she got down on her hands and knees and crawled on the grass and under the window. Alice started to pant as her legs and arms pulled her body weight along the front lawn like a beetle. She made sure to keep low, out of view of the two thugs in the lounge.

"Have you fixed that fence panel yet?"

The voice made her jump, and Alice looked up to see Mrs Mabel standing on the pavement outside her house. The old lady was wearing a grey skirt and black coat and was leaning on her wooden walking stick, glaring down at Alice. Alice made an urgent "shushing" gesture.

"What? What are you doing?" Mrs Mabel called to her.

Why did Mrs Mabel have to be so annoying? Alice tried to focus and kept crawling across the dusty lawn directly below the lounge window. Her knees got dirty, and the keys in her hand dug into her palm, but she didn't care.

"The fence panel is on the left of your garden; that means you're responsible for it."

Please bugger off! Alice wanted to scream; instead she forced herself to ignore the old lady.

Alice made it past the lounge window; a few more metres and she would be at the car. The driver's door was on the far side, so she should be able to slip into her Mini Cooper unnoticed. Then she could drive away, and she would be safe.

Behind her she heard the front door being yanked open.

No!

Panic set in.

Alice jumped up and bounded the final distance to the car. She clicked her keys to unlock the car and quickly pulled the driver's door open.

"You bitch!" she heard being shouted behind her.

She could see a dark figure in her peripheral vision moving towards her.

Alice jumped into the driver's seat, slamming the door shut just as the figure loomed at the window. She locked the door and looked up. It was Mr Flat Nose, and he was extremely angry.

"Open the fucking door," he shouted as he pulled at the handle.

"Who do you think you are!?" Mrs Mabel called out behind him, waving her walking stick in the air.

Alice put the keys in the ignition and started the engine. Mr Flat Nose was stepping back, which was a relief, but then Alice realised he was only doing so to give his fist with what looked like a brass knuckleduster momentum to smash into her window.

The fist and knuckleduster came crashing down, and glass showered her as she put the car into reverse.

A huge hand grabbed for her, and she screamed. She hadn't screamed in fear since she'd been a little girl. His fat meaty fingers were just around her throat when she hit the accelerator, and the car shot backwards. The hand and arm disappeared from the car as she pulled away. Her car screeched off the driveway, and she had to brake and swerve to avoid slamming into the house opposite. She hammered the car into first gear as Mr Flat Nose ran at her. He looked huge and crazy, like some ancient raging devil come to rip her apart.

"You fucking..."

But his words were lost in a screech of tyres as she hit the accelerator with her right foot. Her old Mini Cooper shot off down the road.

In her rear-view mirror she was expecting to see an angry man shaking his fist at her, but instead she could see him running. He was running to his own car. Even before Alice got to the end of the road, the two men were in their car, hurtling towards her.

Her lap was covered with splintered glass, and the wind

whipped her hair through the open window. Her body was filled with a sense of terror.

"What the hell?!" she screamed out.

What the hell was she going to do?

Despite everything, she wondered if they had turned the kitchen tap off.

RICHARD BEEPED his horn at the slow-moving traffic.

"Bloody cyclists."

"So, like, where are we going now?" Sally asked him.

He took a deep breath. She was starting to annoy him already, and they hadn't even got to the boat yet. Would they even get there? The thought made him want to cry. All his planning, all the effort to get this far and he'd fallen at the last hurdle. Richard's hands gripped the steering wheel tighter; no, he wasn't finished yet. Whatever happened, he was getting on that boat.

"We need to go to Brislington. The boat is there."

"Where in Brislington?"

It was a good question. Where would Alice have put it? And why did she move *Seas the Day* without telling him? Did she know what he was up to, know about his plans to leave with Sally? Richard started to suspect that Alice had discovered what he was doing, or trying to do, and that now she was messing with him.

Where could the boat be? There was only one place he could think of in Brislington, and that was Beeses café. It was only five miles away from the harbour, but it would take half an hour in the city traffic. He revved his Ford Focus at the car in front, but of course it did no good. There were roadworks all along the road, and his leg was aching from starting and stopping.

How long did he have to get there? Surely there was no rush, as Alice would be busy with Igor. Or, more likely, Igor would be busy with Alice. A feeling of guilt tried to bubble up inside him, but he squashed it down. Sod her. He'd had enough of her. And, besides, would Igor really hurt her? He caught a sight of his own battered face in the rear-view mirror and pushed away the thought.

"Well?" Sally asked.

Richard had forgotten she was even in the car.

"Sorry?"

"Where are we going?"

He licked his lips and blinked the sweat out of his eyes.

"Beeses café. It's the only place it could be around there."

The traffic lights up ahead turned green, and Richard drove onwards. The sun was beating down, and the air conditioning wasn't working. It was a torturous drive, but eventually they came through the centre of Bristol and into the suburbs.

Sally turned the car radio on. "*News now, and the Met Office has announced that the heatwave currently affecting parts of England and Wales will continue for another week. And, in Sport, we have an interview with Novak Djokovic after his Wimbledon victory over Anderson...*"

Richard stabbed his finger at the controls, and the radio was switched off.

They drove through a housing estate, which seemed a long way from any waterways, but he guessed that was the beauty of Bristol; it was a city built on the coast, with rivers running through it.

"This is it," he said, pulling the car over.

"Here?"

He understood her confusion; they were in a residential street lined with three-bed semi-detached houses. But amongst the houses there was a small alleyway that then sloped down a hill.

He yanked the handbrake on. "Through there," he said as he nodded to the alley.

"That's random. So, is the boat there?"

The alleyway sloped down, and the pathway turned into steps further down as the descent became sharper. From the street above they couldn't see the café building, but Richard did see something that made him grin.

"Look!" He pointed, suddenly excited.

Between the houses, down through the alleyway, there were tall trees visible. And amongst the trees, in the distance, he could see the mast of a boat. He recognised the distinctive blue rope tied to the top of the mast. It was *Seas the Day*.

"The boat is here!" he yelled, the stress and tension of the last few hours leaving him. Sweat trickled down his back as he opened the car boot and pulled out some suitcases.

"Right, let's get this boat loaded and set sail."

He handed her one suitcase and took two himself.

"It's heavy," she said with a grimace.

"Sorry, babe, but we do need to crack on, and you're strong enough for one case."

She smiled at this.

"Let's go."

They set off down the slope towards the boat.

ALICE SPED through the village with the black Land Rover right behind her. This was ridiculous; for a second she thought about pulling over and telling these men off. But then she caught sight of them in her rear-view mirror and saw how menacing they were. Saw violence pulsating out of them. And then her hand went up to her throat.

What if Mr Flat Nose had managed to keep hold of her? Would he have strangled her? Yes, he would. Despite the open window, sweat covered her face and arms. She thought she might vomit.

Alice felt like a helpless rabbit being chased by two vicious wolves. No, this couldn't be! It wasn't her they wanted; it was Richard. But however much her mind tried to make sense of the situation, she knew they would hurt her if they got their hands on her. Those big meaty hands would rip out clumps of her hair, smash her nose, gouge her eyes, break her arms, crack her teeth, batter her to death...she knew her imagination was running wild, but Alice couldn't control the panic and fear flooding through her.

Could she pull over? Tell a stranger that she was in trouble? But then what? She couldn't imagine anyone standing up to these two animals to protect her. So, without really thinking, Alice was heading into the city and in the direction of the boat. But there was no way she would be able to get to the boat, especially with her cases. She needed the police.

Of course! The police. This was England, after all.

Her handbag was on the passenger seat where she'd packed it. Keeping her right hand on the steering wheel, she dug through the handbag with her left hand, her fingers scrabbling through various items.

"Come on!" she yelled.

Where was her mobile phone?

The Land Rover revved behind her, its bumpers inches from hers. The road straightened out, and she tipped her handbag out onto the seat beside her. Then her head became a ping-pong, eyes moving quickly between the road and the seat, back and forth. Tissues, makeup, mirror, little notebook, mints. No phone.

She'd left it in the house!

Alice couldn't phone the police.

Up ahead, the cars began to slow for some traffic lights. She was through Winterbourne and Hambrook villages and coming out onto the ring road that would lead her to the M32 and into the city centre.

Alice was terrified, she would need to stop any moment, and the two men would have a chance to grab her. Her trembling hands adjusted the rear-view mirror. She was forced to slow her car; in seconds she would stop. Alice hit the brake, leaving a gap the length of three cars between her and the car in front; it was the only thing she could think to do. If they jumped out, she could at least drive forward to stop them from grabbing her. Behind her the Land Rover was almost touching her back bumper, the two men glaring at her.

Alice could see them talking to each other, and she thought she spotted a claw hammer in Mr Flat Nose's hand. Were they deciding to jump out and come for her? Surely they wouldn't? Not with this many people around?

To her huge relief, the traffic lights turned amber and then green, and the traffic began to move forward. She would be able to get onto the motorway now.

And then her engine cut out.

"No! No! NO!"

Alice tore her eyes away from the rear-view mirror and

grabbed the car key. She turned it off and switched it back on. The car choked and spluttered but didn't start.

"Please," she begged the car, trying to control the wild panic flooding through her.

The cars ahead of them drove off, leaving the old battered Mini Cooper and the Land Rover alone on the road. A few hundred metres along, the main ring road had plenty of traffic on it, but people wouldn't know what was happening down here on the side road she was on.

Alice turned the key again. The car juddered but still didn't start.

Behind her she could hear the sound of a car door opening and closing. He was coming for her, coming to wrap his fat hands around her neck because of Richard. Richard had given her a death sentence.

"Please," she begged the car again.

Alice took the key out, took a deep breath, put the key back in. She turned it, and the car once again choked and spluttered. This time she kept the key turned, and her foot pumped down on the accelerator.

A shadow came to the open window.

His hand shot in and unlocked the driver's door, then pulled it open.

The car started.

Instinctively, Alice put it into first gear and hit the accelerator pedal with her foot. The old car shot forward, the momentum closing her door.

"Bitch," she heard yelled behind her.

In her wing mirror she could see Mr Flat Nose standing in the middle of the road in a cloud of dirty blue smoke. Alice worked through the gears, picking up speed as she drove onto the ring road. She wiped away tears of fear.

Before she could feel any sense of relief, however, the sight of the black Land Rover filled her mirrors again; all of a sudden, it was right behind her again. Luckily the lights stayed green as she drove out onto the M32. Her car protested noisily as she put it into fifth gear and got it up to seventy miles an hour, but it kept going, with Alice willing it on every inch of the way.

All she needed to do now was to somehow lose the two men chasing her, get to the boat and set sail for the south.

21

LEAVING DAY

Richard wasn't particularly strong; he didn't go to the gym or do anything overly physical in his usual daily routine. The two suitcases he was carrying were heavy, but in that moment they felt light; he was full of excited energy and relief, and he couldn't wait to get them onto the boat.

And now he was so close to doing that.

As they walked down the steep slope, the housing estate disappeared from view, masked by vast trees. Within just a few metres they had stepped into another world; now it looked as though they were deep in the countryside. The river was wide and calm, and both banks were covered by tall trees and thick foliage. The café itself was a hundred metres away from the road at the bottom of the long slope; two single-storey buildings sat snugly against the river's edge.

Surrounding the buildings was bare wood decking that offered a nice place to sit and drink by the river. People were lounging in the heat, each seat was occupied, and a happy murmur of noise greeted Richard and Sally as they got closer.

To one side of the two buildings there was a white marquee. As they reached the bottom of the slope, Richard could see men in light shirts and navy waistcoats, with large pink roses pinned to their fronts, and he realised they were part of a wedding party. *Nice day for it*, he thought even as his legs started to struggle down the path, his arms straining with the cases on the sharp angle.

At last, he reached the bottom of the slope, walked through the outside seating area and continued to the water's edge. As he stepped through the crowded seats, he left the path and made it to the wooden jetty. It was a green and pleasant land that stretched either side of the slow-moving river.

Richard's heart sank.

"Fuck," he shouted as he threw the cases down onto the jetty.

The crowd of people behind him fell silent.

"Oi, mate, there's kids here," someone called to him.

Rage consumed Richard. Anger that he didn't even know existed came bursting through his body and mind. Behind him he could hear Sally tottering down the path and onto the jetty.

"I thought you told me your boat was blue," she said.

Richard didn't answer. He dropped his head into his hands, praying for this nightmare to be over.

"Because that boat's green."

He span around, his mouth open to scream at her. She stood alone, looking hot and confused. Behind her he could see the silent wedding guests watching them.

Richard stopped himself from screaming, tried to calm down before he spoke.

"Our boat *is* blue," he whispered hoarsely through clenched teeth. "That boat," he almost snarled as he pointed to the large sailboat on the side of the jetty, "is green because it's not our boat."

"Oh," she replied, as guileless as ever. "I thought you said it was ours, because of the mast."

"The mast looks the same as ours, but it's not."

"So, like, where's our boat?"

Richard turned away from her, not trusting himself to speak. Instead, he hung his head in his hands again; he felt like a broken man. His mind was spinning; what the hell was going on? This was all wrong.

"Fuck!" he swore again, unable to contain the curse.

Behind him he could hear footsteps as someone else stepped out onto the wooden jetty. Richard turned to see two men carrying half-drunk pints of beer and wearing matching navy waistcoats standing either side of him. If he had to guess, he would say they were rugby players.

"What's the problem, mate? There's a wedding going on, and we don't want to hear you swearing your head off."

Richard knew he should apologise and walk away, but, in that moment, he wasn't fully in control of his anger.

"I'm not your fucking mate," he replied.

The two men had been almost polite initially, but their faces shifted as he swore at them.

"Do you want another black eye, dickhead?" one of them said quietly.

He snorted at them, his chin pushed out, his fist clenched, willing them to come at him. A part of him knew he should walk away, that he was a much older man who was in bad shape, but his head had gone; the missing money, the missing boat and the heat of the day were all combining to make him act completely irrationally.

"Why don't you two bugger off back to the party?"

"Err, babe..." Sally tried to warn him.

The two men looked at each other and nodded. They stepped backwards, and for a second Richard thought he'd frightened them off, but, as he watched, he saw that they were just putting their beer glasses down on the jetty, and they were now walking back towards him.

"Fancy a swim, Granddad?" one of them asked.

The other man laughed.

"Grandad?! I'm only –"

They lunged towards him and grabbed him by the front of his shirt.

"Get your hands off me!"

He was dragged backwards along the jetty. Richard tried to free himself from their grip, but it was no use, and suddenly he realised they were letting go of him...because he was falling backwards. He put his hands out to stop his fall, but they didn't connect with any ground; instead they splashed into cold water, and he was completely submerged.

His mouth filled with water.

The water was so cold and shocking that his mind switched into action mode, compelling him to kick his legs and claw his way back to the surface of the water. As his head came up, he gasped for air.

As he did so, he could hear the wedding party jeer and laugh at him. The two men were standing on the jetty above him with folded arms and big grins.

"While you're there, you should wash your mouth out," one of them taunted.

"Mate," the other added, deadpan.

The two men laughed, and then they left him, spluttering and splashing, as they walked back into the crowd to be greeted as heroes. Slowly, Richard pulled himself out of the water and back onto the jetty.

"You okay, babe?" Sally asked.

He looked up to see an expression on her face that was partly concerned and partly amused.

The water had done as the two men had intended and cooled him off. *No more shouting*, he told himself. Richard spat out the last of the river water and stood up.

"Let's go," he mumbled to Sally.

He picked up the two large cases from the jetty and set off back to the car. The wedding guests grinned and called out at him as he squelched past them; it was completely humiliating. He could hear the click-clacking of Sally's heels tottering behind him as she followed him back up the steep path.

Richard's breathing became laboured as he struggled with the cases, and his wet clothes only added to the weight he was carrying. In amongst the trees the heat was particularly stifling, and he found it increasingly difficult to breathe. He finally made it out of the trees and back to the housing estate at the top of the path. With a final effort he slung the cases back into the car and sat down heavily. He didn't care that he would make the driver's seat soaking wet.

He sat in the hot car and took deep breaths, trying to clear his mind.

His mouth tasted foul.

Alice must have known about his plan. She must have. It was the only explanation: there was no money in the account, and now the boat had disappeared.

Richard took his phone out of his pocket, and although the screen was misted, it still worked. He brought Alice's number up and called her, his wet hand gripping the phone tightly. There was no answer, and he didn't leave a voicemail.

What was he going to do now? He had no money and no boat. He thought back over the whole morning. If Alice did know what he was planning, what would she do? Little innocent Alice, his boring partner. In his mind, all he could imagine her doing was crying and confronting him about his plans. But she hadn't done that. And so, just how had she found out? He couldn't understand it.

Then the back door of the car opened, and Sally flung in the case she had been carrying. She slammed the door, walked around to the passenger's side and got in.

"Thanks for waiting for me," she yelled at him.

Her face was red and covered with sweat. Mascara had run down her cheeks, and her blonde hair, hair that had looked so perfect earlier that morning, was now stuck to her damp forehead.

"Sorry," he said.

"What the hell is going on?"

Richard sighed and put his hand on the steering wheel.

"I think she's worked out what I was doing; she knows that I planned to take the money and boat without her." His voice was quiet.

"What!? There's no way that stupid bitch would know what we were doing."

"Well, she does. And now we need to work out where she's hidden the boat."

"You think she's hidden it on purpose? Is she trying to mess with you?"

"It's the only explanation. The money's not in the

account; she's moved the boat and not told me; I can't get her on the phone. What else could be happening?"

"That cheeky bitch."

Richard snorted. They were planning to do a lot worse to Alice, so it was a little hypocritical to call Alice cheeky.

He felt so drained. He'd been a fool to think he could get away with this.

"So, what are we –"

Sally's musings were cut off by the sound of Richard's phone ringing. He snatched it up from his lap, hoping it was Alice.

The screen told him it was Igor.

Richard's heart sank. That crazy Russian debt collector was all he needed right now. Whatever happened, he needed to leave Bristol. Would Sally come with him? If there was no money? Definitely not.

"You going to answer it?"

Why not? What did he have to lose?

Richard clicked the green answer button. "Hello?"

"You think Igor is stupid?" It sounded like he was in the car.

"Hi, Igor, I was just about to call you."

Igor laughed; it was a terrifying sound.

"We went to your home. What did we find? No Professor Richard waiting for us. And an empty house, all your little things in boxes. So, you're leaving. Running away from Igor and your debts?"

Richard didn't know what to say, he had been caught out, and he just didn't have the energy to deny it.

"I can get you the money –"

"No, no, Professor. It's too late for money. Now there will be blood."

The words sent an icy chill down his back. He looked in the rear-view mirror and out the windows, expecting to see Igor standing outside the car with his hammer. Fortunately, the streets were empty.

"Where are you? Did you speak to Alice? She has money she can give you."

"The little bitch ran away from us." Richard noted that it was the second time in a few minutes that someone was calling Alice a bitch. "But she can't get far. We are following her. And when we catch her, she will tell us where you are."

"You're chasing her? In the car? Where are you?"

Igor chuckled. "You don't get to ask questions. The only way you can save her from a lot of pain is by coming to meet me."

Richard was tempted to laugh, tempted to tell them to do their worst; he didn't care and would certainly not be turning up to save Alice.

"Okay, I'll come to meet you; please don't hurt her," he pleaded with as much mock concern as he could muster. "Are you still in Bristol?"

"We're in the city centre; soon we'll have her. I will text you an address. You'd better be there."

Richard hung up.

They were still in the city; Alice was still in the city. There were only so many places you could moor a boat in Bristol, and he had just been to two of them. There was just the one river running through the city, after all.

Richard brought up the map on his phone. He zoomed into the city centre and harbour. His wet finger slowly traced the river as it snaked through the city.

Where was his boat?

Where was *Seas the Day*?

22

LEAVING DAY

"**C**ome on!" Alice yelled at her car.

At least the smashed window was helping with the stinking fumes coming from her engine. She blinked through her tears. In her mirrors she could see the Land Rover right up behind her. What could she do?

She needed the police, but couldn't call them.

Could she drive around the city until she spotted a police car and flag them down? Alice wasn't sure her car would last that long. Could she drive to a police station? It was her only option. She couldn't call them, but she could drive to the police station and run in and ask for help. But where was the station? Alice had a vague memory of a police station in the city centre somewhere. It was an old stone building, but hadn't it closed down and become a nightclub? Or had she imagined that?

This was ridiculous! Panic was threatening to turn her crazy, and she had to stifle a scream of frustration from bursting out of her. She had one hand on the steering wheel and one hand on her throat, instinctively protecting it.

The M32 took her into the city, and the cars once again slowed down, but this time there were dozens of cars on the roads and people on the streets; surely the men chasing her wouldn't try to grab her now.

The cars crawled along, slow and steady. As Alice stopped at one set of traffic lights, an idea occurred to her. There were several people on the pavement, some walking past, some standing at a bus stop.

"Excuse me," she yelled to the people at the bus stop.

Two women ignored her calls, but a young man looked up from his phone. He raised his eyebrows in a question.

"Do you know where the police station is?"

The young man was wearing ripped jeans and a creased T-shirt. He had a tattoo across his neck and several studs in his face.

"Police station?" he called back to her.

"Yes, please."

He nodded and looked down the road. "Go down here and take a left, drive down a bit, and it's the large glass building on your right."

"Thank you," she yelled gratefully.

"Should only take two minutes."

"Thank you," she repeated with a wave.

Alice wanted to thank the parents of the young man, wanted to thank them for raising a nice, helpful person. Someone who would help a stranger without question.

The traffic moved off, and Alice followed the instructions; she took the left turn and followed the road along. Her rear-view mirror showed the black Land Rover was still behind her. Alice's car was whining now; it was going to cut out any second. Sure enough, there was a huge, glass-fronted building on her right. Alice had always assumed it was an office block. The road was restricted parking with two double yellow lines, but she was beyond desperate, so she pulled up right outside, jumped out of the car and ran towards the entrance. Behind her she could hear the roar of an engine, which she assumed was the Land Rover, but she didn't stop to look back. Her legs pumped, and in a few strides she was inside.

At the entrance was a rotating glass door with a large open reception area. If it weren't for the sign that read "Avon and Somerset Police" she would have assumed it was the offices of a big company.

There were two police officers at the desk: one male and one female.

"Sorry, this is going to sound odd," she said breathlessly, "but there are two men chasing me."

The female officer stood up and smiled at her. "That's not strange at all; are you okay? Where are the men now?"

Alice glanced behind her. Thankfully there was no sign of the Land Rover outside the station. She breathed a huge sigh of relief and started to explain the situation to the attentive officer.

THE POLICE OFFERED Alice an escort to the boat. She had to wait forty minutes, but eventually a small police car turned up outside the station with a police support volunteer officer in it. Not quite a full escort, but still good enough for Alice. During the wait, the police officer had made her a cup of coffee and let her use the bathroom to clean the streaked mascara from her face. Alice knew the police sometimes had a bad reputation, but any time she'd had contact with them, they had been nothing but friendly and helpful, and this occasion was no different.

As she left the station, Alice thanked them, and they gave her several pamphlets on gambling addiction and how to get help for Richard. She didn't have the energy to tell them that she would never see him again.

Outside the station a big woman jumped out of the small car and gave her a cheery smile.

"Hi, my love, I'm Zoe," she said with a strong Bristolian accent. "I just got the call from the station, so I'll follow you down to the harbour."

"Thank you so much."

"All part of the service," Zoe replied.

Before she left the safety of the police station, Alice looked up and down the road, but there was no sign of the Land Rover or the two men who had chased her.

Alice got in her car, and when the road was clear, she set off to the harbour, with the volunteer officer following directly behind her. Zoe had a mass of vividly coloured purple hair, which was piled up in a messy bun, making her look almost comical in her little car, but still the sight of her in Alice's rear-view mirror made Alice feel safer than she had for days.

It was a short drive down to the harbour. Alice continued to the far end of the road, where the Pump House pub was situated. She pulled in, parked her tired car and got out. The engine was emitting a cloud of foul smoke, but it had done its job. She would miss the old tin pot.

The Pump House was a square building next to the harbour water. There was outside seating, and every chair and table was occupied. Alice nervously stared at the mid-day diners, but it all seemed relaxed, just people enjoying some food and drinks in the sun. No sign of any gangsters.

Alice shifted on her feet as the police car pulled up alongside her. Once again Zoe jumped out of the little car.

"There you go; looks clear."

Alice didn't reply; she just stared at the people walking along the harbour walkway and sitting outside the pub. Her hands had stopped shaking, but she felt so on edge.

"What you doing then, going for dinner here?" Zoe asked, nodding to the pub.

"No, I'm here to collect my boat. I'm going to load it up and set sail for Europe; I'm leaving Bristol."

"Oh, that sounds lovely. What an adventure!" The officer peered into the car at the boxes. "You want a hand?"

Normally Alice would decline out of politeness, but she was grateful for the offer.

"Oh yes, please, that would be great."

They set to it. Zoe took the large box of crockery off the back seat, and Alice wheeled the suitcases. They walked past the pub and along the waterfront. At the narrow blue foot-bridge, they turned into a tiny part of the harbour, where there were a dozen small boats moored up. The little waterway was surrounded on three sides by houses and was hidden from the road. At the end of the run of boats, moored up and looking glorious, sat *Seas the Day*. She was exactly where Alice had asked Roger to leave her.

From her handbag Alice took out the boat key and stepped aboard. She had made it! After a terrible, terri-fying morning, and after a gut-wrenching few weeks where her world had turned upside down...at last, she had made it.

"Well, look at that for a boat; she looks beautiful," Zoe announced.

Alice unlocked the main door into the boat's cabin and peered in. She could smell the fresh paint and newly waxed wood. It looked plush and sparkling clean inside. Alice took the suitcases in one by one and carried them through to the main bedroom, where she heaved them up onto the bed. Unpacking would have to wait.

"Where do you want this?" Zoe asked as she brought the kitchen box into the main cabin.

"On the floor, please."

They went back to the car and unloaded the last few boxes, which they then stowed aboard the boat. Alice locked the car, which she'd arranged to be picked up by a scrap merchant in the morning. As she walked back along the harbour path to the boat, she wondered if she would ever see Bristol again. In that moment she wanted nothing more than to leave and never return.

"Well, good luck with everything. You sure you're going to be alright?"

"Yes. Thank you for your help. I really appreciate it." Alice couldn't help but reach out to hug Zoe, who wrapped her arms tight around her.

"Take care, my love," she said with a big grin.

Alice stepped aboard and turned the engine on. She put on a lifejacket, then made sure the cabin door was closed. With the engine purring away, Alice untied the boat and pushed away from the side of the pier with her right foot. Zoe gave her a jaunty wave, turned and left. Alice was all alone now.

Seas the Day drifted out into the middle of the waterway. She had really made it! Alice took a deep breath and took hold of the wheel. She slowly eased the throttle forward, and the boat set off, out into the middle of the harbour. Before she could reach the open sea, she had to pass the swing bridge. As she approached the bridge, she eased off on the throttle and gently drifted in the main harbour channel. Her eyes felt like they were on stalks; she was staring so intently at every person on the harbour walkway.

After a few minutes she could hear the bridge alarm ringing, and a man appeared from a building at the side of the bridge and gave her a wave. She waved back, and the bridge started to turn and open, which would allow her access to exit the harbour.

As Alice waited for the bridge to fully open, she tied her hair back and tightened her lifejacket. Her eyes remained on the walkways, scanning everyone. A jolt of panic hit her as she thought she saw Richard walking along the harbour, but as she focused on the figure, she realised it was someone else, just a stranger out for a walk.

Alice exhaled. "Jeez."

She checked again. There was no sign of Richard or Sally or those two men. She never wanted to see any of them again for the rest of her life.

Once the bridge had completed its turn, Alice pushed forward on the throttle, and the boat rocked forwards, out of the harbour and down the river. Eventually, she left the river behind and reached the open expanse of the Bristol Channel.

She was free!

Free from the pain and stress of the past few weeks.

Free from a tangle of deceit and lies.

Free from the man who would destroy her for the sake of his addiction.

Alice shook her head as if to release herself from it all. Then she turned the engine off, stepped forwards and unwound the sail. The wind filled the sail in an instant, and the boat was propelled forward, the prow cutting through the deep water as the smell of the salt air hit her.

It was the first time Alice had sailed *Seas the Day* out on the open water; she knew it would take some time to get used to her, but already she felt like a great boat to sail. So this was her new home, at least for the next few months. Alice couldn't help but grin in excitement. Thoughts of the last few weeks might still threaten to overwhelm and crush her, but she would push them away and focus on the boat. There would be time to process what had happened, time to mourn what she'd lost with Richard, but at this moment she couldn't face thinking about anything. She just wanted to get away from Bristol.

But even out here, at the thought of Bristol, Alice couldn't help anxiously looking over her shoulder, although there was nothing to see: just the vast empty sea channel.

The wind was a nice seventeen knots, strong enough to push her along, easy enough to work with. To her right she could see south Wales; to her left was the green coastline of southern England.

She sailed for an hour until the sun started to dip in the sky, the hot afternoon on its way out. Alice had no real plan for this first day; she was just going to sail until the evening and then pull into the nearest town or village along the coast; there were plenty to choose from, and she knew Richard would struggle to find her wherever she went. Once she'd docked, Alice would need to buy some supplies from a shop, some food and drink. Top of the list was a bottle of gin.

The thought of getting supplies made her realise she was thirsty.

Alice locked the wheel to follow her course. The boat would be fine to leave for a few moments. With the boat feeling steady, she opened the cabin door, stepped down into the darkness and switched on the lights. The smell of newness was enticing. She knew the fridge would be empty, but in one of the boxes Alice had packed a bottle of water and a bag of bananas. She rooted through the box and found the water and grabbed a banana.

While she was down here, she decided to use the toilet. She put the water and fruit on the side and went to the little bathroom. As she opened the bathroom door, she screamed.

There was somebody there.

Alice stepped back, and in the gloomy light, she peered into the bathroom.

Then she stepped back further as a man burst out to the main cabin.

"What are you doing here?!" she yelled at him.

He laughed and stared at her with wild, murderous eyes.

23

6 MONTHS AGO

Richard knocked back a large whiskey and gasped as the liquid burned his mouth and throat. He was tempted to have another but knew he should keep a clear head, or at least partially. He quietly swilled out the glass in the kitchen sink, wiped it dry with a tea towel, and put it back into the top kitchen cupboard. The whiskey bottle he also returned to the cupboard. The oven clock told him it was 1:30 a.m. exactly.

He would like to think he was ready for this next part, but in reality he would never be truly ready for what he was about to do.

Richard went into the hallway, picked up his car keys and rucksack and quietly left the house. His car wasn't on the driveway but parked further down the street. He got in, started the engine, but left the lights off as he drove slowly down the quiet suburban street. At the end of the road, he switched the headlights on and put his foot down on the accelerator, heading into the city centre.

It was a Wednesday evening in January, and the city was quiet; there were very few cars around and even fewer people to be seen. The car drove unnoticed through Bristol and headed to the south of the city. Eventually, he reached Radleigh Road, but he kept on going until he found a parking spot in the next road. He pulled in between two transit vans and turned the engine off.

The only thing he could hear was the wind blowing outside. He took a few deep breaths. There was still time to drive home and forget this. His eyes looked at his reflection in the rear-view mirror, but he quickly looked away, unwilling to acknowledge what he saw there.

"Come on, arsehole," he said to himself. "Let's do this."

Another deep breath and he yanked the keys out of the ignition and got out of the car with his small black rucksack. He meant to close the door quietly, but it slammed shut in his nervous hands. The rain was already wetting his black jumper and black jeans.

Richard set off with his hands in his pockets, keeping his head down against the wind, which whipped his hair, as he walked around the corner into Radleigh Road. He didn't hesitate, just pulled out the key from his pocket and, as quietly as possible, opened the front door and stepped inside the house.

He was in.

His heart hammered as he stood in the hallway. Richard listened, but the house was silent. He waited for someone to come to the landing, but nobody appeared to disturb the stillness.

In the hallway there was a picture of Van Gogh's sunflowers. Richard stared at it while he waited to see if anyone would appear to investigate his entrance. The streetlights from outside cast a strange orange glow upon the sunflowers, and he blinked and squinted at the picture in the near darkness.

Minutes passed, and he didn't move. His legs ached. He waited to be absolutely sure, but no one stirred.

Finally, he slipped his wet shoes off and opened his rucksack; he pulled out a full-body spray suit and some medical gloves.

They were blue but looked dark enough in the house. Quietly he slipped the suit on and sealed it shut with its buttons so his whole body was covered in the plastic material. Then he pulled on his medical gloves and went to the staircase. He took the stairs one by one, each foot placed carefully onto each step. His heart felt like it was going to beat out of his chest; his breath sounded deafening in his ears. Slowly, slowly he moved upwards until he eventually reached the landing.

That afternoon, when Richard had called into the house to visit Sue and Irene, he had managed to slip two sleeping pills into Irene's tea. As he silently made his way past her bedroom door, he could hear her snoring. It was deep and guttural and real; nobody was pretending to be asleep in there.

Richard passed the door and headed to Sue's room. He pushed the door open with one finger and listened, but there was nothing to hear in the room. The usual smell of urine came to him, and he tried to ignore it.

He went inside.

He could see her lying under the bed covers. Small and frail. Sue.

His hands shook.

He'd played the next bit in his head over and over, but imagining something and doing something were two different things. There was an armchair in the corner of the room with a grey cushion on it. Richard picked up the cushion and held it tightly. In his mind he'd held that cushion a thousand times, but now he actually held it in his hands, he felt sick. Faint. He felt terrible.

It was wool, not cotton as he'd imagined. It was a big cushion but felt as light as a feather in his hands. Richard suddenly wondered where she'd gotten it from. Was it a gift? Had Sue been out shopping one day and seen it, seen the soft grey wool and been attracted to it? She would have brought it home and placed it *the chair, happy with her new purchase. And now Richard held it in his hands.*

He stepped towards the bed. Sue was asleep; he could see that.

Slowly, he moved closer.

He lifted the cushion up and moved to place it on her face.

Goodbye, Sue.

Suddenly her eyes opened, and he froze. Oh God, she was awake. She was going to call Irene; he would be caught. This was a disaster!

But Sue didn't make a sound; she just turned her head to him and smiled.

Now what? He'd planned this with her asleep, like putting down a damaged animal. But now her small eyes were staring at him.

"It all went whoosh," she whispered.

"Yes, Sue," he replied.

As her eyes watched him, he put the cushion over her face and pressed down. Sue didn't resist, didn't stir under his weight. He pushed down harder. His hands were shaking, tears came to his eyes, but he blinked them away.

Under the cushion, he could hear Sue struggling to breathe, struggling to get air into her lungs. It was her body's instinct, her mind might be broken, but the body was still functioning; it still knew that it needed air to survive. It needed air to live.

Richard put his whole weight on the cushion now, his wet jeans and jumper pushing onto the wool. He listened as her breathing became ragged and then stopped, although he kept the pressure on her head for a while longer.

entually he stepped back and pulled the cushion off. He withered face. Some of her grey hair had stuck to her hard softly smoothed it off her face.

* her. She was dead. He'd planned to check*

and double-check that she was definitely dead, but to look at her, there was no need to check; there was no life left in Sue's body. He caught sight of something white in Sue's hand, and he prised her fingers open to reveal a small dried flower.

Richard moved away from the bed and replaced the cushion onto the armchair. That was it, then; he was a killer. He'd murdered someone. He had taken a life. Killed. Murdered.

He was desperate to get the hell out of there. Away from Sue, away from her lifeless corpse. His whole body was shaking now as he quietly left the bedroom. He gave a quick backward glance to check everything looked as it should; then he closed the door. It gave a little squeak, and he paused to make sure Irene hadn't stirred.

Richard moved down the hallway. Outside Irene's room, he waited but couldn't hear her snoring anymore. He heard her bed creaking. No! She was getting up out of her bed. Richard panicked and went back into Sue's room, closing the door behind him. He held his breath and listened.

Sounds filtered through the crack in the door: Irene opening her bedroom door and stepping out into the hallway. What would he do if she came in? Try to talk his way out of it? Or kill Irene too? But then it would look like an obvious murder scene. He was planning on everyone assuming Sue had died in her sleep and not had the life snuffed out of her.

Richard could hear Irene walking down the hallway now, coming closer to him. He was trapped. His eyes scanned the room for a weapon to hit her with. She was a big woman, and he was a slim fifty-six-year-old man: would he have the strength to do it? The sound of footsteps told him she was getting closer and closer. He could see nothing he could use as a weapon. He'd have to punch her, maybe he could punch her and run away, and she wouldn't know it was him in the darkness. The footsteps reached

Sue's room, and he raised his clenched fists. The footsteps kept going. He heard the bathroom door open and Irene turn the light on. Faintly, he could hear the sound of her sitting on the toilet.

With the sound of Irene's piss hitting the toilet bowl, Richard silently left Sue's room, left the door closed as he had found it and went down the stairs. As he reached the bottom stair, he could hear Irene pulling the flush and turning the bathroom light off. Richard knew he couldn't risk leaving the house by the front door whilst Irene was awake, so he went into the lounge. The room was dark and empty and had two different exits if he needed to run away or hide, but there was no need as he heard Irene make her way back to her own room. The sounds of her big bulk getting back into bed confirmed that he was safe.

"Fat cow," he muttered to himself.

Richard was tempted to open the front door and flee, but he knew Irene was still awake, so he sat on the arm of the striped sofa and waited. His mind was whirring, his body continued to give little shakes and shudders, and he had to fight the urge to leave. Every instinct told him to get up and run away. But he waited. And waited.

Eventually, he could hear the distant sounds of Irene's snoring again, and he couldn't help but breathe a sigh of relief. Now he could leave.

Tomorrow Irene would wake up and find her current client dead in bed; she was about to lose this particular job.

Richard left the lounge and slipped his shoes back on. He checked he had his keys, and then he gently turned the front door handle. Once outside, he took a lungful of fresh air. He quietly closed the door behind him and walked down the garden path.

It felt good to be outside, in the darkness and the cold air. Richard went back to his car and drove through the city, down the M32 and back towards Winterbourne. On the way home he stopped on a quiet street with a public bin and ditched his body suit and gloves in the bin. With the car headlights turned off, he parked in the exact spot that his car had been in before.

He let himself back into the house. Alice was away for the night at a biology conference, so he didn't need to worry about making a noise, but he still found himself moving quietly.

The first thing he did was strip off his clothes and put them in the washing machine. There was nothing quiet about that, but it needed doing. Then, naked, he walked upstairs and showered. Richard turned the heat up as high as it would go; he scalded himself until his skin was red. He wasn't a detective, but after so many years as a biology lecturer, he knew enough about forensic evidence, and he was determined not to leave any trace of Sue on him.

After the shower he dried his body and wrapped his dressing gown tightly around himself. Back downstairs, Richard brought the bottle of whiskey and crystal tumbler back out of the cupboard and poured himself a large drink. It went down in one, and he gasped as the burning gold liquid slid down his gullet.

He took the bottle and glass into the lounge and poured himself another. The clock on the mantelpiece told him it was 2:45 a.m.

Finally, he felt himself relax a little. His body was no longer shaking.

That was it, then, murder. He was a murderer.

Except, he didn't see it as a real murder. In a way, Sue had already been dead, her mind was long gone, and all that was left was her body. What Richard had done was put her out of her misery. He'd want someone to do the same for him if he ever had Alzheimer's...probably. There was no quality of life there, he told himself as he sipped his glass of whiskey.

Despite these assurances, as he closed his eyes and leaned his head back against the chair, he could see Sue's eyes watching him as he put the grey woollen cushion over her face. Those eyes. He gulped at his drink and drained the glass. He poured another large one from the bottle. He was officially a killer. However much he knew Sue had a crap quality of life, he'd still killed her. What didn't help was the realisation that if it came to it, he would kill again.

Sue was dead, and he had calculated it would be around six months until her inheritance came through to Alice. Sue's house was mortgage-free and must be worth a lot. He had six months to put a plan in place to get hold of the money. He had a few ideas already, including one crazy idea that involved his new girlfriend, Sally. She was a drama student at Bristol University, completely besotted with him, and, he thought, just perfect for what he had in mind.

24

LEAVING DAY

"**Y**ou know, don't you?" Richard yelled at her.

"What?"

"You know! It's been driving me mad." He glared at her and stepped forward. "I've been going fucking crazy in that cupboard thinking about it."

The movement of the boat was causing him to sway, which added to the air of madness about him. Alice had only seen him that morning. It had been less than a day, but it felt like a lifetime. He looked so different now, wilder and meaner.

Alice stepped backwards.

She couldn't believe Richard was on the boat. Anger flooded through her at the sight of him. But there was something else swirling in her too: fear. His appearance was unnerving. What was he doing here?

"How did you find her?" she demanded, *her* meaning the boat.

"What, after you sent me on a wild bloody goose chase around the city?"

She wanted him off the boat. She needed him off the boat. How could she get rid of him?

"You shouldn't be here. *I'm* taking the boat, not you."

He threw back his head and laughed so the veins bulged in his neck. She'd never seen him like this.

"Oh, no, little Alice. This is my boat."

"No," she insisted. "I've paid for this boat; it's mine."

"It was my idea," he screamed, violently slapping his hands on his chest. "My dream to get a boat, it was all my planning –"

"Oh yes," she screamed back at him. "I know all about *your* planning. Where is your little whore...or should I say *daughter*? Have you hidden her on board somewhere?"

"Ha!" His face was red and distorted with rage. "I knew you knew."

"Obviously I know. What an idiotic plan. What a really stupid thing to do, not to mention something only a complete bastard would think of." She could feel her anger consuming her as she yelled at him. "It's one thing to leave your partner, it's another to plot to steal her money and boat by making your little whore pretend to be your long-lost sick daughter."

"It's my boat," he screamed at her, his voice echoing around the small cabin.

"It's *my* boat," she screamed back at him.

Richard stepped forward, fists clenched.

There was a twisting torrent of emotions battling inside her: anger and fear and heartbreak. But as he stepped forward, her fear won the battle, and Alice became aware just how isolated they were here, out on the empty sea in the fading light.

"You bitch, why couldn't you just do what you usually

do?" he snarled. "Why couldn't you just go along with everything?"

She looked at him, willing herself not to cry.

"You've always walked all over me, taken me for granted. All I've done is love you, and this is how you repay me. You're nothing but a tragic, washed-up and penniless gambling addict."

Her words caused his rage to bubble over.

Richard lunged towards her and slapped her hard across the face. She dropped heavily onto the wooden floor with Richard on top of her. It was a messy fall; pain seared across her back and head as his weight pushed her down.

"Get off," she gasped. "Get off me, you bastard."

His hands were scrabbling over her. He clawed at her, frantically scratching her as he tried to pin her down.

The world span for Alice, the boat was swaying through the water, the fall and the slap to her face all made her head spin, and her stomach threatened vomit. She had to get away from him.

His icy hands caught her wrists, and he succeeded in pinning her to the floor. His face loomed over her, twisted in madness and rage, like a wild animal hungry for blood.

"You bastard."

Alice wriggled her waist, which gave her enough of an angle to bring her knee up behind him. Somehow she managed to knee him hard in the back, which must have hurt because he arched upwards, and that movement gave her enough space to bring her knee up again; this time she used all her strength to smash it into his groin.

She knew she had connected when Richard yelped in pain, and she felt his hands drop away from her wrists. Alice seized her chance and pushed him off her. He didn't resist, and she was reminded that neither of them had really been in an actual fight before.

Alice managed to crawl away from him and get up. She stumbled to the door and pulled herself up the stairs and through the door. The fresh sea air was reviving. She could see that the sun was setting. It would be dark soon. Alice turned to close and lock the door, to trap Richard in the cabin, but suddenly he burst through it. He charged at her, and she screamed. She was too late, and now he was outside with her.

Their bodies connected, and this time he didn't slap her, he punched her.

Pain exploded through her face, and she crumpled to the deck.

The world became blurred and far away, but the pain she felt told her she was being dragged across the boat by her hair. He was pulling her towards the mast, but Alice found she had no strength to resist.

The pain and the spinning became too much for her, and overwhelmed, she threw up, retching with her whole body in agony. The sick was hot and yellow and splashed across the boat's deck. Oh God, she felt awful.

To her horror, Alice became aware of a rope being wrapped around her. Was Richard tying her to the mast? But before she could focus and try to resist, the rope was quickly yanked tight, and she was unable to move. Richard didn't stop there; panting and sweating over her, he bound her wrists together.

She blinked, trying to focus.

Richard stumbled away from her and made his way back to the wheel, which he unlocked. With a hard yank, Richard turned the boat around, and Alice had to keep her head low to avoid the swinging boom pole as it swung across. In a few seconds he had them heading in the opposite direction, and she had to assume they were going back to Bristol. The wind blasted Alice in the face, and the cold against her hot skin provided welcome relief from her nausea.

But the relief was minor compared to the tightness of the rope around her body; she could feel it cutting into her soft skin. Her head was in agony; it felt empty except for a piercing pain that made it hard to focus.

What was he going to do to her? Maybe he was going to swap her for that woman. Would he sail back into Bristol, drop off Alice and pick up his whore?

Alice watched from the mast as Richard went below into the cabin, and she could vaguely hear him rummage around underneath her. The first thing she was going to do was call the police, he might think he was going to get away with this, but he wouldn't be able to take the boat far before the coast-guard caught up with him; he would be charged with theft, fraud, assault. Surely he would go to jail? Earlier Alice had been worried about telling the police too much about this situation, in case she was questioned about taking the boat herself, but this had gone too far now. Now she would tell the police everything.

Next, Richard appeared from the cabin below. He was dragging something heavy, which he hoisted up onto the top deck. It was a chain. A long length of silver-grey chain that was kept on the boat as a spare anchor.

Why would he need that?

"Time for a little swim," he called to her before he disappeared back down below.

Dread caught the breath in her throat. Was the chain for her? Was he going to throw her overboard? No, surely not.

He might be a bad person, an utter bastard, but he wasn't a killer.

Water sprayed her as the boat cut through the sea. She looked around, straining her neck to give her a full view around them, but there were no other boats to be seen. The sea was open and dark and empty. The coastline was a thin sliver of dark green in the distance. They were all alone.

Richard reappeared. He had a mad grin on his face. In one hand he had her wallet; in the other he held a knife. At the sight of the knife, Alice screamed.

"No, you can't do this," she begged.

He stepped up onto the deck.

"Richard, this is crazy –"

"Shut up!" he yelled. "I've had enough of listening to you. Years and years of you moaning at me. Your boring shit." He brandished the knife at her. "The same stuff every day. Nothing to say for yourself, just moaning on and on about the most trivial things."

The force of his anger was shocking to her. Despite everything, despite everything she had seen from him over the past few weeks, in an odd way she hadn't been able to comprehend why he would do what he was planning; she couldn't grasp what his motivation was. But now she could see it, laid bare in a terrifying way.

She knew it then; he hated her.

"What have I ever done to you?"

He tilted his head back and laughed into the evening sky like a maniac.

Alice struggled against the ropes around her wrists and body. And as she moved her body, she realised they weren't as tight as she had first thought. Was there a little movement there?

"You're going for a swim," he repeated, "and I'm going to spend your money."

Richard opened her wallet and grinned at the sight of her bank cards.

"Everyone thinks you're away sailing across the Med, so no one will question when your cards are used to pay for things," he announced triumphantly. "I can keep using them for months."

Seeing a man she once loved acting this way was completely soul destroying. What she felt was beyond heartbreak. Her head was in agony from his punch, her back and sides were throbbing from the fall, and her stomach was truly suffering. But the physical pain racking her body was nothing compared to the agony in her heart. How had she been so in love with this person?

"You're sick."

"Maybe," he agreed.

"Just a pathetic gambling addict."

Thunder filled his face. "I'm not an addict."

Then Richard pocketed her wallet and walked back for the chains. He struggled with the weight of them, but he managed to heave them over to her whilst still clutching the knife.

"Funny," he said with a strange look on his face. "I thought this would be hard, but I'm actually looking forward to it."

25

LEAVING DAY

From the moment he decided to kill her, Richard had thought he would have to build himself up to the task, but now the time had come, he felt quite comfortable with slitting her throat and throwing her body overboard.

He'd killed once, and he was confident he could do it again.

Life had screwed him over in the last few years, so in a way it was only to be expected that he would have to do something drastic. It wasn't really his fault. His plan had fallen through, so he had to make a new plan. Get rid of Alice, go and get Sally, and set sail for the south.

He knew he would have to apologise to Sally; she really wasn't happy that he'd dropped her back to her house earlier. In fact, she had been swearing and yelling at him, but he knew he could turn on his charm, and she would soon come around. Her bags would still be packed, and he was now in control of the boat. In no time at all, she would be there with him, and she would remember to bring her bikinis along too.

Ideally, he would have liked to get the full amount of money from Alice, but this would have to do. What was her spending limit? Maybe £1,000 a day? Within a few months he would have her money withdrawn from different ATMs all over Europe. Of course, it helped that he knew her PIN, but that was what happened when you lived with someone for twenty years.

The chains were heavy, and he struggled with the weight of them, but he knew they were needed to make sure Alice's lifeless body sank to the hidden depths below. His breathing was laboured and ragged, and the rocking boat only made things harder. Maybe he should drag them instead of carrying them, but he didn't want to scratch the new deck and...

Suddenly Richard slipped on the deck, and he stumbled backwards. The knife and chains flew from his hands, down into the pool of Alice's vomit that had led to his accident. Unable to right himself, he felt his head smack against the side of the boat.

The world turned black.

———————

RICHARD'S HEAD THROBBED, and he could feel someone touching him. Without thinking, he waved his hands and pushed away whoever was near him. The sound of wind filled his ears. Where was he? He felt awful. His back was on fire; his head was in bits.

He fought to breathe, and with a great effort he managed

to sit up and look around. *Seas the Day*, of course; he was on the boat.

What had happened? He'd never felt so disoriented.

Alice! He had her tied against the mast and was about to slit her throat. Except he didn't have his knife, and as he looked up, he saw that Alice was gone.

He blinked and wiped his face with his sleeve. He tried to focus.

Where was she?

The ropes around the mast were still there, but he could see they had been cut. Now they were just a useless bundle of frayed and slashed threads. Had Alice escaped? Everything came flooding back to him, including his rage and intent to kill her. Richard realised he must have slipped on her sick that was slick over the deck; he must have fallen and hit his head, knocking himself out and giving her the chance to escape.

But escape where? There was nowhere for her to go, as they were far from the coast. She must be hiding on the boat. He looked around and could see the water was calm and the wind was steady, which was helping keep the boat from rocking too much. It really shouldn't be left unattended for so long, but he had something more important to do.

He had to kill Alice.

Richard stood up.

His head was pounding, and he needed to hold onto the mast to steady himself and stop another fall. Across the deck was the chain he had been carrying, now uncoiled like a dead snake.

Taking a deep breath, he made his way to the cabin door.

The sun had almost set, and it was dark down in the cabin. He peered in but couldn't see any movement. Tentatively, Richard walked down the steps and into the darkness. He kept one hand on the rail and one in front of his face for protection in case she ran at him.

He turned on the lights, and the cabin was illuminated.

It was empty. Where was she? She must be hiding in one of the other cabins.

Frantically he searched around for something he could use as a weapon. There was nothing obvious in sight, so he went through the boxes on the floor. One of them held kitchen items, and as he moved some of the pans and plates out of the way, he found a small vegetable knife at the bottom of the box. It would do nicely. He gripped it in his hand and walked through the cabin, straining to detect any movement.

There were three doors in front of him.

He flung open the door on the left, which was the door to the small bedroom: no Alice. There was a little single cabin bed and several wardrobes in there, and he opened each wardrobe door in turn, but they were empty. He checked the bed, nothing.

Back in the corridor he faced the second door to the main bedroom.

"Alice," he called, his voice sounding odd to his own ears, "come out; let's talk."

As Richard spoke, he gripped the vegetable knife in his hand tighter. This time he wasn't going to bother tying her up; he was just going to stab her. Stab and stab and stab. He was going to kill her. Make her bleed. He didn't care where the blood went, what mess he made, how violent and noisy it all was. No more chances, no more risk.

He was going to kill that bitch.

"Alice," he called again.

He opened the second door.

On the double bed in the middle of the room sat two suitcases. Against one wall was a run of wardrobes, against the other a chest of drawers. Other than the furniture and cases, the room seemed empty. He walked into the room with the knife in his right hand. With his left hand he opened the door to each wardrobe. Each one was empty. Where the hell was she?

The bed was built into the base of the boat; there was no bottom to it, just solid wood. Even so, he checked down the side of the bed. He even opened a few of the larger drawers. Nothing.

Back in the cabin he faced the third and final door. This was for the bathroom, where he had hidden earlier. Of course, she was hiding in the same place he had.

"Alice," he called to the door, trying to keep his voice level, "come on, let's talk about this."

Richard gripped the knife and took a deep breath.

Don't hesitate, he told himself, *just stick the blade in her.*

If she escaped, he was penniless. And she could send the police after him. They could take the boat away. Then what did he have?

But if he killed her, he would get to keep the boat, and he'd have access to hundreds of thousands of pounds. And Sally, don't forget Sally. He could pay to keep her happy; they would have a lavish lifestyle, sailing the Med together.

Kill Alice and his life was good.

He'd killed before, and he could do it again.

Deep breath, his little vegetable knife ready.

He flung the door open and stepped forward, knife slashing at the air.

The bathroom was empty, no Alice.

"ALICE!" he screamed.

Where could she be? He couldn't understand it; she had disappeared. Richard stepped back and slammed the bathroom door. He looked around the cabin, checked under the little table and opened the larger kitchen cupboards, but they were all empty. On the floor of the cabin there was a panel that opened to the engine, and Richard yanked it open. It was a small area, but she could have crawled in there. But that space was empty too. He kicked the door in frustration.

Richard left the cabin area and stepped back outside, holding onto the rail with his left hand, still clutching the knife in his right. Out on deck there was nowhere she could hide. She wasn't on the boat. So where was she?

She must have jumped off. That was the only explanation; she must have jumped and made a swim for it. He looked across the coastline, but it was dark, and he couldn't make out much. Would she have been able to swim that far? Probably. It was just under a mile. But the swim would have been the easy part. Once she had made it to the coast, Alice wouldn't be arriving at a nice sandy beach; no, it was all mud. The mud flats of the Bristol channel were known to be very dangerous; they had claimed many lives in the past.

Could she make her way through the cloying mud? He doubted it. What if she had got lucky and come ashore on a rocky part? The rocks along the coast were as sharp as razors, and Alice would have been cut to shreds. He thought about turning the boat towards the coast, but there was no way he would find her in the darkness.

So that was it? She was gone.

"Good riddance."

Richard went to the wheel and took control of the boat.

Now what? He was nearly back to Bristol and could see Avonmouth ahead. He would press on, pick up Sally and head south. If she'd survived, Alice would phone the police and report him for theft and assault, but would they come for him? Would they be able to find him? He would need to change the name of the boat, sail through the night, get across to France, then to Portugal and Spain, and into the depths of the Mediterranean. There they would be lost amongst thousands of little islands and ports. He could hide out for years without being found, and after a while he couldn't imagine them looking very hard for him.

The real issue, though, was money. If Alice had made it to the shore, she wouldn't waste any time in cancelling all her bank cards.

"Bitch!" he screamed out across the black water.

God damn her, his plan had been so close to working. Now he would have to get a job. Maybe he could borrow a few thousand from his brother; plus he would have the money from his car. What would that be in total? Perhaps £10,000. He could make that last, cheap wine and food, catch his own fish for dinner.

He warmed to the idea. He could make it work. Of course, he could place a few bets, just little ones, and he could turn that money into something big. He thought through the sports events coming up; there were a few rugby games he could bet on. Just a few £100 bets. The thought of placing the bets made him feel better, more energised and optimistic. Yes, a few little bets.

But just as he was working through this bright new strategy, a noise behind him startled him.

Richard let go of the wheel and span around.

THE WATER WAS FREEZING, and Alice shivered. She could taste the sea salt at the back of her throat. Was she doing the right thing?

Nice little Alice, that was what they said about her. Happy little Alice. Loyal Alice. Always reliable. All she'd ever done was try to be a good partner to Richard. She liked gardening, baking and a glass of wine on a Friday after a busy week at work. She loved watching reruns of *The Great British Bake Off* on TV, loved her two holidays a year. Alice had some great friends, and they always supported each other.

Good Alice. Happy little Alice.

Contact with other men was always polite; she would never dream of flirting. Dealings with money were always open and honest. She treated everyone with respect. She believed in humanity; she was always ready to see the best in people, willing to help anyone, to support and encourage without prejudice.

Lovely Alice. Gentle, sweet Alice.

Her passion was flowers. Bright and pretty and sweet-smelling; what was not to like? People thought she was obsessed by them, but she often wondered why people weren't as in love with them as she was.

Yes, that was her, but amongst all that niceness, hidden deep under her gentleness, was a little core of stone. An inner strength that she didn't need to show people. A rock of hardness within. Hidden away.

Until now. Now she was all stone.

When Richard had slipped and knocked himself out, Alice had managed to stretch out and grab the knife that he had dropped on the deck. Her foot reached it, and she gently nudged it towards her hands. Alice had strained and sweated, but she'd managed to get her hand on the grey rubber handle; then she'd turned it nimbly and sawed through the ropes around her wrists. The blade was razor sharp, and the thought that Richard was planning to stick it into her made her shudder. In seconds the rope dropped away. Next, she cut away the rope around her waist, and in another instant she had been free.

Alice had stood up and looked down on the prone body of Richard. Could she hurt him with the knife? Of course not. Instead, she put the knife into her belt.

She grabbed some of the ropes that had been around her body and moved over to Richard. Alice had pulled his wrists together and tried to bind his hands, but he'd writhed on the deck and pushed her away as he began to stir. It was too late, he had started to wake up, and Alice suddenly felt exposed and unprotected. She'd felt a strong urge to get a weapon to protect herself, not a blade that could kill him, but something solid to hit him with if it came to it.

She had gone to the cabin and found a thick length of wood that was used to wedge the door open. Back on the deck she'd been horrified to see Richard sitting up and looking around for her. What should she do? Hide and jump out on him? An idea came to her then, probably stupid, but it was the only idea she had, and she was out of time.

Taking the rope, Alice tied it around the back rail of the boat and threw it into the water. The wooden pole went into her belt before she stepped over the rail and slid down the rope and into the water. She had gasped at the cold. There might have been a heatwave in England for the last few days, but it hadn't been enough to heat the deep waters of the Bristol channel.

She had dropped into the blackness, clutching onto the rope tightly with both hands. Her body vanished as she went in up to her neck. Alice's mind flashed back to being in Bristol harbour when her little Pico had capsized; she thought about the rope being around her neck and the water ready to drown her. She'd had to go down into the darkness to become free then, and it was the same now.

Was this the right thing to do? Hiding in the water? Alice tried to control her breathing, tried to stay calm. In front of her face the painted name of the boat, *Seas the Day*, was large in her view.

She could hear him walking around above her. It had only been a few minutes, but she was already shivering. This was risky, dangerous. But Alice didn't care. Nice Alice had left; now she was determined to win, determined to beat him.

The cold was wretched, but thoughts of what Richard had done to her and what he was planning to do gave her strength.

"Alice," she heard as he called out in the cabin. He was yelling something, but the words were lost on her. She could hear doors being thrown open as he searched for her.

There was a lot of banging and crashing.

And then he was on the deck, where she knew he would take control of the wheel. The boat shot forward as Richard set the sail and headed back towards Bristol harbour. Alice was pulled along on the rope, and her body became horizontal in the water.

"Bitch," she heard him shout into the wind.

She could picture him above her, steering the wheel with his back to her.

Alice pulled herself up on the rope.

Nice little Alice.

The boat was cutting through the water, throwing up spray, making just enough noise. The sail whipped and gave a loud crack. It was loud enough to mask any sounds she made. She was frozen stiff, but her arms somehow still had the strength to pull herself up and out of the water. Despite the cold, in that moment, she felt strong enough to flip the whole boat over.

Loyal Alice.

She pulled the wooden pole out of her belt and silently stepped over the rail, her feet feeling steady as she moved slowly.

Good little Alice.

She raised the wooden pole, and Richard must have sensed or heard her because he span around to face her, but it was too late. Alice swung the pole and hit him on the side of the head. It was a clean strike, hard, direct and on target.

Goodnight, Richard. He slumped, unconscious at her feet.

"Bastard."

26

LEAVING DAY

Bristol harbour was quiet. In the summer's evening it looked magical with the distant twinkling lights of the pubs and restaurants. The bridge that allowed access into the main harbour was closed, so Alice brought *Seas the Day* to a gentle stop on the river and waited for the bridge to open for her.

Despite being completely soaking wet, Alice didn't feel too cold. Perhaps there was enough warmth left in the evening to chase away any chill, although she was still desperate to get changed and put on some dry clothes.

Richard was bound and subdued at Alice's feet as she stood at the wheel, controlling the boat. What was she going to do with him? Calling the police was one option; she could report him. But for what? Theft? It was attempted theft of the boat and her money. What Richard had done, and tried to do, to her was terrible, but in terms of what laws he might have broken, she wasn't so sure. Had he done enough to be arrested? Alice was desperate to get away now, desperate to leave him and Bristol far behind. The last thing she wanted was to spend a few days in police interviews, all the time worrying about the security of the boat.

She looked down at Richard, and he looked up at her.

Alice had tied his hands and feet with rope. The same rope he'd had her tied up with earlier. The cream polo top he'd put on that morning was now creased and dirty.

"I'm going to drop you off at the harbour."

He looked groggy from the strike across his face. His body was slumped against the side of the outer cabin wall, and she could see it was an effort for him to focus on her.

"Why don't we talk about this?" he croaked.

Alice looked at him and shuddered. He was trying to turn on the charm again, slick Richard who could charm anyone, talk anyone into anything. He actually thought he could convince her to take him back.

"There's nothing to talk about. You are a spiteful, horrible man. What you were planning to do to me was disgusting, and the sooner I'm rid of you, the better."

Richard laughed.

Alice hadn't been expecting this, and she narrowed her eyes at him. In the evening light his face looked like a painted mask of hate.

"You silly bitch, you've no idea."

Despite everything, his words still hurt her. Even now, he was putting her down and making her feel small and stupid. She willed herself not to reply.

"You've no clue about what I've done."

"I know enough."

He snorted. "You don't know the half of it."

Ignore him, she told herself.

Alice tore her eyes away from him and watched as the harbour master walked out of his house and into the bridge booth. The barriers on the roads came down to stop traffic coming onto the bridge. It was late enough that there weren't any cars on the road. Slowly the bridge started to open. She watched as it began its steady turn inwards.

"Goodbye, Richard. Don't try to contact me" – she smiled – "not that you'll be able to."

"Bitch."

"I'm sure you and that little whore will be happy in some shitty bedsit together."

Alice tried to control her anger. She couldn't remember a time when she'd sworn so much, and she promised herself that once this day was done, she would stop.

Again, he laughed.

However hard she tried to ignore it, his knowing laugh was like a twisting knife in her gut. "What's so funny?"

"Ask your mum," he whispered.

His words turned her blood cold, and a sickening feeling dropped into her stomach.

"My mum?"

He laughed for a third time. Alice grabbed the wooden pole and stepped to him.

"If you laugh at me one more time, I'm going to knock you out again."

She'd never threatened anyone with physical harm before, but it seemed to be a day of firsts. Alice felt completely drained and exhausted, her body ached, and all she wanted to do was get Richard off *her* boat.

His laughter faded to be replaced by a dark look. Richard's bruised face and dishevelled hair added to his air of viciousness, and Alice was wary of getting too close to him.

"My mum? You're so desperate for attention you'd say anything."

Alice walked back to the wheel, dropped the wooden pole and gripped the wheel tightly. It was dark now. But the tide was still high, and in a few minutes the bridge would be open, and she could drop Richard off and set off south. She wouldn't go far in the dark, but an hour's sailing would get her away from the city. Her plan hadn't changed; she was still going to spend the night in one of the coastal towns and then set off on her long journey. God, she was so close; she couldn't wait to get away. The bridge was almost open.

"I killed her."

He said it softly, as if he were talking to a child. Time seemed to stand still. He had killed her. Richard had killed her mum? She looked at him and shook her head. No way, he was just trying to...

"Held a pillow over her face as she slept."

No. Please no. It couldn't be true. But looking at him then, slouched against the cabin wall with that triumphant look on his face, she knew it was true.

Richard had killed her mum.

Her hands shook. Tears rolled down her cheeks. He was a murderer.

Alice thought she had understood him and understood what had driven him to create such a stupid, horrible plan to steal from her. But this was on a different level; she would never understand this.

"You..." She fought the huge, painful lump in her throat.

He just looked at her. Emotions flooded through her. He was a killer. Suddenly she connected the dots; Richard hadn't just been planning to steal from her for weeks, he'd been planning for months. He wanted to get at her mum's money, at Alice's inheritance, so he had killed Alice's mum, waited for the money to come through, and then schemed to run off with it.

"You evil bastard."

He shrugged. "I just did what I had to."

"No. You can't just shrug this off like it was an accident. You murdered someone..." Her voice cracked. "You murdered my mum."

Alice felt sick. How could she have loved this man? How could he have hurt her poor defenceless mum. Amongst the emotions pouring through her, she felt a black anger come to the surface; it made her breathless and caused a scalding shudder through her body.

"How could you?"

There was something in her voice that made him look up at her sharply.

Alice picked up the wooden pole again, her hands clutching it tightly. His face dropped, and he tried to get up, but his legs were too weak.

She ran at him and swung down hard with the pole. Her views on humanity, cruelty, fairness, justice evaporated under the blazing dark heat of her rage.

"You bastard!" she screamed.

Alice swung and swung; she hit his arms, legs, body. Every strike made a *thwack* sound that was loud out on the quiet river. In that moment, Alice didn't care if the whole world could hear her.

Richard screamed and yelled in pain.

"Stop," he begged.

But she couldn't. She kept swinging. Her arms weren't the strongest, but it was amazing what consuming rage could make you do. Alice ignored the cramp in her hands from gripping the pole so tightly. Again and again, she swung her weapon, smacking it into the man who had killed her mother. One of the strikes cracked his ankle. Another struck his arm, and she thought she heard a bone break. His cream polo shirt was bloody now where the skin had split on his back.

And then the pole broke.

It snapped in two. The pole snapped at an angle, leaving a sharp stake. She looked down at the stake in her hand and looked at Richard. She was standing over him, panting heavily.

Her hands shook as she imagined plunging it into him. He deserved to die, and right then she wanted to kill him. Was that what he wanted? In her first year of university, as part of her biology degree, Alice had studied the human body, and she had a very clear view of where the human heart was. If you were going to kill someone with a wooden stake, then the heart was the place to plunge it.

Alice stepped backwards from Richard's prone body and sucked in huge lungfuls of air. What was she thinking? She wasn't a killer.

She threw the stake into the water.

"I'm calling the police."

Richard groaned in pain and looked up at her.

"They won't believe you," he gasped. "It's my word against yours." He spat out a mouthful of blood onto the deck, and it glistened black in the evening light.

Alice remembered she didn't have her phone, so she dug into Richard's pocket and pulled out his. The screen was cracked, probably from her wooden pole.

Her arms and hands were aching from her attack on Richard.

Alice knew his PIN code, which like his others was his date of birth, so she unlocked the phone. It seemed to still work. There were dozens of missed calls, which she ignored. She typed in the emergency services number but hesitated. Was he right? Would they believe her that he had confessed to her mum's murder? Would they see her as a jilted lover making up a story? Could they prove that an old lady who had died in her bed, supposedly in her sleep, was actually murdered? Would they even bother to try to prove it?

That was why Richard had told her, because nothing could be proven, and it would keep her in Bristol as a witness to his confession. He didn't want her to leave.

Alice tilted her head up towards the night sky and howled like a banshee into the darkness. She had never hated someone so much as she hated him at that moment.

In the silence that followed, Alice stared at him, and he stared defiantly back at her. Her breathing was heavy; she couldn't seem to catch her breath. Her head still hurt, and she just wanted to lie down somewhere on her own and sleep. But then an idea came to her.

She gave him a cold smile.

Alice stepped back towards the wheel and took control of the boat. She could see that the bridge was now open, so she eased the throttle forward so that *Seas the Day* slipped into Bristol harbour. It was cold on the water now, and as the adrenaline drained from her, she shivered. The boat passed the harbour pubs, and as it reached the middle of the harbour, Alice set the engine to idle, making it come to a slow, drifting stop. She caught the scent of beer and cigarette smoke from the pubs.

"Stand up," Alice ordered.

Richard sat up and struggled to stand with his hands and

feet tied. Alice yanked him up by the arm, and he swayed unsteadily on his feet, leaning back against the boat's rail.

"Turn around."

Their faces were close now.

"Alice..."

She took out the little knife from her belt, and the look on her face convinced Richard that he should shut up and do as he was told. He shuffled on his bound feet so that his back was to Alice and he was facing the water. His back made a tempting target for the knife she was holding, but as quickly as the thought of sticking the blade in him came to her, she dismissed it.

Alice held his arm in her left hand, and with her right hand she used the knife to saw through the rope. In a moment the cut rope fell to the deck, and Richard's hands were free. He started to turn towards her and opened his mouth to speak.

But as soon as he moved, she simply pushed him off the boat with both hands. He wasn't expecting the push, and he fell awkwardly into the water. He sank into the dark water, and Alice squatted to peer over the edge of the boat. White bubbles swirled around where he had fallen in. Then the surface broke, and Richard came up spluttering. His arms flailed in the water.

He coughed and spat. "My legs are still tied," he gasped at her.

Alice looked at his phone and once again entered Richard's PIN to unlock it. She tapped onto the missed calls and saw there were dozens from someone called Igor; that sounded very Eastern European to her. Alice clicked on the number, and it was answered on the first ring. She put it on the speaker so Richard could hear.

"Professor?"

Just as she'd hoped, Alice recognised the voice; it was the man who had chased her earlier, the man who had tried to choke her.

"Are you still looking for Richard Barnes?"

"You bitch," Richard called from the water.

"Yes, where is he?" the voice on the phone asked patiently.

Alice looked down at Richard as he struggled and splashed in the water.

"I've just dropped him into Bristol harbour for you. You've probably got ten minutes until he can swim out of here and get away."

"Bristol harbour?" the voice confirmed.

"Alice, what the hell are you doing?" Richard called from the water. "Do you know who that is?"

"Yes, Bristol harbour," Alice said into the phone; she was tempted to give the man on the phone a more specific location but thought she would offer Richard a fighting chance to make his escape.

"I am close. I can be there in ten minutes. Who are you?"

Alice tossed the phone into the water.

She stood up and went back to the wheel of the boat.

"What have you done?" Richard yelled up at her.

"I've given you a chance," Alice called to him. "Which is more than you gave my mum."

Alice yanked the throttle down, and the boat shot forward. She swung the wheel and the boat swivelled in the water so that it was facing the harbour exit. Luckily the bridge was still open; it would only take her a few minutes to leave the harbour.

"Alice," she heard Richard call from the frothing water. "Alice..."

Alice ignored him.

The boat left the harbour, and soon she could no longer hear his calls, just the gentle hum of the boat's engine and the lapping water as the prow cut through the darkness.

27

+1 DAY

Alice woke to the whirr of the engine of a passing boat. She'd slept badly, and her head hurt from the gin she'd drank the night before. After dropping Richard off in Bristol's harbour, she had managed to sail an hour south out of the city before exhaustion and darkness had forced her to dock at Portishead. It was a town just south of Bristol, but its harbour was quiet, and Alice had been grateful to stop there.

Despite feeling drained, she had struggled to sleep, so she had opened a half-bottle of gin she had brought with her. At the time, drinking it had felt lifesaving, but now her head was throbbing with a hangover, and she wasn't so sure it had been a good choice. Alice estimated she'd only had about two hours' sleep. She'd spent the night drinking gin, looking at photos of her mum in an album she'd packed, and crying.

That morning there were so many things rattling around her mind: how she had nearly been screwed over by Richard and his girlfriend, the loss of her mum, being alone. Amongst all of that was the thought of now having to cross the English Channel without any help. Her sailing lessons had been good, and she could sail the boat, but there was a big difference between hugging the English coast and actually crossing the open waters of the Atlantic Sea from England to the coastline of France. She'd watched videos online of the huge waves, and they had looked terrifying. The plan had been for Richard to take charge of the boat during the crossing, but now she would have to do it on her own, and she wasn't sure she could face that.

Thoughts of Richard came to her again, but she couldn't allow herself to think about him, so Alice forced herself to get up from the small double bed. She used the toilet and then decided to brave the shower, it only held a small amount of hot water, and the water pressure was weak, but as the heat hit her skin, she felt a little revived. An image of Richard hiding in the bathroom came to mind, which spoilt what little pleasure the shower was offering, so she turned it off.

Alice dried herself with a towel and made her way to the second bedroom, where she had left the suitcases of clothes on the small cabin bed. She found some underwear, jeans and a navy jumper and got dressed; the swaying of the boat made this simple activity much harder, and she realised it was something she was going to have to get used to.

From the box of kitchenware, she brought out the kettle and made herself a green tea. Then she sat on the padded bench in the cabin, sipping her tea. The space felt small, and the smell of fresh paint only added to her feeling of nausea. God, she felt awful. Her whole body felt bruised and battered from the previous day, and she had the worst headache, a hangover from Richard hitting her and the gin she'd drunk, which was a terrible combination.

Normally, if she felt this bad, Alice would spend the day in bed or on the sofa. But that wasn't an option now. She missed her home, and tears threatened to fall, but she sniffed them away.

Alice finished her tea and searched around for some painkillers, but there were none on the boat. There was also nothing she could have for breakfast, so she pulled on her shoes, grabbed her purse and left the boat whilst pushing away the image of Richard flicking through her bank cards the night before.

It was still early, and there was not a single person in sight. A morning mist covered the water, creeping up and around the harbour so that it seemed the world's colours had drained away. Portishead harbour was surrounded by new apartments, and the buildings in the distance seemed to be floating in the mist. Alice had come here a few years ago to have lunch with a friend, and from the edges of her memory, she knew there was a high street and supermarket nearby.

Walking through the mist and breathing in the morning air helped to clear her head, and when she arrived at the high street, she found a café and went in. She didn't usually eat greasy foods, but she was ravenous, so she ordered a full English breakfast and a pot of tea. The food wasn't as greasy as she'd been expecting, it was hot and tasty, and she surprised herself with how much she enjoyed it.

"Is there a supermarket around here?" Alice asked the old lady behind the counter.

"Down the main road and on your right," she replied.

Alice paid and set off. She walked a few hundred metres

down the road and from the corner of the street and saw the small supermarket ahead.

She could only buy what she could carry, which meant Alice took a basket instead of a trolley. The first things she picked up were two packets of painkillers, the second was a large bottle of gin; she was aware of the hypocrisy, but the way she felt at the moment, Alice knew the gin would be required to get her through the next few days.

Alice filled the shopping basket with oranges, bananas, carrots and kale. There were some large pizzas that looked good, but they wouldn't fit in her little boat oven, so she picked up some kids-sized pizzas instead. To the basket she added a packet of fresh tortellini, teabags, chicken, eggs, crisps, biscuits, cereal, milk, bread, butter and a few tins of soup. There was more that she wanted to buy, but Alice was aware she would need to carry it all back to the boat. The final thing she picked up was a cheap mobile phone. She wasn't even sure it would work abroad, but she still put it in her basket.

The checkout was quiet, so she quickly paid and, with two full bags in each hand, made her way back to the boat. It was only a mile, but she still had to stop halfway to let the blood flow back into her fingers. Finally, she made it.

The second the heavy bags were dumped on the floor of the boat, Alice found the painkillers and took two of them with some water. She then put the food away in the little cupboards, fridge and freezer. Keeping the momentum going, and ignoring her throbbing head, Alice unpacked the large box of kitchen utensils on the floor and stowed everything neatly in the cupboards.

It was tempting to put off the unpacking, but she steeled herself and went to the spare room, where she lifted one of the suitcases and heaved it into the master bedroom. It took her half an hour to unpack both cases into the drawers and wardrobe. Whilst hanging the clothes, she realised there was no iron, and she wondered where she could get one.

Alice walked through the boat. Now that she was unpacked, she tried to imagine living here. Despite everything, she wondered if it would have been better with Richard. She knew it would be better if she were with someone else, not that bastard Richard, but this dream had always been about two people sailing away together, not her on her own. Not only that, but there was still the nagging dread of having to sail into the Atlantic Ocean on her own.

"Damn it!" She cursed herself as the tears came, and she wept.

Forty-six years old and suddenly single. She missed her parents so much. Alice had never felt so lonely. Had Richard really killed her mum, or was he just saying that to hurt her, to punish her? A rush of guilt came at the thought of not contacting the police and reporting him. But what would happen? After her mum had died six months ago, she had been cremated, so they couldn't do an autopsy. Her house had been stripped of possessions and sold. If Alice spoke to the police about Richard's confession, it would mean staying in Bristol for weeks, being questioned endlessly by the police, and eventually it would come down to her word against Richard's. She had no evidence. On the other hand, she had just learned about Richard having an affair, which surely would be considered motivation for her accusing him of something terrible out of spite or vengeance.

It was a difficult decision to make, but her gut instinct told her to take the boat, leave England and forget about him.

She sat and cried for a while, head slumped, arms wrapped tightly around the pain in her stomach. Alice had only ever wanted a nice, simple life. She just wanted to be part of a loving family and to be a good person. But the world had had other ideas for her. Everything had been turned upside down, and it all seemed so unfair. She knew she was indulging in self-pity, but it was a struggle to stop the thoughts racing through her mind.

Eventually the sun pierced the portholes, sending shafts of warm light shining through into the cabin. And then there were no tears left to cry.

Alice forced herself up and walked up onto the deck. It was a perfect day for sailing. So what was she waiting for?

She turned the engine on and untied the ropes. *Seas the Day* chugged out of the port, and Alice set the sails; the wind was strong, but it was blowing north to south, which was perfect for her. The boat cut through the green and blue sea, moving fast towards the south. Out on the water Alice couldn't help but grin at the feeling of the sunshine and sea spray on her face. A flock of birds hovered over the boat and called to her. She watched the sail and the sea, her eyes analysing everything, occasionally adjusting the wheel or loosening and tightening the sail ropes.

In her mind she had always imagined Richard sailing the boat and her being his helper, his second mate. But now she was the captain. It was a strange feeling, although she could feel her confidence growing as she sailed onwards.

THAT NIGHT she docked in a small Cornish village that she didn't know the name of. There was a pub near the dock, and Alice sat in a corner of the pub with her laptop and a bottle of Cornish cider. Connected to the pub's Wi-Fi, she checked the Bristol news, but there was no mention of either Richard or any assault or murder taking place. Did that mean he'd managed to flee from Igor? Or had Igor gotten hold of Richard, but no one knew about it? Alice didn't know, and she decided she didn't care.

Next, she went through her emails. Her old Mini, the reliable old rust bucket, had been collected by the scrapyard and crushed. The furniture removal company had emptied the house, and their furniture was now in storage. At that moment Alice never wanted to see any of it again, but there was no way of knowing how she would feel in the future.

There was an email from Roger, the sailing instructor. He was mailing to say *hello* and to let her know he would be in the south of France all summer and would love to catch up. He gave her an address for a French sailing school where he could be contacted. As Alice sipped her cider, she thought of his easy smile and broad shoulders.

Normally, Alice would have left the email to give herself time to think about it, but with her new-found confidence, plus a bottle of cider in her, she hit the reply button. She told Roger she would love to meet with him and that she would be there in a few weeks. Alice ended the mail saying she would be coming alone, and then she clicked send.

She created a new email to send to her closest friends. In it she explained she was now on the boat alone and was sailing to Europe without Richard. She also added her new phone number, although she hadn't actually turned the phone on yet. Alice hesitated and considered adding an explanation about her and Richard separating, but she decided it was something best done face to face. Again, she clicked send.

That night she slept for twelve hours. The past week had caught up with her, and when she woke up, she felt healed and energised.

She ate breakfast on the deck in her pyjamas; then she got dressed and pulled on her waterproof jacket. Today was the day; she was going to cross the Atlantic.

28

+2 DAYS

It was a bright day, with a mild southerly wind. Alice checked the weather forecast, and the rest of the day was set to be cloudy and dry with a gentle breeze. It was the best she could have hoped for, and she knew it was a case of now or never.

She tied her hair back and began to prepare for the journey. Firstly, she made a flask of tea and a bag of cheese sandwiches for her lunch. She also made sure there were bottles of water within easy reach of the wheel on the deck. The English Channel maps were laid out on the cabin table with pencils and a ruler to track her progress. She checked that her CB radio was working, her fuel tank was full, and there was plenty of spare fuel in the two jerry cans. The satnav was switched on, and she entered her co-ordinates. Finally, Alice clipped on her lifejacket.

She set off, steering the boat on a southwesterly bearing. A feeling of nerves tingled in her stomach, but it felt gentle compared with the emotions she'd had to deal with over the past week. Alice breathed in the sea air, and it helped her focus on the task ahead. The summer sun rose behind her, warming her back and neck. Seawater sprayed the freshly cleaned deck, and several seabirds flew alongside her. At first, she thought they were seagulls, but their calls sounded different, and she realised they were kittiwakes.

Seas the Day left the coast of England and headed south. Out here, in the deep waters of the ocean, the waves picked up, and Alice could really feel the boat rising and falling with them. But the boat was built for the ocean, and her prow seemed at home slicing through the waves with ease.

Alice forgot her nerves as she remembered all the lessons she'd had; in her mind she could hear Roger's calm voice talking her through what she needed to do. Every hour she checked the satnav screen. She also took a GPS reading, quickly ducking below into the cabin to mark her position on the map. Her eyes were everywhere: on the waves, the wheel, the distant horizon and the sails.

Out in the depths she could see huge white jellyfish pass the boat; some of them looked as big as her. Occasionally, the kittiwakes would return and squawk into the wind as they hovered around the sail. Alice could feel the power of the waves and the wind wanting to take control of the boat, but she remained steady and focused and made sure *Seas the Day* only did what she wanted it to.

As the midday sun peaked in the sky, Alice ate her packed lunch. She wolfed down the sandwiches and sipped at the hot tea. The boat continued south, and the further she went, the more she felt comfortable being in control; she could do this. By midday she could see the thin line of the French coast in the far distance. Throughout the day she continued to note her GPS position on the map with her pencil and ruler, and gradually Alice's confidence grew that she would arrive safely at L'Aber Wrac'h, a small harbour town on the northern coast of France.

Despite her attention being set on sailing, thoughts of Richard sometimes threatened to overwhelm her. Still, something strange started to happen for Alice. As she left England behind, as she focused on the boat and the sea, her presence amid the beauty around her, Alice found it more and more easy to dispel thoughts of Richard. She found that she could, quite naturally, be in the moment and enjoy the thrill of sailing from one country to another.

She realised that the trick was to keep the boat's prow angled into the waves and ride them up and down. The waves grew taller, the white edges rising above the edge of the boat, a few even went higher than her head, but she didn't panic. Alice had practised for this. Her arms might be thin, but they were lean with plenty of strength in them, plenty enough to turn the wheel to steer the boat as she wanted it.

She remained alert, kept control of the boat, and soon the waves eased, and *Seas the Day* left the deep waters of the English Channel as the French coast loomed up ahead. Alice managed to have another cup of tea from her flask, and by the time L'Aber Wrac'h came into view, the sun was setting to her right. The journey had taken her ten hours.

Alice turned the boat's engine on, then brought the sails in and tied them to the mast. She stood at the wheel as she casually cruised into the beautiful French harbour. The harbour itself seemed too small and shallow to hold all the boats moored there; however, she knew that the water was deeper than it seemed. Off to the east of the town there were open fields filled with tall sunflowers. Their yellow heads were gently swaying in the early evening sunlight.

A small boat chugged up to her as she entered the harbour.

"*Anglaise?*" a man called to her.

Alice could see the words "Capitaine de Port" on the side of his boat.

"*Oui,*" she called to him. "*Bonjour!* Yes, I'm English."

"Okay. I'm the harbour master. Please bring your passport to the office when you dock. There is space to moor over here," he said as he pointed to the far right of the harbour.

"No problem, thank you. *Merci!*"

"*Bienvenue en France!*" And then he grinned at her before his boat shot off.

Alice moored *Seas the Day* where the harbour master had advised her to. She tied up and stepped out onto the French docks. She had made it! A sense of pride welled within her, and she relished just how nice it was to feel good for a change. She had a sudden image of her mum from years ago, when Alice had graduated from university. That day there had been such an air of happiness and pride around her mum, and Alice thought how proud she would be of her now. Proud that her daughter had survived Richard's clutches and was getting on with her life. Proud that she had single-handedly sailed to France. Alice took a deep breath and exhaled slowly.

She took her passport to the harbour master's office and then strolled around the town. Alice followed her nose to a fish restaurant, where a friendly waiter ushered her to a table outside, overlooking the harbour.

He brought her a menu, and she ordered a bottle of local white wine and a fish dish. The wine was brought and poured, and it tasted amazing – as bracing and crisp as the sea air. The restaurant was small but buzzing with diners, and she couldn't tear her eyes away from the harbour as the sun began its descent over it, turning the sky a hundred different shades of red and pink.

Alice dug the new phone out of her bag and turned it on. Instantly dozens of messages came through and flashed on the screen. They were from her friends. They had all seen her email from Cornwall and wanted to check she was alright. Their concern was touching, and she couldn't help but smile; they were such good people. As she read through the messages, she noted how many of her friends wanted to come and see her, and Alice's smile grew wider at the thought of so many visitors.

As the sun finally set over the harbour, with a broad smile on her face and a large glass of wine at hand, Alice messaged them back. After a while the waiter brought her an exquisite plate of herby lemon sole with summer vegetables, and she put her phone away to eat.

The food was delicious, one of the best meals she'd ever eaten.

VII.VI.MMXXII

THANK YOU FOR READING

Did you enjoy reading *The Adopted Daughter*? Please consider leaving a review on Amazon. Your review will help other readers to discover the novel.

ABOUT THE AUTHOR

JJ Burgess has a degree in Economics and lives in Bristol with his wife and two sons. By day he is the Director of a greetings card company, by night he writes psychological thrillers that ask questions about the world we live in. When he isn't writing, he is usually running through the woods around Bristol, thinking of new characters and dark plots.

ALSO BY JJ BURGESS

The Donor

The Adopted Daughter